JAW

The Banker (Starling Key book #3)

Edit by The Word Tank

Cover image by Wander Aguiar

www.januaryjamesauthor.com

For Seema.

The sunshine to my soul and the medicine to my mind.

PREVIOUSLY ON STARLING KEY...

Isaac

I'm deep in numbers when my radio buzzes, letting me know the Birds have arrived on Starling Key. I reluctantly close down the spreadsheet I still need to complete for Connor. As the unofficial financial whizkid of the luxury beach resort, it's my job to make sure all legitimate (and illegitimate) business is taken care of, and the books look slick. Connor, the Head of Security (and unofficial Head of Resort) runs a tight ship. I stretch out my legs to get the blood circulating again and stand. Here we go.

I walk out of my office, past the reception desks and out to the main foyer where I see the trail of back sedans arriving in a long line. A team of events guys are waiting, like groupies, under the guise of showing the drivers where to park up.

"Which one is she in?" I ask Rupert, the guy closest to me.

"No idea. The windows are totally blacked out. Second one, maybe. I'm guessing security are up front."

As if to confirm his assessment, the doors of the first car open and out step four—*four*—security guards, wearing blank, serious faces, flashy earpieces and bespoke, tailored suits. I'm no fashion expert but I'm guessing those were not off the rack—they look designer. One of them spots me wearing my SKS shirt and gives me a cursory nod before walking across to the second car. Rupert's assessment here wasn't totally on point. Instead of a girl barely out of diapers stepping out, it's a man, twice, maybe three times her age.

Alana, Connor's newly appointed Head of Talent rushes over. "Mr. Bird," she says, holding out a hand to the father and manager of our latest star attraction, pop star Aurelia Bird. He shakes it, somewhat lazily. "Welcome to Starling Key. How is your stay in Miami?"

Ah yes, Starling Key isn't quite good enough for the Birds and they've opted to take over suites at the Ritz-Carlton in Miami instead. Mind you, looking at the number of people along for the ride to simply recce the place, we probably wouldn't have had enough space—they'd have taken up most of our accommodation.

"Great, thanks," he replies, without even looking at her. "Where's the boss?"

"Connor Johnson, sir?" Alana asks.

"Starling," the man grunts. "Eric Starling."

Little does he know, Eric Starling is the boss of this place only on paper. In reality, he doesn't care a great deal about the daily running of the resort. As long as the golf lawn is in outstanding condition and the caddies are good, he doesn't pay much thought to whatever else we do to make him money.

"Um, he'll be over soon, I believe. The plan is to visit the concert hall first so you can have a look at the place, get a feel for the resort, then we'll take lunch in our private dining room, where Mr. Starling plans to join us."

"Where's the bathroom?" he barks, making Alana take a step back in surprise.

"It's just through here, sir. Let me show you."

She plasters a generous smile to her face and leads Mr. Bird into the reception, shooting me a slight eye roll as they pass.

Great. Not one prima donna, but two. This is going to be huge amounts of fun. Thanks Connor.

Another two security guards have appeared, along with what looks like a mother, two small twin girls and two harassed-looking nannies. Mrs. Bird stands as the two children are ushered away by the nannies and two members of the events team. She stands erect, elongates her neck, closes her eyes and takes a dramatic breath in.

"God, I love the sea," she says, breathy and wistful. Older women are my poison. I would usually go for one of her age and means, but not this one. One of the advantages of being well-acquainted with women of this social stature, wealth and caliber is that I know authenticity when I see it, and this woman has none. Her face has been contorted with excessive surgery, and she looks almost the same as every other rich person who has become obsessed with getting work done. Her hair must be caked with so much lacquer it doesn't even move in the breeze, and her outfit is completely over the top. I ponder briefly if it's a bid to draw attention away from her daughter, to herself. She's certainly relishing having everyone's eyes on her right now as she pretends to appreciate her new surroundings. My guess is she's barely even looked. She may not even know where the hell she is, and she may not even care.

"My bag," she calls out, to no one obvious. Then a thin, overly expressive young man snakes his way backwards out of one of the cars and runs on tiptoes to Her Majesty, proffering a tote small enough to hold little more than a stick of gum. "And my Versace pumps," she adds, looking down her nose at the young man who doesn't seem at all affected or offended by her manner. "I can hardly wear these, here, can I?"

My eyes drop to her feet and, indeed, she is strapped into spindly red heels about a foot high. I'm amazed she was able to get out of the car and take the three steps to where she now stands preening at her immaculate, dust-free blouse.

"Of course, Charlotte," the man replies, scurrying back to the car.

I'm so absorbed in the otherworldly scene unfolding before me, I almost don't notice what's going on by the car at the end of the line. A young guy and a girl are clamoring around the rear of the car, leaning into the passenger seat, talking quietly. I step to the side, to focus my full attention on them. I'm not working in my security guise now but I can't turn off the urge to be aware of everything going on around me, especially anything untoward. Mrs. Bird is oblivious as she leans her weight on the boy who's changing her shoes with deft efficiency.

My eyes flick to back to the car and a small head of blonde hair steps out. Her face is concealed behind the two people who appear to be talking to her softly, coaxing her out of the vehicle. The girl leans forward and seems to run her fingers across the blonde's cheeks, before the boy leans forward and wraps his arms around her. They stand for several minutes comforting the girl who's got out of the car, whose face I still can't see, then step to each side of her and the three of them walk towards us. The girl to the left is sweet and homely-looking. She's dressed in dark, casual clothes, nothing special, with a long braid down her back. The boy is also casually dressed, his kind face marred slightly with pimple scars. He puts his arm around the girl in the middle, who is facing him and mumbling quietly as she walks. Then, as they come within a few feet of where I'm standing, adjacent to the mother, the girl in the middle turns her head towards me.

I'm taken aback slightly by the innocence in her wide, hazel eyes. Her lips twitch into a small smile and she nods hello, as would any well-bred celebrity who knows being nice to everyone is their bread and butter. As she looks away again, I take her in. She's slim but not skinny, with baby blonde hair that dances around her shoulders. Her curves are not substantial by my standards, but her shortness in height keeps all her features in perfect proportion. As much as I begrudge it, I can see why the world has become enamored with this pretty young girl, based on her pleasing, youthful looks alone. She's watching her mother, her expression giving nothing away, but her fingers grip those of the girl and boy standing at her sides.

"Who are they?" I whisper to Rupert, sidling back over to him.

"I think they might be Ana and Billy, her oldest friends. They go almost everywhere with her. So I've read, anyway."

"Right," I reply, curious.

My phone buzzes in my pocket and I slide it out to look at the screen.

Paris.

I hesitate for a second then cut the call and shove the phone back in my pocket. For some reason, I'm more interested in knowing how this arrival, this scene, is going to play out.

"Aurelia!" Her mother snaps, throwing a glance back over her shoulder. "We don't have all day!" Then she stomps off, as best she can in dainty pumps, with the doting man-child scurrying behind, wafting imaginary pieces of air away from his mistress's clothing.

"You ok?" Ana says quietly, dipping her mouth to Aurelia's ear.

Aurelia simply nods and I see her squeezing her friend's hand.

As they walk past, the girl in the middle flicks her eyes back up towards me again and stops.

"Excuse me," she begins. "I don't suppose you can tell me who my security is going to be while I'm here?" She dips her chin slightly, looking almost embarrassed to be here. "I'd just like to introduce myself. Start off on the right foot, you know? Before… before anyone else can get to them."

I frown at her comment. What a weird thing to say. Not only do celebrities of this stature generally not care less who's going to be on their detail, but why and in what way would anyone 'get to' the guy in question?

"Um…" I start, slightly thrown by the way she's looking up at me with an innocence I've never before seen, and a strange feeling starting up in my gut. I'm experiencing an odd need to protect this young girl whose parents clearly don't give a shit about her, and who feels the need to take her childhood friends everywhere, if only to help her get out of a car. My thoughts are interrupted by a loud bellowing.

"What are you standing out here for? Get inside that building, Aurelia. Money doesn't earn itself."

She chews her lip, waiting for my answer. Unfortunately, I don't give her the right one. I give her the only one my mind will entertain in that very second.

"Me. I'll be your detail while you're here. I'm Isaac," I say, holding out my hand. "It's a pleasure."

A gush of air leaves her lungs and her shoulders soften.

"Aurelia," she replies, putting her small, nineteen-year-old hand in mine. Her lips twitch into a genuine, half-embarrassed smile. "I'm glad it's you."

I blink, surprised. Maybe it's just the fact I came here to see her arrive that's given her some reassurance, I don't know. But whatever the reason, when she follows her father's orders and walks out across the grass to the concert hall, I can't help but hope there's more to it than that. That maybe I make her feel safe. My mind has already decided, without any conference at all, I do need to protect Aurelia Bird. Not least from her ridiculous parents.

I sigh, resigned to my new predicament. Guess I better go break the news to Jax. Aurelia Bird has just landed herself a shit hot bodyguard, and it's not him.

PROLOGUE

saac

"You're bored?" My director stares back at me, his eyes wide, his mouth hanging open.

I don't flinch. "Yes, sir."

"You're a practically untouchable operative in the CIA and you're… *bored*?"

I know Emerson doesn't take kindly to repetition so I don't respond. He knows the answer.

"Let me get this straight. You've risen to the top of your paygrade faster than anyone else from your intake; you led the operation to take down the Qatari Finance Minister after several others failed; you masterminded the operation to nail the Libyan terrorist hacker group… And you're FUCKING BORED?"

I bite the inside of my cheek to stop a grin forming. That wouldn't earn me any Boy Scout badges. And to Emerson, this isn't funny. I know how inconvenient this is for him. He's already lost four operatives at my level—two got hit in a random attack in Mexico, one retired early, and the other left after suffering a mental breakdown. Let's face it, if I stay, the odds aren't good. But, that's not why I'm leaving. I'm leaving because it's true: I'm bored. Everything I do is to further the interests and successes of the Agency, and rightly so. But I've given them ten years, a couple hundred international criminals and several dumpsters of blood. I deserve a bit of time to go do whatever the hell I like.

"You know what this makes me, D'Amico, you prick?" His face has turned a putrid shade of red and sweat is beading out of his forehead. "Disa-fucking-ppointed."

Spit lands on the desk beneath him as he delivers the sentiment every operative dreads. But, it rolls off me like water off a duck's back because this is one of the reasons I want out. It doesn't take much to disappoint a superior in the CIA. I haven't had the misfortune of disappointing anyone in all my years here, but others have and I've seen how debilitating it can be. The self-doubt it inspires can cripple a man, especially one who goes to battle with his mind, not his muscle.

"I'm sorry you feel that way," I reply, my face as blank as a fresh covering of snow.

"Do you realize what you're throwing away?" he continues to seethe. I know what this is. He's processing the five stages of grief. First, denial, then anger, now comes the bargaining. "You'll never be able to come back at this level, you realize that, don't you?"

"I do, sir. I'm not planning on coming back."

"That's fucking hasty, D'Amico. You're not thinking straight. How about I give you a sabbatical? Let you think it over, come to your fucking senses?"

"I appreciate that sir, but there's no need."

"One year? Two years? How long do you think you'll need, to get this crap out of your system?"

"There's no crap in my system, sir. I simply want different things."

"D'Amico," he glares at me, practically panting. "You leave, there's no turning back."

"I know."

"Ah, Jeezus!" He claps his palms over his face and throws his head back in defeat, finally. Just when I think he might actually be crying, he removes his hands and stares back at me with a mixture of sadness and mild panic. "It's a shitshow, Isaac. I need you."

I lean my forearms on the table and breathe out. I feel him watching me with a disproportionate sense of hope.

"Emerson… I really am sorry to leave you when you're so many men down, but I've done my time. I need a break from the agency. I need to use other parts of my brain…"

"Seriously? It doesn't get any more challenging than this."

"I want to be a part of a business where I can reap the profits of a job well done. I want to be able to see the fruits of my labor. I want to be able to clock off and enjoy the sun and a few beers without having to constantly look over my shoulder. I want to be a part of the normal world for a change."

"The world out there ain't anywhere near normal, kid."

"I'm willing to take my chances. Besides, I want to relax, kick back with a few women, you know?"

"You haven't been deprived of women, D'Amico. Look at you for fuck's sake. And I wasn't born yesterday—I know what you boys get up to in your downtime."

"I don't mean those kinda women, the ones in the clubs, still living off their parents, still at school in some cases. I mean *real* women, Emerson. I'm going somewhere I know there are plenty, and I'm going to enjoy them, one hundred percent."

Emerson shakes his head. "And where are these '*real women*?'" he says with an eyeroll.

I sit back again, a small smile creeping onto my lips. "The Florida Keys."

"You kidding me? That place is full of retirees."

I arch an eyebrow in reply.

"Really, D'Amico? That's what floats your boat? The older woman?"

I nod, lightly. "*Real* women, Emerson. The ones who've been around town a few times, know what they're doing. They take care of themselves, they have class. They don't want to get attached."

"You know what? It sounded pretty good until the part about them not wanting to get attached. I never came across a woman who didn't want to be attached."

"The women I like don't want to be. They don't need to be."

"And why's that?"

"Well," I say, relaxing my shoulders. "They're already married."

Emerson collapses back in his chair with a half-laugh, half-sigh. "Ah, man. I thought I had you all worked out, D'Amico, but I barely scratched the surface."

I smile wryly. No one knows the real Isaac D'Amico. Not even my mother. "Isn't that what makes a good operative? Someone who can assimilate into different environments, become different characters, get into different peoples' heads?"

"Yeah. Yeah it is." Emerson sighs heavily. "You sure I can't convince you to stay?"

"I'm sorry, man. It's my time."

"Fine," he shakes his head. "Fine. You got a job lined up already?"

"Yeah, an old friend recommended me for a security job at one of the resorts."

"Security? Fuck, D'Amico. You're going from the CIA to a shitty security job, to become a beach bum drinking beer and chasing cougars?"

"Yup," I grin. My new gig isn't quite as low level as he thinks it is. I'll be orchestrating the books for the entire beach resort and managing some not-entirely-legal-but-entirely-lucrative side hustles below the radar. But, I'm enjoying winding the guy up.

"I really don't know you," he says again, his eyes burrowing into me as though he's reassessing everything he once thought about CIA Operative, Isaac D'Amico.

"How well do we ever really know anyone?" I shrug.

Several seconds pass as he ponders. "Fair point."

"Here." I pass him my new business card.

He picks it up and flicks it back and forth between his fingers. "Starling Key," he mutters. "Sounds like a wildlife sanctuary."

I ignore his jibe. "You should visit. Bring the wife and kids. I'll get you a discount."

"Hmph," he mutters in reply.

I stand up to leave his office, not bothering to take a last look around it. I won't miss this place. "Thanks for everything, sir," I say.

"Whatever."

I grin back at him, open the yellowing door and walk straight out. No looking back.

CHAPTER ONE

saac

I TRAIL a finger along her delicate collarbone, then down her chest to the valley between her breasts. She's laying on her back but the surgeon's genius ensures her breasts remain pert and bulbous. I bend my head to press the flat of my tongue against the surprisingly soft and taut skin, and lick from the right side of her ribcage up to the deep pink of her nipple, which I suck softly into my mouth.

"God!" She gasps, her back arching, pressing the firm dome into my face. "Isaac, baby, you're killing me."

I push her chest back down to the floor and shift my weight above her. We're lying naked on the deck of the Hemingway Villa, the most luxurious sea villa on the resort, and my cock wastes no time in resting between her legs.

"Keep still, my love," I say, my tongue lapping at the hard peak, my cock nudging at her entrance.

"I'm going to come before you're even inside me," she moans.

"It wouldn't be the first time," I reply, licking down into the valley and across to her left nipple.

Her head flips to the side as though she's in pain. I gently bite down on the skin of her left breast, eliciting a gasp of frustration.

"Please, Isaac. I mean it. You can't do this to me."

"You're so impatient, my love. I'm just getting started."

She grinds her hips against me in an attempt to hurry me along, so I take both her hands and pin them to the ground behind her head.

"Patience," I growl at her.

A tear rolls down her cheek. "Please…" she whispers.

I lean forward and lick the salty track away. "You break my heart."

She lifts her head and bites into my neck, chasing it with hot kisses. The mixture of pain and her expert caress sets me on fire, and for a second I forget my need for control. My hips jut forward without thought and she seizes the moment. Her legs spread and she hooks her ankles behind my back, pulling herself up and onto my cock with a cry of release.

"You fucking—" I splutter, as the sensation of being inside this gorgeous woman overtakes me.

"What, Isaac? What am I?" she pants, as she meets my thrusts with her strong, Tracy Anderson-toned hips.

"You're a fucking vampire," I groan, working her faster. "Biting my neck like that."

"You asked for it," she replies, breathily. "You know you shouldn't tease me. I lose my mind."

I move inside her, hard and deep. This is what I love about older women. They know exactly what they're doing. There's no nervous fumbling, no fear of asking for what they want, no second-guessing what they need. Older women know the language; they speak it fluently. Especially this one, Paris Navitsky. And they don't take any shit. I can skip the tasting stage and go straight for the full bottle. I get better quality sex, all the time, unlike the other guys who go for women with hardly any experience at all. That's not for me. The idea of breaking in a virgin positively turns me off. No. *This*. This is what I live for. A good woman who wants good sex and nothing else.

"This is incredible, Isaac," she breathes out.

"You are incredible," I reply, slanting my mouth across hers. I know when she's about to come. Her voice turns all breathy and desperate-sounding, and I live for it. "That's it, my love," I say, coaxing the climax out of her. That's another thing I love about older women. Their orgasms seem to be more powerful; they can be felt a mile away. When Paris finally erupts, she comes off the floor. Her legs unravel and I raise myself up on my knees, one hand spanning her lower back, supporting her as I thrust my way through her climax. She clenches down hard with a cry and I go from zero to sixty in half a second, dumping myself inside her with the force of a ten-ton truck.

I remain on my knees, the muscles bulging out of my thighs as she comes down from her high.

"You made me come too fast, Paris," I snap.

"Then we'll have to reconvene again soon," she replies, lazily, her face smug and sated. "I have to meet Roman at the gate in thirty minutes."

I pull out and wipe her and me with the Egyptian cotton Starling Key branded towel lying beside us. "Where's he dragging you to today?"

"Lunch with Jamaica Miles, she's the wife of a potential investor and a supreme bitch. She's from New York society.

Thinks she's better than everybody else. It'll be a win if I can get through lunch without spitting in her food."

"Sounds like fun. Wouldn't mind being a fly on the wall to watch you play nice with someone you don't like."

Paris lowers her eyes to my face and reaches for my hands. "I wish you could be a fly on the wall. I hate leaving you to go and do Roman's dirty work."

I lean forward and brace my hands either side of her head, taking her in for just a little longer. She has the kind of face I could stare at indefinitely. She's fifty-two-years-old—twenty-two years my senior—but could pass for thirty-five and has the spirit and libido of someone far younger than that.

"Is he coming back here with you afterwards?" I ask, stroking an immaculate blonde hair from her eyes.

"I don't know," she sighs. "I hope not. But, he has an appointment tomorrow in Miami before he heads back up to the City, so maybe."

I lower my lips and brush them against hers, feeling her sigh into my mouth. "Tomorrow?" she whispers. "Can I see you tomorrow?"

For a second I'm completely lost in the sensation of her words against my skin, then I remember. I sit up and rub my eyes with no small amount of annoyance at what I've landed myself in.

"I'm busy tomorrow," I sigh, heavily. "I have to be around for Aurelia Bird."

"The singer?"

"Yeah. She's doing a residency this season, remember?"

"Right. Of course." If I didn't know Paris better, I might have mistaken the look that flashed across her face as one of jealousy, but knowing Paris as I do, it wouldn't have been. I've known Mrs. Navitsky for six months and I've been fucking her behind her husband's back for five months, three weeks and six days. It was lust at first sight and it hasn't abated in the slightest. I haven't even entertained any of the other golf-obsessed guests' wives, as I normally would, since Paris arrived on the scene. She gives me everything I want, everything I need. Space, no strings, sex like I've never known, and the smugness of knowing she would rather be with me, a low-paid security bum, than a billionaire Russian oligarch. Well, up to a point. Paris and I have an unspoken agreement. She will never leave her husband and I will never ask her to. It's perfect. Ok, so Luca has asked me one too many times if it bothers me she wants the money more than me—because that's what it's about at the end of the day—and I reply honestly every time: not one bit.

I know who Paris is and it's not her heart I want, it's her body, her vibrancy, and the little part of her soul that reveals itself at the peak of her climax. That's what I want.

"Is she going to be staying here? On the resort?"

"No. Starling Key isn't good enough for her social-climbing idiot parents. They're staying at the Ritz Carlton."

"Nice," Paris replies, her face serene once more. "So, when can I see you again?"

I think quickly. "Well, I need to make sure Aurelia and her parents know where everything is, introduce them to the events team, work out the schedule for her security detail while she's on the island…"

"Who's the lucky guy?" Paris asks, with a wry smile.

Fuck, I thought I'd told her. "Um, well, me."

Paris pushes herself up and slides her legs away from my thighs. "What?"

"Yeah, I'm leading her security. It's no big deal."

"Why didn't you tell me?"

"I thought I had, to be honest."

"Um, no," she says, slowly. Her breasts stay completely still as she hops to her feet.

"It's no big deal," I repeat.

"So you keep saying."

"I've said it twice." I grasp one of her hands as she attempts to walk away. "What's the problem, Paris? It's work. It's my job. She's a child."

Paris whips around and if her surgeon hadn't done such a fine job with the filler, her frown would be saying everything in one long sentence. "She is *not* a child anymore, Isaac. She's a grown woman, and a beautiful one at that."

"Really?" I say, almost to myself. "She looks about twelve."

"You're just saying that to make me feel better," Paris pouts before looking away to the sea.

"I always want you to feel better, my love, but it's what I really think. I met the girl once. She's incredibly young, she can't go anywhere without her childhood friends trailing beside her, she's being used by her parents. That's why I put myself forward. She needs someone like me to look out for her, because her fucking parents don't."

"Wait, what?" Paris spins back to face me, and filler or no filler, she looks horrified. "You *put yourself* forward? You actually offered to be her *personal security* while she's here? For FOUR MONTHS?"

Ah, sheesh, when she puts it like that. "Look, Aurelia Bird is nothing more to me than an investment. She's bringing valuable publicity and high-paying visitors to the resort. That's all I care about. The way her parents spoke to her… I can't be sure she'll get through a full four months without breaking down, and I can't risk that happening as we'll lose a lot of fucking money. Ok?"

Paris grinds her teeth, delicately. "But, you'll be with her the whole time she's here, right?"

"Only when she's rehearsing and performing. I don't think she'll want to hang around here much when she's not actually working. So, I won't even be with her really. She'll be up on the stage or with her dancers." I don't actually know that for sure, but it seems to make Paris feel better as she turns her whole body towards me and steps forward, bringing her pussy to my face.

"You owe me," she orders. I oblige happily, rubbing my nose over her clit, breathing in her possessive scent, before my tongue acts of its own accord. I don't even care that I came inside her only minutes earlier. I want to please her. I want to feel her shudder against my face, make her scream so loud they can hear her on the golf course. I dig my fingers into the cheeks of her smooth ass, feeling the skin bruising beneath them. She's small enough that I can inch my thumbs around and part her, easing the way for my mouth. I make a point of French kissing her slow and deep, until I feel her knees weaken, then I hook her left knee over my broad shoulder, bringing her closer still.

"God, Isaac," she chokes.

I move my lips decadently, sucking her in then circling her with my tongue, as though it's her mouth I'm plundering.

"Promise me nothing will happen with her," she gasps, holding back her impending orgasm. "I know I can't… with, well… I'm not in any position…"

"Shut the fuck up," I murmur. "I only want you."

The tremors start the minute I return my mouth to her and I focus intently on her clit as she grips my head, her nails digging into my scalp. Even when her shuddering abates, I don't stop. I lighten my touch, I blow and I caress, until the sensitivity has passed, then I French kiss her again, deeply, drawing another climax from her core.

CHAPTER TWO

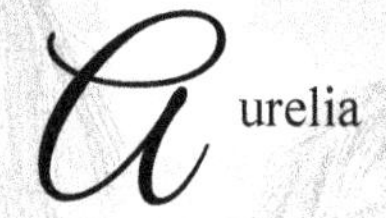

urelia

I GATHER UP THE BROCHURES, writing pads and pens and slide them into a drawer to make space on the dresser, then I carefully place my good luck charms in a row, one at a time. The verbena candle Ana bought me to invoke some sense of familiarity wherever in the world I am. The small trophy I won at my first talent show, aged eight. It reminds me of what I love about music and dancing, why I keep at it, despite the way this industry turns the people you love into near-strangers. Lastly, the gold locket my grandmother gave me before she died two years ago, to remind me to always keep my head in the clouds and my feet on the ground.

"Well, here we are, Grams," I say, opening the locket and looking in at the face I knew more intimately than my own mother's. "Miami. You always wanted to come to here. Well, this is it. And the Ritz Carlton, no less."

"Did she want to stay here?" Ana says behind me, pausing between hanging outfits in the closet.

I laugh out loud, dragging my gaze away from the locket to my best friend, and the closest thing I have to family. "No, not Grams. She would actually be turning in her grave knowing we're here. She hated all this… *materialism*. Would have called it vulgar. She'd have preferred to stay in some beach hut somewhere, floating around in a kaftan, smoking a joint or something."

Ana chuckles and returns to smoothing down my favorite Stella McCartney dress and placing it in the closet alongside a Thierry Mugler gown. "She sounds awesome. I know I always say this but I wish I had met her. I can't believe I never did."

"She lived too far away. And she never liked Chuck, so when Mom married him, she refused to visit. She knew Mom and Chuck were off doing their own thing, especially in the early days, and I was on my own a lot. She asked me to move in with her so many times. Part of me wishes I had."

"But, then you'd have moved away and we probably wouldn't have stayed besties," Ana replies, turning to lift another packaged outfit off the bed.

"Exactly. These things happen for a reason."

Ana stops and glances down at the locket in my hand. "I'm so sorry she's gone, Ray," she says, using the nickname she gave me, like, forever ago.

"I know," I say, sadly. "Me too."

Ana puts the packaged outfit back down on the bed. "Do you want to go for a walk? Just the two of us?"

I almost snort. "Yeah. I'd love that. Never gonna happen."

"I'm serious," Ana says, diving across the bed to her own bags. She pulls out a brown wig, a pair of Jackie O sunglasses and a Burberry mac. "I came prepared."

"It's beige," I pout. "I would never wear beige."

"Exactly," she says, bouncing back up to her feet. "It's a disguise. You're not supposed to look like you."

I shake my head. "Tried that before, remember? It didn't work. It never does. And they know I'm staying here, don't they? Chuck made sure of that. The whole damn world knows the Birds are staying at the Ritz Carlton."

I stride across to the window, pull back the curtains and gesture out the window without even looking. Ana rolls her eyes and reluctantly follows my pointed finger. I can hear the crowd gathered below so I know what she's looking at.

"Yes," she nods. "This does complicate things. But, come on, Ray. How good will it feel to sneak past them all, none of them any the wiser? We could go to a little café, or a quiet park, just… somewhere outside and not cooped up in this stifling building."

"You feel it too, huh?"

Ana steps towards me and takes hold of both my hands.

"Ray," she says quietly. "I always feel it. It's claustrophobic; it's oppressive. You are pushed around like cattle at a market, and worked to the freaking bone. These hotels that I used to think were so glitzy and decadent, they don't shine anymore for me. I've seen what lies behind them, and it's not happiness. It's deep dissatisfaction. It's a ravenous need to be better than everyone else, and that's miserable. You're miserable."

"Not all the time," I say, defensively.

"No, that's true. When you're up on that stage, or at the meet and greets, you are incredibly happy—you come to life. But all the other times—and there are *a lot* of other times—you're miserable, you're lonely, you're creatively starved. I'm the only person in the world who doesn't envy your life."

"But I'm not lonely," I protest. "I have you and Billy."

She smiles, sadly. "You do. You really do. We love you Ray, so much. But, you know we won't be here forever. Billy has to leave for school in a few days, and I can only stay long enough to help you settle, then I have go help Mom in the store."

"If it's the money, Ana, I can pay you…" I say, clutching at straws.

"I know you can," she replies, sternly. "And you know I'd never take it. Mom needs the help. Ever since Aunt May stepped down, she hasn't been able to find anyone reliable to do the deliveries. I just need to help her get back on track and find someone decent to take over Aunt May's work, then I can come back, ok?"

I would offer Ana's mom money too if it wouldn't totally offend her, because I'm desperate. When Billy and Ana leave, I will have no one. No one except my parents, who have both become strangers to me over the five years since the success of my first single. Our relationship now is all business. Chuck, my stepfather, is my manager. I was fifteen when I first hit the number one spot with *Break His Heart* and I had no idea about managing the finance side of things, or my schedule. In a way, I was lucky my mom met him—he took over the business of being Aurelia Bird.

But then my time was taken up rehearsing and recording all the new material he arranged for me, making appearances on talk shows and networking with anyone he saw fit to boost my career. I was to be the next Britney Spears. It didn't matter that I wasn't even born when she got her first number one. When my best friends leave, it will be just me. Me and Grams, who lives in a bloody locket.

"Where is Billy?" I ask, changing the subject. "He took off while I was in the press briefing."

"Oh, he just found out one of his cousins is staying downtown. He's gone to meet them for a coffee. He'll be back later. Anyway, what do you say?" she asks, reaching for the wig and waving it in my face. "Fancy being someone else for an hour or two?"

I sigh in surrender. "Fine. I'll give it a try. But it won't work. Don't say I didn't warn you."

TEN MINUTES LATER, Ana has transformed me into a sophisticated French woman with a glossy chestnut bob, thick black shades, a crisp beige trench, ankle grazer jeans and white sneakers. She's dressed the same, but with a navy jacket, a blonde elfin wig—a total change from her usual long dark plait—and geeky red-rimmed glasses. Ana has been with me for so much of my career, she's almost as recognizable as I am, so we agreed she should disguise herself too.

"No!" I hiss, as she propels me through the lobby towards the main entrance. "Are you crazy? There are about a thousand people out there."

She turns and lowers her voice. "We can't exactly take a back exit, can we? It will look so suspicious. Like, who are these two girls sneaking through our kitchens? The best deception happens right under the nose."

"Whatever you say, Sherlock," I groan. I follow her but make a point of seeking out one of Chuck's security team standing near the entrance. At least I can run to him if this doesn't work.

"Chin up," Ana hisses under her breath as we near the doors. "If you look as though you're hiding something, people will suspect you are."

I hold my breath as a doorman opens the heavy glass doors and Ana steps through, me following close on her heels. We may be wearing disguises, but they are eye catching ones at that, so we attract a few glances as we make our way through the crowd. But, I do as Ana says and keep my chin up, looking straight ahead, willing my heart rate to slow the hell down. I haven't ventured anywhere without security since I first hit number one and almost immediately, half the state of Massachusetts seemed to be camped out on my doorstep. That was five years ago. I haven't been without security for a quarter of my whole life. But now, with the crowd thinning out, and no one having seen through the disguise Ana has wrapped around me, I'm beginning to feel an unnerving combination of excitement, freedom and almost paralyzing fear. Ana seems to sense this and reaches behind her to hold my hand. I take it gratefully and she tugs me through the last row of fans all waiting for a glimpse of the popstar who's just managed to sneak past them all unnoticed.

We make it two blocks and turn a corner before we cover our mouths and scream at each other.

"Oh my God, Ray. I didn't think we'd do it!"

"What?" I squeal. "You thought it might not work? And now you tell me?"

"Blind optimism," she giggles, taking my hand and pulling me along the sidewalk. "It'll get you everywhere."

I let her drag me another two blocks until we reach a park with a large marina beyond it. Ana leads me to a quiet spot on the outer edge of the park and we sit down beneath a cluster of palm trees. I breathe in deeply and stretch my legs out in the shade.

"This couldn't be more different to Middlesex County."

"Right? The vibe for a start. It's just gorgeous here," Ana sighs. She removes her giant sunglasses and rests them on the grass beside her.

I watch her close her eyes and hold her face up to the sun peeking through the leaves. "I envy you, you know."

She snaps her head back to me. "Why?"

"You can just take off your glasses like that and, I don't know, be yourself."

She looks around. "You can do it too. No one'll see. It's really quiet here."

I feel both courageous and petrified as I do the same, removing my glasses and placing them on the ground. I lean back on my elbows and relish the anonymity, the freedom of my face being uncovered and open, in public. "This is awesome. Thank you, Ana."

"What for? Thank Miami, not me," she grins, laying back and stretching her arms overhead.

"I would never have done this if you hadn't been so persuasive."

She gives me a sidelong glance. "I was as desperate to get out of that place as you were."

I lay back too, relaxing into the warm grass. "Are you looking forward to going home?" I ask, quietly.

Ana rolls onto her side to face me. "Would you be upset if I said yes?"

"Of course not." I stare up at the palm leaves dancing in the blue sky. "I'm sad you're leaving but I think it's great your mom has you to help her out. Will you give Mrs. Willis a big kiss from me?"

"You know it. She sends her love—I can tell you that already," Ana grins. She rolls onto her back again and takes a breath. "I hate leaving you," she whispers.

"I'll be fine." She doesn't answer but I can hear her shallow breathing. "I honestly will be. Starling Key is beautiful. It has a really cool, laid-back vibe, and the staff seem nice."

"Yeah," she breathes out. "They do. And I think you'll be

safe with Isaac. He doesn't look like he'd be easily bought by Chuck. And he was soooo hot, girl."

"Who, the security guy?"

"Um, yeah." She fans her face to emphasize her point.

"Right. I didn't notice. I guess I was more concerned about the way he was with my parents. You can tell a lot about how someone's going to turn out by how much they suck up to the management, you know?"

"Yeah, I guess. He didn't seem too impressed with your mom and Chuck, actually."

"No," I giggle. "I liked that."

Ana sits up and brushes blades of grass from her elbows. "I think you'll be fine. I have a good feeling about it."

I sit up too and we both stare out at the marina. There's something about being near open water that soothes my soul. I can't wait for more of this when I get to Starling Key.

"Excuse me," a small voice ventures behind us. Ana and I spin around to see a young girl, and who appears to be her father, standing behind looking at us expectantly. "It is you, isn't it? Aurelia Bird?"

"Shit," Ana mutters under her breath.

"It's ok," I mutter back. "She's only young."

I get to my feet and walk over to the young girl who instantly flushes beet red. "Hi, I'm Aurelia," I say, bending down to her level. She is shaking like a leaf. "What's your name?"

"Ag… Ag… Ag…."

"It's Agnes," her father answers.

"Agnes? What a beautiful name."

The girl sniffs and I can sense tears brewing behind her eyes. Even after five years, I still don't get why people react to me this way. I'm a living, breathing human being exactly like them. I just sing on a stage for a living, that's the only difference.

"Would you like a selfie, Agnes?"

I look up at her father to check it's ok and see Ana in the corner of my eye pacing on the spot. Her father nods and offers his phone. I crouch next to the girl, holding the phone up to face us. "Smile!" I say, softly. She manages a very small one before she bursts into tears. "Hey! It's ok," I say, putting my arms around her. "It's ok, Agnes."

A couple minutes pass and I can sense Ana having a conniption behind me. "It's so nice to meet you," I say, pulling away from the hiccupping girl. I stand and give the father an apologetic smile, then join Ana to walk out of the park.

"Put these on," she orders, handing me my sunglasses. I do as she says and we walk quickly back along the road towards the hotel. "I have a bad feeling."

"A bad feeling about what?"

"As nice as those people were, they have your photo. It's probably on social media already, location tagged and all."

We get one block away and the sound of stampeding feet freezes me to the spot. The source of the sound is not yet visible. Ana and I look at each other. Even behind the sunglasses, I can tell she is freaking out. She spins around to scan the area; Ana was always quicker on her feet than me.

"Down there," she hisses, pointing to a back road filled with dumpsters. "Go hide. I'll send someone to find you."

I stare at her. *Is she out of her mind?* The sound of running feet gets closer. "Go!" she hisses.

I spin in my sneakers and run down the back alleyway, keeping as close to the dumpsters as I can in case I need to dive behind one of them. I turn back and see Ana looking straight ahead, her posture rigid. I keep running, dodging bits of trash that have likely been dragged out of the dumpsters by vermin. I look back again and Ana is nowhere to be seen. Instead, there's a giant mob of people in her place. *Shit.* I keep running until I realize I'm close to the end of the alley and right around the corner from the Ritz Carlton. I can hear chanting so there is still a crowd outside the hotel. I take a left, hoping to get in through a back exit, then I hear someone yell. "She's there!"

I turn to see another group of people appear in the alley to my right. It's one thing to be courteous to a lone fan, a young girl who chances upon me in the middle of a quiet park, but I've been in the business long enough now to know it's a whole other thing to find yourself mobbed by a group of people fanatical enough to stand outside a hotel for hours—days even—waiting for a slight glimpse. My legs burn as I run as fast as I can to the back of the hotel. I look over my shoulder to see the group flying up behind me, and when I spin back around, I slam into something large and solid. An arm wraps around me, lifting me up and over a thick, broad shoulder, and again we're running.

"I've got her. I need back-up. Side exit. Five seconds."

I would cry with relief if I wasn't hyperventilating so badly. We burst through a fire exit and keep running down a concrete corridor. Three security guards pass us heading for the exit. I can't see them but I hear commotion as the group of fans slam against the closed door. A gun fires and finally, my tears fall.

I doubt anyone is going to be hurt but to think all this is my fault almost cripples me. We eventually reach my parents' suite on the top floor and the security guard—who I now recognize as my stepfather's number one, Franklin—lowers me to the couch, where I sit, trembling.

Chuck emerges from another room and comes to sit opposite me, frown lines indented on his brow, and waits until my sobs slow a little.

"What the hell were you thinking?" His voice is low and menacing.

"Ana..." is all I can say.

"Forget Ana," he rumbles. "What *the hell* were you thinking?"

"I wasn't... I wasn't thinking," I stammer. "I was stupid. I shouldn't have gone outside. We were stupid."

"Damn right you were. Who's idea was it?"

I look up at Chuck, finally, to see him glaring at me with a venom I haven't seen before. "Does it matter?"

"So it was Ana's."

"No," I fluster. "No, it was my idea. Don't blame Ana for this. She tried to talk me out of it."

"So why was none of this..." he scans his appalled eyes over my outfit, "*shit* packed in your bags? Huh?"

"I knew that you or someone else would probably find it. I made Ana pack it."

"You just said you hadn't thought about pulling this ridiculous stunt. But now you're saying you two had planned this?"

I look back at him, sheepishly. I know I've landed us both in serious trouble. The best I can do now is say nothing.

"She leaves. Today. And you will not see her again until after the residency."

"What? That's in almost five months!" I gasp.

"Exactly. She is a bad influence, Aurelia. I will not have anyone put you at risk like that again under my watch. Do you understand?"

"Wh—what about Billy?"

"Him too. I need complete focus from you. I don't need idiot kids from back home who have no idea what it's like to manage a multi-billion dollar music career, getting in the way, thinking they know what's best for you."

My voice feels squeezed. "They don't get in the way," I whisper.

"Of course that's what you think. You can't be objective. That's why you have me."

"Where's Mom?" I ask, sheepishly. Maybe Mom could get Chuck to see reason. Not that she really helps on that front anymore. She's more interested in shopping and lunching with her so-called friends than defending me to my stepfather.

"She's out. And she will agree with me anyway, so don't even think of trying to get out of this through your mother." He gets up to end the conversation. "You'll thank me for this one day."

He gives me one last disappointed glare then walks out of the room as smoothly as he walked in.

I watch him leave then drop my gaze to my fingers which are still trembling. He's just removed the only support I had. I doubt that the 'one day' he refers to will ever come.

CHAPTER THREE

Isaac

I WALK into the offices early, determined to get a bunch of stuff out of the way before Aurelia Bird arrives. It's been two months since she came to recce the place—not nearly enough time for me to get my head around what I've set myself up for, let alone the wrath of Paris Navitsky that I've incurred along the way. I walk into my office, put on the light, and jump the hell out of my skin.

"Carter? That you?"

A large lump is laying on my couch with its back to the doorway. I hear it groan. At least it's alive. I walk past it to my desk, sit down and boot up my computer, entering a gazillion different passwords to get through the gazillion different security walls Jaxon installed.

"Time is it?" The lump grumbles.

"Five-fifteen," I reply, opening the team planner. I'm going to need someone to take over my shift in the casino this afternoon; I don't know how long Aurelia is going to want to stick around. It's her first day; she might want to make the most of it. Or at least get away from her parents.

"And you got up this early out of *choice*?"

I spin my chair around and Carter is sitting up now, rubbing his eyes. When he's finally done scrubbing at himself, he looks up. His bloodshot eyes could stop traffic. "Man," I chuckle, "that is an ad for rubbers if ever I saw one." He and his girlfriend Seleste just had a baby. Gorgeous little thing. Has her mama's golden Cuban skin and her dada's crazy long eyelashes. She's only a couple months old and she's already breaking hearts, and grown men by the looks of poor Carter.

"Asshole," he huffs.

"I'd ask how it's going but the bags under your eyes tell quite the story."

"Are you gonna stop being an ass and get me some coffee?"

"Oh, I'm sorry. This is an office, not the Four Seasons. You really are tired, bud." He sighs and sinks his face into his hands. I relent. I don't have it in me to be a bona-fide dick, not when my friend is going through such a hard time. "Black, triple shot?"

"Fuck. Yes."

I get us two coffees from the machine, hand one to him and turn back to my screen. "How's it all going, seriously?" I ask, running through the planner looking for anyone who might be free later.

"Man, it's the weirdest thing. She's amazing. I mean, like nothing else. I love her more than I've ever loved anything in my life. But that whole thing about sleeping like a baby? I don't know where that came from, dude. Not my baby. She's allergic to sleep, Isaac. It's killing me."

"I'm sorry, man. I don't know what to say," I reply. I notice Luca has a free afternoon and I fire him a quick email, before turning back to Carter. "How long do you think it will go on for?"

Carter is taking large gulps of his coffee, like it's a life-saving elixir. "No one knows. We've been Googling all kinds of shit. Some people say they grow out of it after a few weeks, others say they never do. Man, if nothing changes soon, I'm gonna go insane."

"You're doing great, Carter. Trust me. You're raising a whole other human. How's Seleste doing?"

"Better than me. She's a natural with Safia, but she's struggling with tiredness too."

"Is there anything you can give to Safia? Like, I don't know, do they do sleep tablets for babies?" I take it from the glare Carter is shooting me, that's a no. "Ok, listen," I level with him. "Is there anything I can do? I want to help."

"I could really do with a couple more hours' sleep," he says, weakly. "At least if I get some rest before my shift, I can go home with a bit more energy to help Seleste. She's managing on her own all day."

"Is the triple strength injection of caffeine you just took really going to help with that?" I'm skeptical.

"Isaac, I could fall asleep on speed right now."

"Ok," I grin, sympathetically, undocking my laptop. "I'll go sit in the café. You sleep here for a while. There's a blanket under the couch."

"Won't the café be closed?"

I jangle a set of keys at him. "Not for long."

"Isaac," he says, as I open the door. I turn back to face him. "You are the biggest fucking lifesaver, you know? I owe you big time."

"I'll remember that," I wink, then softly close the door.

I SIT at the back of the café, out of view of the main seating area, so I don't have to bother moving when the early risers descend in a couple of hours. I bury my head in figures, moving money to and from various accounts, covering tracks and metaphorically cleaning it as I go. Our biggest under-the-radar client and Miami mobster, Mario Bianchi, asked me on the sly to do a little laundering for him. I'm good, I'm discreet, but above all, with an esteemed career in the CIA behind me, I'm connected. Connor and the boys know what I'm doing, and as long as it's a short term gig, they're happy for me to do the work. The few extra grand in their pockets doesn't do much to dissuade them either.

"Working hard, as always," comes a familiar voice. I look up to see Elijah, the barista, standing over me holding a steaming cup of coffee. "You look like you need fueling, honey," he winks.

"You're too good to me, Elijah," I say, winking back. We have a mild flirtation thing going on, even though he knows guys don't float my boat. I love him, regardless.

"I can't have my favorite bodyguard passing out from exhaustion now, can I?"

"That's not going to happen anytime soon," I smile.

"Not if you keep pounding those weights at the gym," he purrs, his eyes crawling over my biceps.

"I do it for you," I say, taking a grateful sip of the coffee.

"Oh, stop it, you do not," Elijah says, flicking his head and pretending to stomp away in a huff.

I return to my screen and immerse myself once more. I shift a few things around in Starling's end-of-week report, then turn my attention to the ticket sales for Aurelia's residency. We sold out a three month run and had to add more dates only last week. I'm hoping to God she has the strength and the stamina to perform for such a long period. She looked to me like she'd blow over in a gentle breeze; I have my doubts she can maintain a residency for longer than twelve weeks.

"Honey, did you let it go cold?"

"Shit, I'm sorry, Elijah. I got carried away with this stuff. Any chance I can get a fresh one?"

"No problem," he says. "Oh, by the way," he adds, "that young starlet of yours is over by the window attracting her fair share of attention."

"Aurelia Bird?" I ask, surprised. "She wasn't supposed to be here for another three hours." I crane my neck to follow Elijah's gaze. I recognize her instantly. She's sitting, like a ray of glitzy sunshine, baby blonde hair framed by the light from the window, chatting to two female guests. She's wearing tiny shorts, a tank top that exposes her midriff and thick black sunglasses. She looks about thirteen. I roll my eyes as it dawns on me again what I've signed myself up for. I'm basically looking after a toddler for three, actually, no, *four* months. At least she's being polite to our guests, though, and not diva-ish like some of the other A-list celebrities we've had on the island.

"Forget the coffee, Elijah. But thanks."

I shut my laptop and stand, tucking it under my arm, then I make my way over to her.

The closer I get, the more I take in. Her glittering laugh and bright teeth, slender shoulders and enthusiastic bob of her head as she talks. I stand behind the guests, waiting for them to finish their chat. I can't tell if Aurelia has seen me because her sunglasses cover her eyes like a shield. Eventually, the women thank her for talking to them, take a few selfies with their phones and shuffle away with their take-out lattes, chattering excitedly.

"Hi," I say, facing her. "I wasn't expecting you for a couple more hours. How was the journey?"

She pushes her sunglasses up her forehead where they rest on a soft cushion of almost-white hair. Her rich hazel eyes are warm and I notice she wears no make-up at all. There's a smattering of freckles over the bridge of her nose and her lips elongate into a delicate smile. If I was ten years younger, I might have thought she was cute. She's true to her brand image—squeaky clean, perky, and virginal. For most men, the dream girl.

"It was great, thank you. Please, sit," she says. I take the chair opposite her.

"How are you feeling about the residency?" I settle back. I'm not officially on duty so I decide to take some time to get to know this girl I'm going to be shadowing for the next few months.

"Good! Really good," she beams. "I haven't done anything like this before. The closest thing was the world tour last year. It wasn't back-to-back like this will be, but the traveling was pretty exhausting. It's going to be nice to settle in one place for a while."

"And I can think of worse places to settle for a while," I grin.

"Right? This place is idyllic." She looks out of the window giving me a view of her profile—a dainty, slightly upturned nose, perky chin and long, natural lashes. I'm not used to seeing youthful features since I'm mostly fixated on older women. I'm fascinated.

Catching myself, I turn the conversation straight to business. "What's on your agenda today? You father sent me your schedule—"

"My *step*father." She turns back to me with a thin smile. "But I prefer to have him referred to as my manager if that's ok?"

"Of course. Your *manager* sent me your schedule, but there was some detail lacking that I'd like to discuss with you, so we can plan a sufficient protection detail while you're on site."

"Of course. I'm happy to fill in any gaps."

"Your first live performance is two weeks from today," I begin. "The concert hall has been closed off for rehearsals. When do you plan to start?"

"Today," she replies. "My dancers should be here by ten and we have rehearsals after lunch. My voice coach is arriving at four, and my publicist in an hour or so. Will you be able to accompany me to my PR meeting? It might give you a bit more insight into what I do." A smile tugs at one corner of her mouth. "But you don't have to stick around for rehearsals as Benji is here today too."

I figure Benji is the big, suited guy sitting in the far corner of the café watching us closely.

"No, it's fine. I can be with you until five p.m., then I have an appointment I can't miss, I'm afraid." *Otherwise, Mario Bianchi will ensure that is all the cover she's going to get from me, ever.*

"Great!" She seems delighted as she takes a delicate sip of her water.

"Will your friends be joining you? I'll need to know who's going to be around and when."

Her faces falls. "No. They won't." She casts her eyes down so I can't meet them, or attempt to read them. I don't press further; it isn't my business.

"What about your parents? I mean, your mother and your manager?"

"My mother will be staying in Miami until the first live show. My manager will probably come and go. I have no sight of his schedule so it's difficult to know when he'll be here."

"Do you have an assistant?" I ask, surprised at how small her entourage is compared to the last time she showed up.

"Yes," she nods. "Sort of. I share her with my manager, but most of the time I tend to look after myself."

It strikes me as odd how alone this girl appears to be, despite having millions of fans around the world who would kill to be around her. And I don't use the word 'kill' lightly. I've been in this business long enough to know to what exact lengths some people will go to get close to their idols.

"Have you eaten?" I ask, changing the subject. She unclenches one of her hands and reveals an empty protein bar wrapper. "That's it?" No wonder she's as slender as a rake.

"For now," she grins. "I'd drop dead if this was all I lived on."

I narrow my eyes, confused.

"Have you seen any of my performances?"

I refuse to feel mortified by the fact I haven't. Knowing exactly what she does on stage does not make me a better bodyguard. "No."

She doesn't seem at all offended by this. "Well, I dance a lot. So I eat a lot. You don't need to worry about that. All you need to worry about is whether or not someone's coming up behind me with a machete." She bursts into laughter, clearly having cracked herself up.

I allow myself a grin, then get straight back onto more professional footing. "It's not machetes you need to be concerned about—they're hard to miss. Have you ever had a problem with stalkers? Or have there been any threats I need to be aware of?"

She takes another sip of her water then closes her eyes in thought. When she doesn't open them for a while, I ask if she's ok. Her eyes ping open. "I'm counting."

"That many, huh?" I shouldn't be surprised. This kind of thing is par for the course for someone as high profile as Aurelia Bird.

"Since my first single, *Break His Heart,* came out five years ago, I've had forty-nine stalkers."

"*Forty-nine*?" I feel like my eyes are popping out of my head.

"Ten a year, on average, some more threatening than others. They definitely got worse this last year though when I began to make changes to my image."

"What kind of changes?" I ask, clueless.

"Changes that reflect the fact I'm no longer a kid, you know? I can't continue to be this cutesy, do-good, girl-next-door 'til I'm fifty. No one wants to see that," she laughs again. "My lyrics are more mature now, I got a new choreographer, and a new stylist. Sometimes it's just subtle things like, I don't wear pigtails on stage anymore." She flicks her hair about to make the point. "And my make-up is a little heavier."

My mind is reeling trying to take in this whole other language I've never been interested in before. Coming of age, I guess it's called. I came of age earlier than most, after Mom left. I didn't have to put strategic thought into it like Aurelia is doing; it happened seemingly overnight. Then again, I wasn't confronting a potential billion dollar impact on my income.

"So, anyway," she continues, "Turns out some people *really* don't like that. They want me to stay virginal forever." She shakes her head. "And of course, they think because I'm in the public eye, they own me. Not all of them, just a select few."

I want to say I can't imagine what that must be like, but I don't. I've worked with other celebrities who've struggled with stalkers and threats, but never in such high numbers. I don't want her to think I'm not qualified to be her detail, so I say nothing and instead open my laptop to take down some notes.

"We managed to get restraining orders out on most of them, a couple are serving time," she shrugs. "There are a couple I need to keep an eye on."

"Like who? Have they made specific threats?" I ask, my fingers flying over the keys as I catalog every word.

"Not yet. At the moment, it's mainly name-calling. I'm a whore, and a slut, of course."

"What makes you say 'not yet'?"

"Because there's a pattern most stalkers follow. They start out nice, pledging their undying love. When you don't respond in the way they want, they get intense. '*But we're meant to be together. I'm your soulmate; it's fate*.' She says this with a whiny voice and a curled lip and it's almost comical. "Then, you know, it's time to cut all communication with them, which obviously, they hate. Then, it's all '*you're talentless, you're nothing without me, you're making the biggest mistake of your life*', blah blah blah. And then they move onto the name-calling, and then come the threats."

I watch her talk, conscious my eyes are wide. What this girl has seen and become accustomed to, by the mere age of nineteen, is mind-blowing.

"Depending on the stalker, the threats can be relatively harmless. You know, '*I'm going to write to the local paper and tell them all your secrets*', etcetera. But others graduate to the death threats pretty quickly, and that's when we have to get the cops involved."

"You only get the cops involved at that point?" I'm stunned.

She cocks her head to one side, her expression one of mild amusement. "It's the only way they'll take me seriously. If I called the cops every time someone called me a whore, they'd get tired of me pretty quickly. It's like the boy who cried wolf. I don't need the cops to roll their eyes at me when the real wolf shows up."

I can feel the hair on the back of my neck bristle, and can't help but admire her maturity. She lives with this every day, I think. And Joe Public out there has absolutely no idea.

"How do they make the threats? Do you have evidence?"

"Oh, various ways. Some are old school," she says, reaching into a duffel bag by her feet. "Some are handwritten —different pen types and styles, of course—while others are made from letters that have been cut out of magazines and glued on. I kinda like those," she says, shaking her head. "They make me feel like Whitney Houston in *Bodyguard*. Like, someone cares so much, they've gone to all the trouble of cutting out individual letters and words and sticking them all together to make a message." She slaps a pile of notes on the table and looks out of the window, wistfully. "All I need now is my very own Kevin Costner."

"Doesn't he part ways with Whitney Houston at the end?" I ask, taking the notes and flicking through them, carefully.

"I don't remember," she sighs. "Doesn't matter anyway. It's a fairy tale. Happy endings don't happen in real life, do they?" She drinks the rest of her water while, for some reason, I commit those words to my memory. They resonate, and I don't know why.

CHAPTER FOUR

Aurelia

I WATCH Isaac quietly as he reads through the threatening notes. I can sense he is not a fan of the *Bodyguard* reference, and I don't doubt he's had his fair share of female clients wanting that same storyline from him. But I am not one of them.

I just want to be protected by someone I can trust. Someone who is not affiliated with my stepfather for once. He's always been strict and more business-minded than fatherly, but his refusal to let me see Ana and Billy was a step too far. I have the horrible feeling he did that out of spite and not for my protection or benefit.

"I'd like to make a change to the contract, before we begin." I feel nervous saying this. I've never dealt with the money side of my business before—that has always been Chuck's domain. But, since his refusal to let me see my friends, I've decided I need to carve out a little independence. Paying for my own security is priority number one.

Isaac looks up. "What kind of change?"

"To the payment. You'll be paid directly from my personal account, not the company's."

His face betrays nothing. "Fine. Just email me the new details and I'll make the adjustment."

"Thank you. And if I may, can I ask that you don't notify my manager of this?" I hold my breath, waiting for his reaction.

His eyes soften. "Of course." He rests his forearms on the table, bringing his face closer to mine. He has a face that I would be happy looking at every day for the next four months, I decide. Sure, he's a lot older than me, and has clearly lived a whole other life, but his features are sharp, his skin is that pristine shade of olive with the glow that comes with Italian blood. And his eyes… I've never seen such arcs of darkness that are both terrifying and reassuring all at the same time. "Aurelia," he says, softly. "Is there anything I need to be aware of?"

I shake my head, timidly. I've never spoken about this with anyone. "No, it's just that, I don't have access to my money yet, really. Most of it, my rights and royalties, are being held in a trust until my twentieth birthday—five years from the launch of my first single. That's when it will transfer to my company, Bird Holdings, Inc. In the meantime, Chuck manages the money I make from live performances, merchandise and the like, to pay for staff and the various agencies that work for us. He gives me an allowance so I can buy stuff for myself. I'll pay you out of that."

"Of course. I don't mind how we are paid. But, surely there are tax benefits to paying us from the company accounts?"

"I guess." I have no idea, really, but I know one thing for sure. The further away I keep Isaac from my manager, the less likely it is he'll feel obliged to do Chuck's dirty work. I lower my voice and my eyes. "But, I want to have full control over this contract. My security needs to be in my own interest, not anyone else's." I know it's a cryptic response, but I also know Isaac isn't stupid. He'll know there's more to my reasoning than I'm letting on.

My phone buzzes. "It's Carla," I tell Isaac. "My publicist. She's at the gate. Where should I tell her to go?"

"Tell her to head for the main reception. We'll go there now and we can use one of the meeting rooms."

I type out the brief message while Isaac finishes reading the notes, then we walk out of the café. I'm grateful there is an older clientele here during the day so I'm not likely to be hassled too much. We pass Benji on the way out and I tell him to come back for me at five p.m. He nods briefly, unsmiling.

"So, have you always worked in security?" I ask Isaac as we walk across the immaculately preened grounds.

"Yeah, in some capacity for the last fifteen years. Before I came here I was with the CIA for ten years."

I stop short. "The CIA?" For some reason, my chest just did a somersault. "That's kinda hot," I say, before I can stop myself.

He laughs at that while I force a blush from my cheeks. "It's anything but hot when you're in it."

"I can imagine." I chew my lip. "Actually, I can't imagine. It's so far removed from anything I've ever experienced."

"Well, you make a living being very, very visible. I made a living trying to be the exact opposite. It's just different."

"Why did you leave?" I watch his face as he thinks through his reply.

"I wanted a change. It's easy to burn out doing that kind of work. I got out before that happened." He blinks down at me. "I'm glad I did. You get to see a lot more sun when you're not hiding out in some basement for weeks on end."

"I'd love to hear more about it," I say, honestly.

"Well, you'll have plenty of opportunities." He arches an eyebrow as he politely holds open the door to the main building.

"I'll hold you to that," I wink as I pass.

Carla is already in the reception lobby when we arrive, talking to a pretty young woman with gorgeous red hair piled on top of her head. She introduces herself as Tawny, and tells us she manages events on the island. Not the big ones—concerts and the like—but smaller ones like excursions and seasonal holiday events. She tells me that someone called Alana looks after the larger scale events and will be my point of contact.

I remember Alana from our last visit. She was obliging, and handled my stepfather with a light, professional touch, but she was sharp too. She had an answer for everything and a nerve that never wavered, even when Chuck's attitude towards her was borderline insulting. I remember him instructing her to refill his coffee after lunch. Her reply was epic. *Oh, Mr. Bird, don't tell me you're not itching to take a look around the place? The coffee pot is just outside, sir, and I won't tell if you happened to take a little detour around the grounds, maybe to the spa…* She smiled sweetly and he was at a loss for a response. He disappeared and didn't come back for a good hour and a half. A short window in which we were all able to relax. Mr. Starling included.

I liked Mr. Starling. His jolly laugh and strange British way with words made me giggle more than once. He was clearly well-liked among his employees. But something didn't add up. Starling didn't appear to have a clue what was going on across the whole resort, while, weirdly, Connor and Isaac knew everything. It seemed as though it's not Starling who runs this place; it's the security team.

"I'll let Alana know you're here," Tawny says, before politely leaving us to attend to a small group of guests.

"Follow me," Isaac says, leading us through the double doors into the business suites. He shows us to a spacious room looking out to the ocean. There's a small, oval boardroom table which could seat maybe eight people. I don't get to sit in many boardrooms—Chuck has always insisted I focus on the performing—but this isn't my first. I walk to the window and imagine myself swimming out to sea, away from this life, towards something completely unknown. The feeling elicits not relief, as I would have expected, but sadness. Because I still love this life. I still love the singing, the dancing, the entertaining. I just dislike everything else that goes with it.

"Can I get you drinks? Snacks?" Isaac asks.

"I'd love some sparkling water," Carla replies. Isaac disappears then returns with a server in tow. He brings two large bottles of iced water with glasses. A bowl of freshly sliced tropical fruit also appears on the table. I sit and turn my attention to Carla.

"How are you, Carla?" I try to be as pleasant to my publicist as possible, but there always seems to be something in the way that I can't quite put my finger on. She reports to Chuck, really, and I know they will have had a briefing before she travelled down here. I reassure myself Carla is harmless and just doing her job.

"We've got an interview with Miami Beach Radio, in…" she checks her wristwatch—a brand new Rolex, I notice, "twenty minutes. They're so excited you're finally here on the Keys, rehearsing for your residency."

"That's great! Over the phone?"

"I spoke to Connor Johnson," she nods towards Isaac. "He offered me the recording suite in this very building, and someone called Jax is going to help us with the levels."

"Fantastic. What's the key message?"

Carla flicks back her expensively blow-dried shoulder-length curls. "This one's not a biggie. They just want to hear how much you love Florida and the Keys, and how it's the perfect place for your first residency. The local fans you've met so far have been the best and you're looking forward to meeting more of them. You know, that kind of thing."

"Sure," I say, making notes on my tablet.

"Oh, and maybe drop a hint about the compilation we're releasing in eight weeks. It wouldn't hurt to get some buzz going for that."

"Compilation?" I look up, surprised. "What compilation?"

"Chuck updated us all at last week's huddle. The record company is releasing a limited edition compilation of all your top ten hits."

"R—really?" I sink back into my chair, feeling metaphorically slapped. "Why hasn't anyone thought to tell me?"

I sense Isaac, who's sitting by the door, watching and listening intently, and I half-wonder what he's making of all this. I also feel embarrassed. It's obvious my management and the teams around me don't value my opinion, or even care that I have one. Maybe a couple years ago I would have happily let something like this slide, because performing really was all I was interested in. But now, as I've gotten a little older, I've started to question things, like, what is my money being spent on? Why aren't we marketing this next single in the same way as the last? Why has the number of dancers in my shows halved?

"I, um, I don't know," Carla says. "I thought you knew. I'm sorry. It must have slipped someone's mind, I'm sure it's an innocent mistake."

"Are there any plans to record new material for this record?"

"Not that I'm aware of." Carla's face has warmed so much I could fry an egg on it.

"I don't like the idea of putting out a new record with only old material," I say. "My fans deserve better than that, surely."

"I don't know. I guess so."

"I wasn't asking," I say, surprising myself with the firmness of my tone. I let the silence linger—another new feeling for me. Normally, I hate silence, especially of the uncomfortable kind, but I want Carla to realize how I feel. This is my career we're talking about, my image and my fans.

"Is there anything else?" I ask, finally.

Clara looks relieved. She reaches into her bag and pulls out a folder. "No other interviews this week. That will all build up next week; I'll send you a schedule. But here are some of the latest clippings we've had." She opens the folder at a page marked with a pink post-it note. "Some positive ones," she explains. "But mostly, they're, um, I hate to say this… A little critical of your latest album. It seems your new style hasn't gone as well as you—*we*—had hoped. I believe this might be another reason why a decision was made to release a compilation—to remind fans… um… why they like you."

"That's strange," I say. "My sales don't seem to have suffered."

"The view of the record company is that fans bought the

new album purely out of curiosity and loyalty, but if they don't like the new material, they won't continue to buy in future. They're worried."

"But critics received the album well," I argue. I know this isn't about the fans. It's about Chuck's fear that anything but a saintly, virginal, people-pleasing pop princess is going to crash and burn, effectively cutting off his financial supply.

Carla takes a deep breath and passes the folder across the table, pausing conversation. I leaf through all the pages, not just those marked out by pink post-its. It doesn't take me long to see she isn't giving me the whole story. "What about this one? Vanity Fair?" I say, pointing at a small opinion column. I read out some of the quote. "*'It's a brave move from someone so young, but it seems to be paying off. The lyrics are intimate and insightful, the performances electric. Bird's confidence is clear and the crowd is hanging on her every word.'* I wouldn't necessarily call that 'critical', would you?"

"Well, um, there are a few positive ones, like I said," she mumbles. "I'm referring to the majority. Anyway, we should probably go and get set up." She stands and reaches out a hand for the folder.

I grip it firmly. "I'll hold onto this, if that's ok?"

"Oh, but, I…"

"Is this not for me?" I ask, innocently.

"Well, yes, I suppose it is."

I stand and look to Isaac to show us the way to the recording suite. He turns to lead us out, but not before I catch his attempt to cover up a wry smile. That small gesture, however disproportionate to the size of my challenge, elicits a giant sense of relief. He gets it. That's all I need for now. He gets it.

CHAPTER FIVE

Isaac

THIS IS MY HAPPY PLACE. This is why I gave up the CIA. I'm sitting on the Starlings' private beach, the jewel in the island's crown, with nothing but white sands and blue seas before me, a good woman at my side, my brothers—aka the Starling Key Security Team—around me drinking cold beers, and the delicious smell of a barbeque sailing past my nostrils. The Starlings have returned to Europe for a break so we've sneakily taken over their private patch of paradise to enjoy a little luxury of our own.

"Isaac, catch!" I look up to see a cold beer flying in my direction. I grab it and snap the lid off with my teeth, catching the bubbles before they overflow. Paris snuggles into my side and runs a manicured hand down my thigh. Tawny is sitting with Carter, Seleste and baby Safia under the shade of a palm, while Connor, Jax and Hud sit behind them arguing about the latest Buccaneers game. Luca is wielding metal cooking utensils like weapons, flipping burgers, lobster and corn, and Maisie, the receptionist from the spa, is walking out of the Grand House with two large bowls filled with potato salad and coleslaw.

I put an arm around Paris and feel her lips against my neck. "So soft," she murmurs.

"You can't still be horny," I whisper. I gave her at least three orgasms before we came over here.

"I'm always horny around you." A finger trails back up my thigh, threatening to stand a certain part of me to attention. I jab my bottle into the sand and place my cold hand over her errant one.

"You really have to learn some patience, Paris," I say, keeping my voice low.

Her big eyes look up at me, innocently. "Why?"

It reminds me who she is and, more to the point, who she's married to. Paris Navitsky never has to wait for anything. If she wants a night out in London, *that evening*, a private jet will be laid on within the hour. If she wants a quick nip and tuck, Roman clicks his fingers—or, his Amex—and it can happen that day. If she wants a brand new Bentley imported, she'll be bumped to the top of the waiting list. She doesn't know what patience is. She doesn't need to.

"Because…" I want to say that I can't be bought like everything else, but instead I say, "It's not often we get to sit on this beach and I haven't spent time with the guys in a while."

She withdraws her hand. "And we both know why that is, don't we?"

"Paris," I sigh. "We've been through this. I hadn't expected Aurelia to take up so much of my time. I'm sure as she settles in, and the live shows get underway, she'll want to spend more time with her family."

"You're sure. Right. We'll see."

I shake my head, feeling the return of the familiar dark cloud that has been hovering over Paris and I since Aurelia arrived.

Things have been going well otherwise. Connor has found someone to take over the bulk of my other duties while Aurelia is here, and working with the young pop star has been surprisingly ok so far. She's sweet enough, she's hardworking, and she's nothing like the diva I expected her to be. She's obviously aware of her fame, but she hasn't let it go to her head. Not like her parents seem to. She's been prompt, polite, considerate and friendly with me. She's been utterly lovely with the small team she works with every day—her choreographer, her backup dancers, her costume assistants and stylist. She's always asking how they're feeling and if there's anything they need. Some of them are a long way from home and even younger than she is. She displays a maternal streak beyond her years towards them and I wonder if she is the same with her young twin sisters. I find myself wondering about a lot. More than I had expected to. I put it down to the fact she's blown all my assumptions out of the water, and I actually respect the girl.

The only thing that gets me down is Paris. Well, not Paris herself, but her feelings about the arrangement. She's jealous, even though she knows she has no right to be, but she's having a hard time keeping a handle on her feelings. I've already had to replace a porcelain dish, two champagne flutes and a crystal tumbler after she threw them at the wall of the Hemingway villa when we navigated the first few days of Aurelia's arrival. What I love about Paris—the passion, the fire, the frenzy—are becoming things I find I don't have a lot of patience for anymore. Ironically.

My mind drifts back to that morning. I was watching Aurelia rehearse for the fifth day in a row. The choreographer was correcting the steps and the moves every two seconds, but to me, the whole performance looked perfect, seamless. Despite the repetition and the sweat, Aurelia didn't falter once. Her dancers took turns to sit out of some rehearsals, but not Aurelia. She kept going like a long-life battery. And on the rare occasions I diverted my gaze from the surrounding area to her face, I saw immediately why. Every time she flipped around, ducked and weaved, spun, kicked, gyrated her hips, she looked the happiest I'd ever seen anyone. And so utterly in control. The sweat poured off her, but she didn't care, she didn't stop. She just laughed, took a giant swig of water and hopped back to the starting position every time.

Halfway through rehearsing, they took a break and Aurelia wandered across to me.

"So, what do you think?" She took another long glug of water.

"About what?" I replied, avoiding her eyes while maintaining a watch of the surrounding area, the doors, the roadies.

"The dancing?" I heard a grin. "You think we're getting any better, or should we just quit now?" Her laugh lit up the air around us and I marveled at how infectious her energy was when she was immersed in her work.

"I can't say I've noticed," I said, teasing.

"Are you telling me, Isaac D'Amico, you haven't even snuck a peek? There are some hot dancers up on that stage."

I dragged my eyes to hers and arched an eyebrow. "I'm

working, Aurelia Bird. But, if you want my opinion, which probably doesn't count for much since I don't know squat about dancing, I would say you couldn't get any better."

She tucked the bottle under her arm and clapped her hands together gleefully, as though a dear uncle had just given her the biggest compliment ever. It made me feel old. And strangely warm. I resolved to keep my eyes on the floor and the doors after that.

"YOU DODGED THAT BULLET, HUH?"

I'm shaken out of my reverie to see Luca crouched beside Paris, nodding towards Seleste and baby Safia.

"I sure did," she replies, thinly. "Roman was never interested in having children."

"You get to sleep instead," Luca chuckles. "Or not," he grins across at me.

I playfully punch him and he lands on his ass in the sand. I like how Paris gets along with the team. She might be worth a billion or so dollars but she isn't a snob; she doesn't let her wealth stop her from associating with low-paid security guys.

"What about you, Luca?" she asks. "Think you'll ever have kids?"

"Sure, one day," he says, nonchalantly. "I'm still a baby myself. Not like these ancients," he says, gesturing towards the rest of us guys.

"You're twenty-six—hardly a baby," I retort. "But, yeah, you have plenty of time yet. Enjoy yourself, bro'."

"I plan to."

"How is Autumn these days, anyway?" I know this is going to irritate the hell out of him.

"For the hundredth time, I am not attracted to Autumn Lockhart." His frown and slight flush tells me otherwise, but

I don't ever press. He's loved Autumn forever. Well, at least since she arrived here a couple years ago. She's completely oblivious though and seems to have a weird penchant for stiff, corporate guys in suits, not laid-back surfer dudes in board shorts.

"I'm heading back," Jaxon announces.

"I'll go with you." Hud says, grabbing one of the bags of empty bottles.

"I'm going to walk Seleste back to reception," Tawny says. "A few guests have left gifts for the baby so I'm going to go fetch them."

"A sleep machine by any chance?" Carter sounds hopeful. He bends to kiss the baby on her head then lands a long one on Seleste's lips. "I'll catch you up, chica," he says and a glint appears in her eye.

"Don't you boys let him out of your sight," Seleste calls over her shoulder. "I'm pretty sure he'll jump in a boat the second you turn your back."

"I would never do that." I've never seen Carter pout, but his expression now comes close to it.

"I'm heading to the dive center," Luca announces. "Help Autumn close up."

"I'm gonna leave you boys to it," Paris says beside me. I can detect a hint of defiance in her tone. She's not inviting me to go with her, back to the Hemingway, the most luxurious villa on the island. Her Russian billionaire husband hires it for most of the season so he can keep his wife happy while he carries out his dirty dealings in Miami. She knows I would never invite myself back to the villa; I'm still a member of staff at the end of day. So I suspect I'm being punished, yet again, for taking on the role of Aurelia's full time security.

"Ok, you sure?" I turn to face her fully.

"I am." She gives me a dazzling smile which makes me

question myself. "I need some sleep before Roman comes back tomorrow."

"Of course." Roman's impending returns usually drive Paris into my arms, not away from them, but not this time it seems. I sigh inwardly. I don't know what else I can say to her. I am not attracted to Aurelia Bird, but the money is good, and keeping Aurelia secure will ensure no controversy hits our first residency on Starling Key. My arm stretches out as Paris walks away, until finally, our fingers disentangle and my wrist falls to my thigh. I watch her leave, with mixed feelings. I'm pissed that I won't be spending the night with her, enveloping her tiny body with mine, but I'm annoyed that she feels she has to play me.

So now, it's just me, Connor and Carter.

"So, who's this guy you've found to cover Isaac for the next few months?" Carter asks.

"His name's Axel…" Connor starts.

"Dude—" Carter laughs. "What kind of a name is that? There's literally only one Axel in this world, ok? Axel Rose. No one else can carry that name off."

Connor arches an eyebrow. "When you meet this guy, I guarantee you'll change your mind."

"Who is he?"

"He's friends with a buddy of mine from the Marines. He was a SEAL…"

Carter hisses through his teeth. "Great."

"…but he got kicked out."

"What?" We'd started walking around the side of the Grand House towards the drive, but my grip on Connor's arm stops us all. "Why?"

"He smuggled drugs into Iraq."

"Drugs? How?"

"I'm not sure exactly. There was some distribution

network, he was involved… Well, he actually masterminded the whole thing. I know that much, but I don't know the details."

"Connor, we can't bring that kind of heat to Starling Key." I hope the warning tone in my voice is unambiguous.

"We can hardly talk. Besides, it was five years ago. His rep has been blemish-free ever since."

"What's he been doing in that time?"

"Well…" Connor stalls. "He served time for some of that." I groan and rub my eyes. "Then he just did regular security work and some manual labor. Basically redeeming himself, making an honest living."

"What makes you think he's qualified to do Isaac's job?" Carter says, frowning his doubt.

Connor looks at me pointedly. "Because he has a math major from MIT."

"Are you kidding?" My eyes are wide. "That's hardcore. So, his parents are loaded too, I guess?" As far as I know, MIT is not easy to get into, but money talks.

"Far from it. The guy's an orphan, but a scarily brilliant one. He won a scholarship."

I let out a whistle. "This guy's gonna be better at this than me."

"At math, maybe. But you do so much more than that, Isaac," Connor reassures me. "You will still be missed."

"Yeah, I mean, who are we going to advertise in the brochures now as the complimentary lady sitter?" Carter chuckles. "Not that you've lived up to that role lately, with you and Paris being a thing, and all."

"Yeah, I'm not sure about that," I grumble, as we resume our route up the drive.

"Trouble in paradise?" Carter asks, with a grin.

"You could say so. She's convinced I'm attracted to Aurelia Bird."

Carter snorts. "Dude, doesn't she know you?"

"Hey! As far as she's concerned, she's the only older woman I've had a thing with on the island. I haven't exactly broadcast to her the number of mature ladies I've been in bed with. She assumes she's different—special. And she also can't understand why a red-blooded security guard like me wouldn't find a young, sexy popstar like Aurelia Bird attractive."

Connor and Carter are silent. Connor bites his lip.

"What?" I huff.

"You just called her sexy," Carter grins.

"Only because… well, that's what everyone thinks, isn't it? I mean, I don't. You know she isn't my type."

"You sure about that, Isaac?" Connor asks in a low voice.

"Yes!" I answer, loudly. "Don't you start. Seriously, I've got enough on my plate with Paris."

"But, you gotta admit," Carter says, kicking at the gravel. "You've been kind of a different person these last few days."

"What do you mean?" I frown.

"Like you're less stressed, more easy-going. I don't know, it's hard to explain. It's like you've been feeling lighter, in a way."

I shrug off his observation. "That's just because I have only one job now and I don't have to worry about the balance sheet, or which shift I'm on next, or which petulant reality star I'm going to be covering this week. Life is a lot simpler when you have only one client."

"I guess," Carter replies, but I can hear the doubt in his tone.

"Guys," Connor starts, steering us to the side of the drive. It's dark now and we're standing under one of the lamps we've got dotted along the drive. "I need to talk to you about something."

I look down and notice his hands are shaking and sweat has reappeared on his forehead even though the sun went down hours ago.

"Is everything ok?" I ask.

"Yeah, yeah, everything's fine. It's nothing to worry about. It's just… it's…"

Carter's frown deepens. "Spit it out, Connor."

"I'm going to ask Tawny to marry me," he rushes out.

"What?" Carter gasps. "That's huge! Congratulations! How? When?"

I roll my eyes inwardly. Everyone knows I am of a specific marriage type. I like the *marrieds*, not the *marriables*. "Why so drastic?" I grumble.

Connor glances at me. "I knew I could count on you for support." Then he turns back to Carter. "Well, this is the thing. I know I want to do it, but the idea of *actually doing it* scares the hell out of me. So, I have no idea how and when, just that I know I've found my soulmate and I want a piece of paper that says we're committed. You know?"

"Yeah, I do," Carter says, shooting me an accusatory look.

"I am supportive," I say. "Whatever you want to do, Connor, I'm right behind you. It's not what I would do, obviously, but that doesn't mean I can't be happy for you, man."

"Thanks," Connor replies, looking relieved. "I need help. Seriously. I have no idea how to go about this."

"Have you bought a ring?" Carter asks.

"No. Like, how do I even know what she'll want?"

I break into a smile. For all his perfectionist genius and supposed sex appeal, Connor actually has very little clue about women. "Does she have a favorite stone?"

"Fuck knows. Diamond? Isn't that what they all want?"

Carter shakes his head, fervently. "Not all of them. Seleste likes sapphires. They remind her of everything she's come through to get here, with the trek across the sea and all. Plus, she has a diamond on her ass. My diamond. We got it inked before she left for Miami. So, for her finger, she wants one big sapphire with a small diamond either side, and a yellow gold band. Not platinum."

"You've discussed this?" Connor asks, shocked.

"Yeah, sure we have. I mean, it's not going to happen for a long time. I need some fucking sleep and a win on the lottery first, but we both want to do it at some point."

"Oh fuck. What do I do? I want it to be a total surprise, and it won't be if I have to ask her what kind of ring she wants."

"Leave it with me," Carter says, slapping Connor on the shoulder. He's no more familiar with women than Connor is, but I'm sensing some gleeful superiority on his part for having had *the* conversation already. "If it's ok with you, I can ask Seleste to do some digging. She'll ask Tawny the right questions, she won't raise suspicion. Trust me, she's great at stuff like this, and they've become pretty close."

"Ok," Connor nods, gratefully. "And what about where and how? Proposals are a big deal, right? Do I need to take one of the boats? Hide the ring in a slice of cake?"

No one is particularly interested in my opinion on this matter, which is totally fine by me, but I give it anyway. "That's way too clichéd."

"So, what then?" Connor asks.

A thought springs to mind. I might know exactly how he should do it. Connor will absolutely hate the idea, but Tawny will recognize it as a gesture of epic proportions. But I need more information first. "When do you want to do it?"

"On her birthday. It's eight weeks away."

"Ok," I say, thinking. "I have an idea, but I need to talk to someone before you get your hopes up."

"Thanks guys." Connor lets out a sigh of relief. "What would I do without you two, huh?"

I grin and cross my fingers. I have a very good feeling this might work.

CHAPTER SIX

Aurelia

I FEEL Benji's eyes on me as I make the last few steps down the hotel corridor to my suite, hoping my parents aren't around to notice I'm back a little early. But, the turn of a door handle, followed by a gush of air as it swings open forcefully, tells me I shouldn't feel too optimistic.

"Aurelia, just the person." I turn around to see my mother in her complimentary hotel robe and slippers, her wet hair swept back into a ponytail, her face slick and greasy with various expensive oils and creams. Makeup-free and stripped almost bare, there's a glimmer of the woman she used to be five years ago, before *Break His Heart* turned our lives upside down.

"Come in here. Your father needs to update you on a few things."

I follow her voice, obediently. I know better than to object to the invitation—or command—and the inference that I'm biologically related to Chuck. She holds the door of their suite open as I walk inside, immediately spotting Chuck at the far end of the room, reclined in a chair, his head back and eyes closed as a massage therapist rubs his feet.

"Here," Mom says, nodding to the sofa opposite Chuck and handing me a sheet of paper. "Your revised schedule for the month."

I run my eyes over it, not expecting too many changes since the residency is set to take up almost every night for the next three and a half months. But the absence of the few empty dates—my days off—that previously existed makes me suddenly aware of my pulse. "What are these new shows?"

Chuck slowly raises his head before making a wafting motion with his hand which I interpret to mean he is dismissing the therapist. She assumes this too and gets to her feet, nods, and walks right out of the suite. It appalls me to think that type of gesture is a form of language she's accustomed to.

"Private performances. Corporate. Your bread and butter."

"But, I hardly have any days off," I say, not quite believing what I'm seeing.

"Every day of this residency is a day off, Aurelia." His voice is stern, his tone bored. "All time outside of the three hours you spend performing is time off. You think we don't know what you do during the day? All that sunbathing, loitering around the resort, hanging out with the *staff*?" He spits out the last point as though I've brought shame upon the family. I haven't been hanging out with anyone. I've had the occasional conversation with Tawny, Alana and, of course, Isaac, but most of it has been work-related.

"I've been rehearsing every day," I counter. "I've only

had a couple hours off here and there." *And what does he know anyway? Does he have people spying on me?*

"How many times do we have to tell you Aurelia? Young artists like you have a shelf life. It won't be long before no one wants to buy your records anymore, or pay to watch you perform. You have to make hay while sun shines. There's no such thing as time off in this business. This train you're on might only run for two more years, tops. Then you'll have as much time as you could ever need to take a break. Until then, you need to work every chance you get."

"Chuck, I need some time off. Performing every night is going to be exhausting. The rehearsals alone are intense, I can't do more than this. I have to focus on the residency, nothing else. I thought that's what we'd agreed."

"Nonsense, Aurelia. You are nineteen, not ninety. You can easily perform every night. It's every little girl's dream, this job, and you get to do it. Are you seriously telling me you would pass up the opportunity to perform again in front of more adoring fans, so you can sleep a few extra hours? Those are hours you'll be paid hundreds of thousands of dollars for. What's a couple of hours when you could use that money to buy houses for your two little sisters, or pay for their education, or—" he visibly squirms on his seat, "donate to that animal charity you never shut up about? You owe it to your family to do this. You owe it to your fans, to the people who work for you."

I peer again at the sea of scheduled nights with no gaps for respite in between. "But, Chuck—"

"Will you stop calling your father that," Mom snaps.

I glance up her and see genuine hurt in her features. "I'm sorry, Mom, it's just, this is a business conversation… I find it easier—"

"Let her call me whatever the hell she likes, Charlotte,"

he says, not taking his persistent eyes off me. "I am her manager and this is what she pays me for."

Mom visibly glows at Chuck's display of authority. It's what she loves most about him. I used to hate the way she fawned over him like this, but now it's not worth the energy.

"I need time off," I plead.

"And you'll get it," he says, glaring. "Every *day*."

My shoulders drop, resigned.

"But every *evening*," he continues, "you work."

"Who are these gigs for?" I ask, quietly. I'm not going to win this battle.

"One of the biggest energy companies on the East Coast. They're holding a series of events for its employees and they're paying a lot of money to have you perform at them. They are so keen, in fact, they are happy to work around your residency."

"How generous," I mutter.

"Indeed they are," Chuck says, standing. This is how he ends conversations with me. He simply gets up and walks away. He knows I'm too polite to do the same, too highly trained to the etiquette of this business, too nervous of pissing off the fans, and possibly creating more stalkers. "To the tune of five-million dollars—one mil per show. Enough to give your sisters just a tiny sample of the life you have. You'll do well to remember that when you're performing for your adoring fans and hating every minute of it because you're supposedly exhausted." He turns away but I don't miss the sneer on his face. I watch him walk to the bar, help himself to a scotch on the rocks, then saunter out to the balcony. My mom watches him too, before turning to face me.

"He just wants what's best for you. What's best for all of us." Her voice is almost kind, a small hint of the mom she used to be. She was never the best but at least she used to care about my feelings. These days, she's more concerned with whether her top L.A. hair stylist is going to be able to fly out to whichever glamorous locale I'm performing in.

I can't meet her eyes. "I don't hate it," I whisper. That insinuation is what hurts the most. I can live with him forcing these extra dates on me, knowing I am indeed going to be exhausted. If Chuck tried even one of my dance routines, I know for a fact he'd keel over halfway through. But, I can't accept any implication that I don't love what I do, that I don't enjoy giving the fans what they want and more.

"We know that," Mom says, reaching out tentatively to rub my back. She hasn't done it for so long it feels almost alien.

"So, why does he always throw that at me?" I ask, turning my body to face her. "He knows I live for this, that I'd never jeopardize the future of this family, my sisters…"

She finally looks at me and a ghost of a frown appears, despite the care her facialist and cosmetic surgeon put into her features. "Your father does not 'throw' things at you. He says things for a reason, to motivate you, to get you to see what the right thing to do is. You know it already, but he says things a certain way to get you to the right place quickly." Her eyes wander away wistfully. "He's a genius, really. I wish you would recognize that. He's doing it for all of us, Aurelia. And he's right, you won't always be flavor of the month, you know. We have to capitalize on your popularity while we can." She sighs, somewhat irritably. "Especially now we're asking your fans to accept the drastic changes to your image—"

"Drastic?" I stand up to face her. "The changes I've made have not been drastic. They've been subtle, Mom. And they are way more appropriate than me getting older and still wearing pigtails and singing about 'boys'. I need to dress my age, I want to sing about issues that affect other people my age. If it offends anybody, surely it's their problem, right?"

Her lips narrow. "The record company apparently doesn't see it that way."

I feel a hard resolve form in my belly. "Then let *me* talk to the record company."

Her face pales and suddenly the confidence her frown previously exhibited is gone. "Aurelia, don't be ridiculous."

"Why not? I'm officially an adult. I can have a conversation about my own career and livelihood with the record company execs without my manager being in the room."

She clasps both my hands. "Don't be silly. You don't know the first thing about business. And you've just said yourself, you need time off. You don't need to be using any time you have when you're not performing or rehearsing to sit in boring board rooms discussing numbers. That's why Chuck does it. To protect you from the stuff you don't care about, and don't need to care about. It's all in hand."

"What if I do care about it?" I challenge. Something inside me is turning a little sour. Why all of a sudden is she so animated about not wanting me to be privy to the business side of my business? I'm getting the horrible feeling something is being hidden from me, and I don't like it. I don't like it at all. "Why can't I defend my decision to evolve my image?"

"Aurelia, the record company is on board. They are just... nervous, that's all. The smallest of changes can cause the biggest losses."

"I don't believe that. Female artists in particular are always having to change up their image. They have to, to stay relevant. It's not fair but it's the reality."

"It's different with child stars, Aurelia. But, you don't

have to worry. Your father has it all under control. You just need to focus on the performances, ok?"

I'm not listening. My thoughts have returned to the revelation Carla dropped on me during our publicity meeting. "And what's this about me releasing a compilation album with no new material, Mom? I didn't approve that, and I don't approve of it. No one wants to buy a collection of only old material."

Mom straightens and wipes an irritated hand across her oiled forehead. "I don't get involved in these decisions Aurelia. But, if I remember correctly, your father said there will be some reworking on certain tracks. Nothing you'll need to go into the studio for. He's concerned that the residency will take you off the radar for a while and he wants to keep your music front of mind with your fans."

I can't argue with the rationale but it still bothers me that I had no say. "I just wish I'd been included in the discussions, that's all," I say, weakly. "It is my career, after all."

"Yes." Mom's voice is clipped, as though she's finally run out of patience. "But you can't do it all on your own."

I look away, so many thoughts flooding my head I can hardly see. One crystallizes more than any other. Something doesn't feel right, but I'm too close to see what it is. I need distance. I need room to breathe. I need a plan.

It's time.

CHAPTER SEVEN

saac

FLOODLIGHTS SWAMP the concert hall as the opening bars of Aurelia's latest single, *Clandestine*, vibrate against the walls. Screams and shouts of "*Aurelia, Aurelia*" compete with the music, until the object of the crowd's obsession appears on a raised platform at the back of the stage. The music stops, allowing only for the squeals and cheers of adolescents and their secretly appreciative parents to be heard. Then the bass crashes in and Aurelia's dancers go nuts.

Fortunately, half the security team and a bunch of agency personnel are guarding the event, so I don't reprimand myself too harshly for being unable to drag my eyes away from the glittering star as she descends the neon stairway to the main stage, belting out a catchy, powerful song I am now more than familiar with. I was impressed with the way she commanded the stage and the performances during rehearsals, but seeing Aurelia now, center stage, holding thousands of pairs of eyes, strutting with the kind of confidence I'd expect from a president, not a nineteen-year-old girl, I am stunned.

The stage is awash with throbbing lights and sweeping imagery, creating a kaleidoscopic, fantastical vision. As Aurelia flashes through, her voice bending, swaying, elongating, she becomes otherworldly. A completely different person to the one I've been slowly, quietly, contentedly getting to know. I am now a hundred percent certain of my idea for Connor's proposal to Tawny. It's going to frighten the living shit out of him but there will be absolutely no better way to make a splash of a proposal. And knowing Aurelia a little more, I think she'll be as excited about this as I am.

I'M WAITING outside Aurelia's dressing room when the door opens and Sherry, the assistant Aurelia shares with her stepfather, appears.

"She wants to see you inside." Sherry says this with an eyeroll and I immediately like her a little less. I spin and step through the door she's holding open. Aurelia is standing at the back of the room, next to her dressing table, looking a lot smaller than she did on stage just thirty minutes ago. I wait for the door to close and it's just me and her.

"Is everything ok?"

From several feet away, I can see movement in her throat as she swallows hard. Then her eyes flick to a sheet of paper lying on the dresser. When her eyes flick back to mine, they're coated in unshed tears. It takes me two strides before I'm inches away from her. I want to take in more of her face but my professional curiosity has become instinctive, and I look down at the note. It's an intricate collage of letters glued together to form words, sentences. Not many, but enough.

Congratulations, my angel
You're on my territory now
Think of me when you blow out your candle before bed
And enjoy these nights, because they won't last

"It was in my bag, the one I packed in my hotel room," Aurelia says, her voice as meek as a child's, in stark contrast to the exhilarating range and power she just demonstrated on stage.

"Who's had the bag in their possession since you left it?"

"It was loaded into the trunk of one of the cars by Franklin, my father's security. I assume he took it from my room. But then I didn't see it again. I got out of the car and was ushered straight here, to the concert hall."

I can feel the familiar, impeccably restrained urgency building my chest. "I'll speak to him now—"

She puts a hand on my arm. "Whoever it is has been inside my hotel room."

Her fearful eyes stop me in my tracks. "What makes you think that?"

"They know I burn a candle every night."

"Isn't that prohibited in hotel rooms?"

"They turn a blind eye to certain people, and even if they didn't, I'd do it anyway. I do it for my grandma, it helps me to feel as though she's with me. That's what freaks me out. I burn a candle every night for my grandma, and only two other people know this: Ana and Billy. And they wouldn't tell anyone or do anything like this."

"Have you spoken to them?"

She shakes her head. "I've been banned from contacting them for a while."

"What? Why? By who?"

"By Mom and Chuck. It was after Ana convinced me to go out in Miami in disguise, but it didn't work and I got mobbed. It was just before I started rehearsals here."

"I didn't know about that."

"It was all over the media."

"I don't tend to believe much of what is reported in the media."

"That's reassuring."

Her confidence is returning and her replies have picked up tempo.

"So, what, your parents think Ana is a bad influence?"

"That's their story, and they're sticking to it."

"Bullshit."

Aurelia steps back in surprise, and I realize I said that with a little more aggression than I'd intended.

"I only saw Ana once," I say, explaining my outburst. "But it was clear she was looking out for your best interests. It was obvious she is a genuine friend. I doubt she got you into trouble on purpose."

Aurelia dips her head and I follow her gaze to her glittering thigh high boots. The saliva disappears from my mouth for a moment. The boots are extraordinarily sexy. "She knew I was being suffocated under that roof. She figured I'd feel so much better if I got out from under everyone's glare, if only for thirty minutes. And she was right. For a split second, I felt freer than I have since I was fourteen-years-old."

The thigh-high boots suddenly look very different. They look like beautiful shackles. All glamour and glory on the surface, but harsh and punishing at the core.

"I need to speak to your father's security," I say, bringing the topic back to the reason I'm standing over her in her dressing room feeling like I want to kill whoever is behind this threat. "I'll go do it now. Is there anyone who can stay with you? One of your dancers?"

She shakes her head. "They need to rest."

"It doesn't sound to me like they're resting. More like they're having a party next door."

"They're kicking back right now. The adrenaline after a concert runs very high. They need to let off steam without the boss around. Give them an hour or so, they'll pass out."

She says all this without humor, just pure business. I feel like I'm speaking to a thirty-year-old, not a teenager.

"Is Sherry coming back?"

"I doubt it."

"Why not? She's your assistant, isn't she? Shouldn't she be making sure you're not alone?"

Aurelia looks up at me. Her eyes seem to get bigger each time, or something. All I know is it becomes harder to look away the more she directs them at me. "She prefers to make sure there's someone else who isn't alone," she says.

"Your father?" I shouldn't ask. This is personal, none of my business. But, knowing the answer might help me protect her better. She nods once, her eyes searching mine for a hint of judgement. I don't betray any because that's not who I am. It hits me. This girl is completely alone. She might have great camaraderie with her team, but they're her employees, the bond can only stretch so far. Her family give even fewer than two shits about her, and on this night of all nights, when she's just killed the first residency to hit the Florida Keys with an absolute knock-out performance. And they've banned her from seeing her only two friends. I, it seems, am the only person who cares about Aurelia Bird, and that's only because

I need to protect the reputation of the resort. I'm as bad as her parents, I think. I'm only here right now because I'm paid to be.

That thought knocks me into action. If the best I can do is protect her, then protect her I will. For the next few months, Aurelia Bird belongs to Starling Key. Her real family has failed her so she's going to become part of ours. And we will embrace her just like we embrace everybody. No one will care that she's rich, or that every pre-pubescent boy—and girl—likely has a poster of her in their bedroom. No one will care that she owns a soulless mansion in LA, and a closet containing every expensive label known to man. They will only care that she's ok. Sure, they might ask her to sing occasionally, but that's only because we like good music here on the Key. But, they'll be more concerned she's happy.

"Aurelia, you are not obliged to say yes to this, but I'm going to advise that you stay here on Starling Key for the duration of the residency. It's the only way I can protect you. There are limited routes onto the island and we have security personnel based here who know the island like the back of their hands. I can arrange for you to have one of the sea villas. It may not be the Ritz Carlton but it will be safe, I guarantee it. I can be with you around the clock, and if I need to rest, one of the team—each of whom I would trust with my life—can step in."

The tension in her face falls away like melting snow. "Starting when?"

"Now."

I can't help a small smile form at the corner of my mouth at the look of elation on her face, then when she leaps forward and throws her arms around my neck, I am engulfed. My face becomes damp from the sweat on her neck and hair.

My hands move to her waist instinctively and my mind registers a million things at once that it will process later. Her hard body, her feather-light build, the soft elastic fabric of her stage outfit, the rub of her thigh-high boot against my right leg, the smell of her perfume mixed with dry ice and concert halls. When she slides back down to the floor, it's a few seconds before she looks up, and her face is different. Her cheeks are delightfully pink and I notice her bottom lip is slightly larger than her top lip when she pulls it between her teeth.

"That… that's great," she says. "Thank you Isaac. I knew you'd be different."

I can't help the slight frown. "What do you mean?"

"I knew you wouldn't be like the others, so eager to please my stepfather that he becomes the priority, not my safety."

"I'm a security guard, not a politician."

"That is music to my ears," she smiles, reaching for a jacket to pull over her shoulders.

"And I guess that's saying something coming from one of the best singers in the world right now," I grin.

She stops suddenly, her jacket hanging between her fingers.

"You really think so?"

I actually have no idea. I listen to rock music and wouldn't be able to tell Taylor Swift from Martha damn Stewart. But I've heard a lot of people say this about Aurelia Bird, so I figured it was a widely-held belief.

"Well, yeah, sure," I say, kicking myself because I know I sound unconvincing.

She tries to stop another smile forming but fails. "It's ok, Isaac. I know my music isn't your thing. I kind of like that it isn't."

I don't hide my sigh of relief. "Really?"

"Yeah," she says, pulling her jacket on. "That way I know you're interested in me as a person, not me as a popstar."

I stiffen without thinking and she becomes flustered.

"I don't mean *interested* interested, I mean, like, you know, the way you see me. As a person, not a popstar—"

"I know, I get it," I say, feeling flustered too. I force myself to regain some composure. "Let me know when you're done here and I'll take you to the villa. I'll ask Tawny to pull together anything you need for the night and we can have the rest of your things brought here in the morning."

She nods and right at that moment, there's a knock at the door. "That'll be my meet and greets," she says.

Carla, the PR woman, opens the door a crack and peers inside. When she sees me, she pushes it open wider. "Are you ready, Aurelia? The fans are waiting in the Dolphin suite down the corridor. They're giddy to meet you."

As much as I dislike the PR woman, the excitement on her face lights her up. It's clear she very much enjoys this part of her job. But then, who wouldn't enjoy giving a bunch of young kids a once-in-a-lifetime opportunity to meet their idol?

"I'll come back in one hour," I say, following Aurelia through the door. "Luca will accompany you to the suite." Luca is already standing out in the corridor, prepared to provide any back-up if needed. He arches an eyebrow seeing me emerge from Aurelia's dressing room, which I ignore. Then I turn on my heel and go to make arrangements for Aurelia to stay on the Key. I know, without having to voice it myself, I will have to move in there with her. It's the only way I can provide round-the-clock security. The villa I have in mind, the Morrison, has four separate suites, so we'll both have plenty of privacy, and this won't be the first time I've provided live-in security for a guest. But it will be the first time since Paris, and that is one conversation I'm not looking forward to having, especially since the Morrison villa is right next door to the Hemingway. I sigh, preparing myself for the inevitable explosion, and pull out my phone.

CHAPTER EIGHT

Aurelia

THE BLACK SKY is alight with thousands of glittering stars and there is no noise around apart from the soft sound of our feet on the boardwalk as I follow Isaac and Luca to the Morrison villa—the place I'm going to live for the next fourteen weeks. Chuck was livid when I called to tell him about the new arrangement, but at least he agreed not to tell Mom about the threat. Neither of us want to have to deal with another one of her emotional breakdowns.

We reach the door and Isaac swipes it with a key card. We all go inside. Bright lights come on automatically and Isaac gives a command for them to dim. The villa is deceptively spacious and has every top-spec appliance I could possibly need. The far wall is made entirely of glass and all I can see beyond it is blackness and sparkles, from the sky and the reflection on the water. A tranquil calm soaks into my skin and I let out the deepest sigh of relief in a long time. A few weeks in this place and I won't need my therapist or my masseurs ever again.

"This is heavenly," I breathe out.

Isaac and Luca glance at each other. "It really is," Luca says. "We're so lucky to see this every day, but when we see someone else taking the view in for the first time it reminds us just how special it is."

"It's not just the view though, it's the villa, the quiet, it's everything."

No one says anything else. Isaac and Luca busy themselves testing cameras and monitors while I press my nose against the glass and breathe. For the first time in forever, I feel like I have space and freedom. It's ironic because I'm actually being hidden away in a remote part of Florida, a boat being my only true means of escape.

"Ok, I think that's everything," Luca announces, facing both Isaac and me as we stand in the shared living area. "I guess I'll head back to the dorms. Just let me know if you need anything else, Isaac, I'll bring it over."

"I got everything, but thanks."

"Night," Luca says as he lets himself out, leaving me and Isaac alone.

"Thanks for doing this," I say to Isaac. He looks up and seems to notice me for the first time since we left the concert hall. Until now, he's been all business, talking on the phone to organize the shipment of my stuff, shift changes so he can take breaks, new security devices for the villa. He was focused and efficient, and such was his fair, no-bullshit tone, people bent to his will. Even Luca, who I gather is a close friend as well as a colleague, moved quietly around him, checking Isaac had everything he needed, asking if there was anything else he could do to help. Isaac was juggling a ton of balls without barely moving his hands.

Something stirs in my chest, catching my breath. Nerves are a part of my job. Stage fright is a very real thing I've had to confront, and continue to confront with the help of my therapist. So, nerves have become second nature and I rarely notice them anymore. But, being alone in a room with a man who commands such attention and respect with very little effort is making me very much aware of them.

"You can retire to bed if you want," I offer. "You don't have to stay up for my benefit. I'm just going to look at the stars a while longer, then I'll go to bed myself."

"I don't sleep a lot," he says. "Perils of the job. Would you like some company?"

I hesitate, then smile. "I'd like some quiet, actually. But company is good too."

"I can be quiet," he replies. "Let's go on the deck."

He leads the way out through a sliding glass door and pulls back a chair for me to sit. Then he pulls out a second chair but sets it a little away from me. "I won't crowd you," he smiles, before sitting.

We sit in silence and at first it's painfully uncomfortable. It's human nature to want to fill the space, but I push through it. Once I'm out the other side, I feel like I can breathe more freely than ever before. I'm alone and quiet in my own space, with another person beside me allowing me that freedom. I sneak a look at him out the corner of my eye and he appears to be somewhere else. He's leaning forward, his elbows resting on his knees, looking out at the sea with the slightest of frowns resting on his brow. Every now and then, his eyes flick to the west, and he lets out a shallow breath.

"I really appreciate this," I whisper, and he whips his head around, bursting out of his trance. "I know you've got a life and there was a lot more to your job before I came along and bought all your time. So, I just want you to know, I appreciate it."

He looks resigned when he answers. "There's nothing to appreciate. This *is* my job. It was my idea to bring you here, to this villa. I could have left your stepfather's security to handle everything outside of the Key, but that's simply not how I like things. I don't work well with other security teams. I don't trust anyone else, and this threat demonstrates exactly why I don't. If I'd been your twenty-four security before this, that threat would have never reached you. You are not safe anywhere but here. As I said, I don't sleep a lot, but knowing you're here will make the small amount of sleep I do get a little easier."

"Why don't you sleep a lot?"

"I don't know," he shrugs, looking down at his feet. "Never did. Even as a kid."

"Man, I'm envious. I need a lot of sleep. Otherwise I can't perform, and my voice goes all cranky. And so do I."

"I find that hard to believe," he says, smiling.

That weird flutter returns and I realize it's the third time I've felt it this evening. "Just wait 'til you get to know me," I laugh. "I'll ask you again in a couple months."

We both turn to look out at the sea again, and the silence stretches, more comfortably now.

"Did you like the show?" I look sideways at him. I want him to say yes. I don't need him to be a fan, or a sudden convert to pop music, but I do want him to have liked what he saw and heard.

When he faces me, his smile is wide. "Are you kidding? It was amazing."

"Really?" I can feel my face reddening and I'm thankful we're sitting in darkness.

"Sure. I mean, I've been to some pretty good shows, you

know, rock concerts. But, I've never seen anything like that. It was so… I don't know… physical. You never stop moving. And you sing while you're moving. I can barely talk when I'm pumping weights, so I can't imagine how you do it all."

My throat dries up as the vision of Isaac pumping iron flits across my eyelids. "You don't have to say this, you know. Just a simple 'yes' is fine," I laugh.

"A simple 'yes' wouldn't do it justice," he frowns. "It really was amazing. I mean it. I feel very privileged just to have been in the audience."

"Well, you're going to be in the audience a hell of a lot more. You'll be so bored of me by the end of this residency." I look away, smiling.

He pauses before answering. "I doubt it." I feel his eyes on my face and I can't bring myself to face him.

The flutter in my chest has quickened, and I swallow hard, my mind going blank. I only felt this way once before, when I first met my ex-boyfriend. At the time I put it down to the fact he was a member of Jinxed, the boyband I'd had a crush on since I was twelve, and I was simply starstruck. But Isaac is not a star, so this feeling doesn't make any sense.

"Some new shows have been added to my schedule," I say, changing the subject.

"Where?" Isaac asks, understandably confused.

"They're private gigs, up in Miami. Chuck put them in."

"Are you sure about doing them? I mean, watching your performance this evening, you already have a lot on your plate. Aren't you going to be exhausted?"

I laugh under my breath, almost bitterly. "I will have all the time in the world to rest in a couple years, according to Chuck. I need to capitalize on my popularity now."

"Do you agree?" Isaac doesn't sound so sure.

"Not really, but he's family. It's—it's hard."

"You don't have to do them if you don't want to," he says, slowly.

"No, it's fine. I'll manage. And it makes more money for my sisters, you know, for when they're older and want to go to good schools and have nice homes. I just… sometimes I wish I could have more of a say in my career. They won't even let me speak to my record company. I'm not suspicious, but… I sometimes feel like Chuck isn't telling me everything."

Isaac gives me a lop-sided grin. "That's kind of the definition of suspicion."

I laugh, realizing he's right. "I guess."

"Listen," Isaac says, leaning forward and resting his weight on his knees. "I don't know you very well, but I know this much. You've got a good head on your shoulders. If something doesn't feel right to you, chances are good that something isn't right. I won't say anymore, just that if you want me to help in any way, I will."

I don't say anything but I roll his words around in my head. The fact he believes me and doesn't think I'm some stupid teenager with anxiety, ungrateful for a stepfather who wants the best for me, is more than I could have hoped for.

"I'm glad you enjoyed the show," I say, forcing out the words. "I'm going to go to bed now. Thanks for… bringing me here."

He stands when I do. "Sleep well, Aurelia," he says, smoothly.

I nod and give him a brief smile before forcing myself to turn and walk back inside the villa, towards my own suite, where I lock the door behind me and let out the longest breath. I hope it takes the flutter with it, but it doesn't.

I WAKE at eight and I shower and throw on a short beach dress that Tawny must have put in my closet. I actually prefer the unbranded, non-showy clothes she has provided and I wonder if they are her own. I make a note to ask her where she shops.

I have most of the day off before tonight's show, and I want to explore the island. I walk out of my suite into the living area and see Isaac sitting at the kitchen island with a laptop open, his head buried in it. Until he hears me, then he turns and gives me a brief nod.

"Hey. Did you sleep ok?"

I walk around the island to face him. "Yeah, like a baby. The peace and quiet here really helps."

"Good." He looks up, his face all business, in contrast to the more relaxed and casual demeanor he exhibited last night. "What's on your agenda today?"

"I'd like you to show me around the island." I help myself to juice from the fridge, and a banana.

"Didn't you see it all the first time you came here?"

"No, I just saw the concert hall, the backstage area and the reception building. My stepfather got a tour while I had iced tea with Billy and Ana inside the venue."

His gaze lingers on me for a few seconds while a range of emotions seem to glide across his face. Surprise, followed by annoyance, followed by resignation.

"Aren't CIA operatives supposed to have good poker faces?"

He drops his head in exasperation, then flips it back up, showcasing a heart-stopping smile. "It was always a weakness."

I turn away and busy myself with the banana skin, feeling my appetite slowly disappear. "Well, is that ok?"

"Of course," he replies. "It's a beautiful island. It will be my pleasure to show it to you."

My chest flutters again and I force the banana down with a glug of juice.

"Great. Well, let's go," I say, putting the juice box back in the refrigerator.

He snaps the top of his laptop closed and gets to his feet. I notice he's wearing the exact same uniform as last night—a black suit, shiny shoes, and an earpiece.

"Can you wear something else?" I ask.

He looks confused for minute. "Like what?"

"Like, something less formal. You'll roast in this heat."

"I'm a bodyguard," he sighs. "This is what we wear."

"No," I correct. "You're *my* bodyguard, and you will wear what I ask you to." I smile, cheekily, so he knows I'm not pulling rank. "Something more casual. You may as well be wearing a neon arrow sign pointing right at me. I don't need people spotting a celebrity from the other side of the island."

His jaw clicks and that damn flutter starts up again. "Whatever you say, ma'am," he bites out and walks back towards his suite.

"And you can stop that right now, too," I call after him. "Ma'am makes me feel like an eighty-year-old grandmother."

He ignores me and returns a minute later wearing something that takes the breath right out of my throat. Calf-length combat trousers, large black training shoes and a fitted back t-shirt with the SKS logo emblazoned across the front. I can see the sharply cut outline of his upper body, and it has made my mouth dry. Finally, I know what this is, what this freaking flutter is telling me. I'm attracted to my bodyguard. I mentally kick myself. *What a damn cliché you are Aurelia Bird. And what the hell have you done? You've just agreed to live with this guy for the next three months and you've got a freaking crush on him. Plus, he's old enough to be... well, ok, not my father, but not far off.*

I finally find my voice. "That's more like it," I mutter. "Let's go."

He doesn't smile at my reaction, but his eyes do, and they taunt me for a few seconds before he opens the door and steps out onto the boardwalk, then he stops sharp and I walk straight into his solid back. My forehead smacks against his shoulder blade.

"Ow!" I say, rubbing my head. When he steps to one side, I see why he'd pulled up so abruptly. A woman, about my height, older but beautiful, is standing opposite us, staring at Isaac. Her expression is indecipherable but they look at each other for a long time before she finally speaks.

"Isaac," she says, simply.

"Mrs. Navitsky," he replies. I hear something like an apology in his voice, but it doesn't make sense. Her eyes dart to me and she looks me up and down with the merest hint of a sneer on her lips.

"Aurelia Bird," she states.

"Nice to meet you," I say, holding out my hand. She takes my fingers, limply, then whips her hand back, as though I've burned her. She says nothing further, but looks back to Isaac and clenches her jaw, before spinning around to the sound of a door closing in the next villa along. A large, blonde man with a hard expression walks towards us. Mrs. Navitsky takes his hand, he nods to Isaac and they walk together down the boardwalk, both looking distinctly unhappy, neither of them looking back.

CHAPTER NINE

saac

*F*UCK.

I watch Paris holding Roman's hand—she *never* holds his hand—as they walk back to shore. My initial guilt about her seeing me emerge from the next villa along from hers with the one person she doesn't want to see me with, quickly morphs into defensiveness. If she'd answered her damn phone last night instead of screening me, which she seems to be doing a lot these days, this would not have come as such a big surprise to her. There was no way I was going to tell her about this development by text; I owe Paris that much. But she didn't pick up.

"Right then," I say, a little snappily, and start walking in the same direction back to the shore. I hear Aurelia walking softly behind me. She must have sensed something back there, but wisely, she doesn't say anything.

"Where first?" she asks, brightly, as I close the boardwalk gate behind us.

"We'll go west," I say, nodding in that direction, "to the marina and the dive center. Then there's a nice beach over that way, just south of the spa and gym, then the golf course. You've seen most of the main building, with the concert hall. I can show you the casino, if you like. Otherwise, we can head east and south, past the staff accommodation, down to Reef Street and the main beach."

"Sounds great."

We take off along the path towards the Grand House.

"Is that where the Starlings live?" she asks, pointing to the large white building.

"Yeah. Eric, Maria, and their daughters when they're not studying in England."

"What a life," she sighs.

"The grass is always greener," I reply. "Think of all the people who want your life. I'd bet it's most people."

"Even you?" I feel her looking up at me.

"Nah. I'm probably one of the few that don't. But I've had the privilege of seeing what it's really like, you know? This job takes me behind the scenes where it's not all that glossy and glamorous. Everyone else sees the picture painted by the media. The big shiny houses in the Hollywood Hills, the glowing faces coming out of expensive restaurants. They don't see the tears that come the minute the doors are closed, or witness the panic attacks that can happen at random, only to be covered up by a good PR."

I can hear her breath turn shallow. "Yeah, you've summed it up pretty accurately."

We pass the house and head in the direction of the marina.

"What a beautiful place to dock," she says as we

approach. There are three boats in slips at the moment—two yachts and a cruiser.

"It's quiet right now. We can take up to eight and we're usually fully booked."

"That doesn't surprise me."

"Would you ever have a superyacht?" I ask, trying everything I can to drag my mind away from Paris and her rapidly diminishing opinion of me.

"A superyacht? God no, way too ostentatious. I have a great smaller one though. I named it the Esmerelda, after my Grams. Chuck convinced me to buy it last summer, although I hardly ever use it. He takes it out a lot, sometimes for days at a time. If he didn't, I would probably sell it, to be honest, let someone else enjoy it."

"Yeah, I'm not sure I see you as a boat person," I say, without thinking. She spins around, a look of mock horror on her face.

"Why ever not? You can't see me reclining on a sun-kissed deck, in a skimpy bathing suit, sipping a glass of champagne?"

The image actually makes me swallow and I wish I hadn't said anything. "Well, when you put it like that," I say, a little meekly, then change the subject. "What would you spend your money on, if you could have anything you wanted?" I genuinely want to know the answer. What makes Aurelia Bird really tick?

"I don't know. There's nothing I want more than simply health, happiness and comfort. I've bought houses for me and members of my family, and I've taken them on some nice vacations. But I don't want *stuff*. I'd rather my money be used to help people who don't have anything."

"So, you want to be a philanthropist?" I like the idealism but I take it with a pinch of salt. When people say they don't want anything, it's generally because they don't want *for* anything.

"Yeah, something like that."

"Would you give to any particular cause?"

"Absolutely!" She reels off the names of about seven different charities and campaigns.

"Do you donate already?" I don't know why but there's a part of me wants to prove to myself it's all talk, that she has these ideals but she'll never follow through, because at the end of the day, she does want the money. Because for some reason, I don't want to bring myself to believe otherwise.

"As much as I can," she says, vaguely. "My stepfather controls most of it. It'll change when I reach my twentieth birthday though. That's when my rights and royalties are transferred to my company, and when Grams figured I'd be able to manage my money responsibly."

"You seem pretty responsible now," I challenge.

"Yeah, you say that, but I really would give it all to charity if I had access to it. Apparently that's not the best way to manage it." She grins at me.

We step onto the deck and walk alongside one of the yachts. I stand and watch as Aurelia reaches out to touch the beautifully sloping side. She presses her palm against it and closes her eyes. "They are beautiful aren't they?" she sighs, opening her eyes again. I nod in agreement. "How far is the reef from here?"

I point out to sea. "About six miles that way."

"I'd love to see it."

"Well, the dive center is our next stop, so we can ask about scheduling a trip for you."

"Really? That would be amazing." Her face lights up and her blonde hair bobs about her shoulders as she skips back down the deck to the path. For a moment, I forget about bumping into Paris and find myself feeling the way I felt last night while I sat next to Aurelia in silence. It wasn't the first time I'd sat in the company of a client without speaking. In fact, it is pretty commonplace in this profession to be unseen and unheard. But, there was a weird feeling in the air that I couldn't put my finger on.

We reach the dive center and chat to Autumn and Clark about organizing a trip for Aurelia. Seeing the framed photographs of the reefs in all their technicolor glory only serves to further excite Aurelia, and I watch, curiously, as she seems to glow from the inside out.

We continue up to the spa and I introduce her to Maisie and show her some of the available treatment rooms and the yoga studio. Then we make our way towards the golf course. We walk along the lower side towards the northeast wall.

"That's where I usually live," I say, nodding towards the steel security gate.

"Behind that wall?" Her voice is full of intrigue as opposed to judgement.

"Yeah. The northeast wall. It's where the real fun happens," I say, raising an eyebrow conspiratorially.

"Can I see?"

"Really?" I backtrack. "There's not much to see. Not right now anyway."

"Then when?"

"Sunday nights are quite vibrant," I say. "And we have beach parties three times a season. Things can get a little… debauched."

"Debauched," she repeats. "I like the sound of that. It's a shame I'm going to be performing Sunday nights."

"The parties go on into the early hours," I say, then without thinking, I add, "I could bring you one night after your show."

She claps her hands together. "I would love that!"

I smile, knowing the team would love that too.

We stop for some lunch in the café, then head back out towards Reef Street. I tell her about Barbie and Fitz, two of our famous ex-Hollywood residents, and she says she can't wait to meet them. We bump into Esme, Tawny's friend from Housekeeping, and chat about other singers we've had stay on the island. Thankfully, Esme remains tight-lipped about some of the shitshows she's had to clean up after. It wouldn't do to bitch about people who are effectively Aurelia's peers.

Finally, we walk back along the boardwalk, and as we approach the Morrison villa, I hear Aurelia take a deep breath. "Who was the woman we bumped into earlier?" she asks. "Paris somebody?"

I swipe the key card and open the door. "Paris Navitsky. Roman Navitsky's wife."

"Roman Navitsky? *The* Roman Navitsky? That was *him*?"

"Yeah. His wife stays here a lot."

"Right. I thought she looked familiar. And that would explain how she knows you."

"What do you mean?" My heart has started to thump.

"It's clear you two knew each other. She didn't look very happy with you."

I shrug it off. "She looks like that a lot," I say, thinking how true that has been of late.

Undeterred, she continues. "Don't take this the wrong way but it was obvious there's something between you two."

I spin around. "There isn't," I say, a little too quickly. "She's been a guest here for a long time."

"Isaac," Aurelia smiles and heads off to her suite. She keeps talking even as she's out of sight. "We're going to be living in the villa together for quite a few weeks. You have to realize I'm probably going to learn things about your life that other clients wouldn't. I don't want you to have to shut yourself off. I'm asking a lot of you; I want you to feel as though you can be yourself. If something is going on between you and Mrs. Navitsky, you don't have to keep it a secret from me, ok? I'm not going to judge you."

Part of me is relieved, but a much weirder part of me is pissed. I understand the first part, but not the second. Until she walks back out of her suite.

Then, I understand it perfectly.

There's a lot I like about Aurelia Bird. She's bright, she's kind, she's witty, she's perceptive. And now, as I try hard not to stare at her impeccable figure dressed daringly in a white lace, almost transparent bikini, I finally admit she's hot. I feel the heat rise up my throat and into my jaw as it dawns on me, I might actually fancy Aurelia Bird, and I might actually be old enough to be her dad.

CHAPTER TEN

Aurelia

SO MUCH HAS HAPPENED since I first arrived on Starling Key—the rehearsals, the first live show, the threat, the move into the Morrison villa. But I'm not struck by any of it as acutely as I'm struck by the moment Isaac first lays eyes on me in my white bikini. He hardly says a word as I walk past him onto the deck and dive straight into the sea. His eyes burn into me so hard my skin sizzles when I hit the water.

I swim back to the surface and push my hair back off my face. When my vision clears, I see him standing on the deck; he'd followed me out.

"Do you want to come in?" I ask.

He shakes his head. "I can't when I'm working."

"So, you won't be able to swim out here the whole time I'm on the island? That doesn't seem fair."

"I can't do my job if I'm in the water." He folds his arms

across his chest and I can't tell if he's annoyed with me or bemused.

"Will it be easier for you if I come out?"

"It's not up to you to make my job easier. Success for me is that you get to live your life the way you want to, without being afraid."

I swim to the ladder and grip it with both hands. He steps closer to the edge and looks down. I notice the fine, dark hairs on his muscled calves, and swallow.

"I feel safer now than I've felt in a long time," I say, quietly, pulling myself up the ladder.

He frowns and seems to do a double take. "What do you mean?"

I take a breath in and wonder if I should tell him. He is my bodyguard, not my confidante. But something tells me he is genuinely interested and I figure more knowledge might only help him to protect me better. I watch his jaw tick as I lift myself out of the water. "It's a long story."

"I have time on my hands if you do," he says, stepping back and handing me a towel, his eyes diverted.

I wrap the towel around myself and walk to the nearest chair. I sit down and curl my legs up beneath me. A glass of sparkling water is already sitting there, so I take a long sip. Isaac sits in the chair opposite. He doesn't say anything but leans forward, resting his elbows on his knees, giving me his full attention.

"Before Chuck came along, it was just Mom and me. She was a different person back then. We used to do so many things together. She always loved her spa treatments and girly brunches, but she would often take me with her. I learned how to sit still, be polite, eat my food with good manners. I loved those times. It felt as though it was just the two of us in our little bubble—friends, really. And she was always so supportive of my career."

"Did she push you at all?" Isaac asks.

"Yeah, of course, but no more than any other showbiz parent, I guess. She took me to singing and dance classes, entered me into competitions. She worked really hard to pay for all these too, as she keeps reminding me." I add.

I notice the sweat beading on Isaac's forehead. As if reading my mind, he wipes it away and pushes his hand through his hair, then rests his chin on it.

I continue. "She found me a manager, some small-time guy who talked the talk but didn't know what he was doing. He got us a deal with the record company but the contract was terrible. After *Break His Heart* hit number one, Mom met Chuck. They dated for a few weeks before he offered to look over the contract. He studied law in school so he at least knew a little bit about it. He pointed out to us all the clauses that didn't work in our favor at all. Any lawyer could have done that, but Mom was just in awe of him. So, you know, he became my manager pretty quickly. Then he and Mom married soon afterwards."

"So, he assimilated into your family and business pretty quickly," Isaac says with a frown.

I sigh. "Yeah. It wasn't long after that Mom started leaving us a lot to go do her thing, whatever that was. More frequent—and expensive—spa treatments, more lunches with friends and people from the industry. That was her job I guess, to schmooze with the execs and their wives, and she loved it. But I used to watch her leave and wish so hard that I was going with her. I really missed our lunches and spa days together. I felt as though I'd lost my best friend, you know? But Chuck was giving her money to go treat herself. More money than I ever saw from him. I don't know, it was like he wanted her out of the way."

"Do you think she realized that?"

"No, and I would never say it to her. She worships him."

"Then, there was this one time when she eventually did take me on a shopping trip. I didn't particularly want to buy anything; I just wanted to spend time with her. She went into a changing room with an armful of clothes and left me outside. I sat and read a book while I waited for her. But, when she came out, she'd completely forgotten I was there. I had my head deep inside my book, so I didn't notice her come out. She walked straight past me, paid for her clothes and went home."

I stare at my feet while I tell the story. When I look up, Isaac's jaw is set hard.

"At the time, my face was everywhere, but thankfully, we'd managed to get into this shop without anyone recognizing me. I had no security at the time, and even then, fans were persistent and could get quite physical. When I realized she'd gone, I had a panic attack, my first one. I didn't know what was happening. My heart beat so fast and I felt like I could hardly breathe. I'll always remember the lovely sales girl helping me into a back office and calling Chuck. And I'll never forget the feeling of being forgotten by my very own mother. I was fifteen, but as this young famous singer who everyone wanted a piece of, I was vulnerable."

Isaac's head moves slowly from side to side. "Did your mom realize what she'd done?"

"Not until Chuck called her. He was pissed and I think that's what bothered her the most." I shrug. "When I eventually got home, she yelled her head off at me."

"She blamed you?" Isaac says, slowly.

"Of course. Everything was always my fault. I knew

though. I knew she'd forgotten me and probably felt guilty as hell. Fortunately for my mom, she had a close relationship with the local sheriff so no charges were brought against her for 'irresponsible parenting'. The incident was never mentioned again, and Chuck gave the sales girl a tip big enough to buy her a new car and keep her quiet, but it changed me for good. I insisted on having security from that point on, which Chuck controlled of course. And then Mom had the twins."

Isaac doesn't say anything and I feel as though he's really hearing me. "Things still didn't change, though. It wasn't like Mom became the homely Mom again after that. Instead, two wonderful nannies arrived and Mom continued to go out for her treatments and her social events. Chuck was never that interested in fatherly duties either. He was more interested in my career, and bossing me about," I add, with a weak smile.

"I noticed the way he spoke to you when you first visited the island," he says, choosing his words carefully. "Does he speak that way to you a lot?"

"All the time. If it wasn't for the money I make, I don't think he'd want me around at all, to be honest." I have never admitted this to anyone before, not even Ana and Billy. I don't know what it is about Isaac, but I feel like I can tell him anything. There is no judgement there and he appears to genuinely care. I have to catch myself occasionally. He is on my payroll, of course he has to appear that way.

"But, wait. Your name, Bird?"

"It's my mom's name. Chuck changed his name when he married her."

Isaac shook his head.

"What about your dad? Your real dad?"

"I've never had one," I say, with a bitter laugh. "That's the weirdest thing. I was a sperm bank baby. My mother actually went and got herself pregnant, on her own. You would think she wanted to actually be a mother." I shake my head, the bitter laugh lingering.

"I never heard that about you. Is it common knowledge?"

"No. I mean everyone knows I was raised by a single mom, but no one knows why. No one. Only you. And Mom. Chuck thinks my dad left my mom high and dry; I think she prefers it that way."

Isaac sits back and lets out a long breath. "Fuck, Aurelia."

"I don't want pity, Isaac," I say, firmly.

"I'm not pitying you," he says, with a slight snap in his voice. "I am… I…" He rubs his eyes in frustration. "I'm in awe of you, to be quite honest."

Almost immediately, my heartrate picks up and my cheeks flush again. But this always happens. Whenever anyone gives me a compliment, I hang onto it for dear life. The fact the giver of the compliment is a strong, fit, good-looking security guard who's devoted the next few months to keeping me safe, only intensifies the feeling.

"Remember you said you'd help me if I needed it?" I venture, unable to look him in the eye.

"Yes. What do you need?"

I take a deep breath. "Bank statements." I still can't look at him.

"Bird Holdings?"

"Yes."

"And Chuck Bird?"

"If that's possible."

"Anything's possible."

He says all this with no emotion, no judgement, and I'm so grateful I could hug him, but I've already made that mistake once. After the first show. It didn't help the burgeoning warmth I felt and have been trying ever since to deny.

"Thank you," I conclude, taking another sip of water to cool my veins. "Now, that's enough about me. Tell me about Paris Navitsky." I finally raise my eyes to him.

It is alarm that flashes across Isaac's face before resignation. "There's not much to say," he replies. It's his turn to look away as he speaks. As he gazes out at the sea while I take in his profile. He isn't just tall and dark; he is downright handsome. *And* a bodyguard. Most girls' dream. But he's complicated too. I can tell before he utters a word about it.

"Yes, we have a bit of a thing going. But, as you know, she's married." He doesn't wince as he says this, but he doesn't look at me either. "She's alone a lot. We like each other. That's it really. Neither of us want anything more, and I'm pretty sure Roman knows. I doubt I'm the first."

When I don't say anything, Isaac turns to gauge my reaction, but I know my face is blank. "It won't get in the way of my job," he says, narrowing his eyes, darkening them further.

"I didn't think it would," I reply.

"In fact, I'm pretty sure it's over," he says. There's a hint of sadness in his voice that I guess even he doesn't realize is there.

"Why is that?" I noticed the way she stared at him when we walked out of the villa together.

"She, um… It doesn't matter," he says, avoiding my face again.

"It's ok, you don't have to tell me."

A few seconds pass then he turns towards me and his face is different somehow. "No, I… It might be a good thing that you know."

I uncurl my legs to return the full attention he'd given me

earlier and I don't miss the way his eyes dip to my bare legs as the towel slips away.

"She um, she doesn't trust me with you."

My eyes almost pop out of my head right there. "With me? That's insane! Why?"

For a moment, he looks as though I've slapped him, as though I think there's no way in the world the two of us would be attracted to each other, but he composes himself quickly. "I don't know. You're famous, you're talented, you're attractive…" I feel the blush deepen at my collarbone, so much so, I put a hand to my chest. Isaac follows it with his eyes. "She can't understand that a man can be around you and not, you know… want to be with you."

I choke out a small, nervous laugh. "I'm flattered she thinks that."

"Well, anyway, that's kind of why it's over. She doesn't trust me around you."

I want to ask him if he trusts himself around me, but he's already said, in not so many words, the idea alone is a load of rubbish. Instead, I simply offer my apologies.

He throws his head back and laughs, instantly lightening the dark mood that has been descending slowly. "It's hardly your fault, Aurelia. I mean, she's a married woman. She has no claim over me and I have none over her."

"Does that bother you?"

"Not at all. I'm not the 'relationship' type," he says, making quote marks with his fingers. "I don't see myself ever settling down."

"Is that why you've gotten involved with a married woman? Because she doesn't want commitment from you?" I know my questions are way too personal, but I suddenly want to know.

His smile broadens. "You a shrink now?"

"I guess I am," I smile back.

"Then, maybe. I don't know." He chews his lip then eyes me sideways again. "She isn't the first married woman I've been involved with."

"She isn't?" My heart is racing and it takes all my effort to keep my voice from quivering. The fact he's opening up to me at all makes me feel strangely warm.

"No. It's kind of, my thing. I'm not proud of it."

"So, why do it?"

"I guess you're right. I don't want to commit, and these women don't want that from me."

I want to ask if he cares about potentially breaking up families but I get the distinct impression the women are as invested as he is, possibly the husbands too. It seems to be a convenient arrangement all round.

"Well, I suppose, as long as no one gets hurt," I shrug, surprising myself. I've always been resolutely against cheating, but I've never come across this type of cheating before, where everybody seems to be on board with it. It's weird and it's not for me, but that doesn't mean it's not for other people.

I eventually go back to my suite to shower, feeling as though a weight has been lifted. Not only has Isaac agreed to get me what I think I need, but we've shared something of ourselves with each other. We're each that little bit more invested in making this arrangement work. I come straight out of the shower, curl up on my bed and fall fast asleep.

THE DOORBELL RINGS and when I open it, Tawny is waiting to take me to meet Barbie and Fitz. I've been looking forward to this since Isaac first told me about them. Apparently Barbie is a huge fan. We head out to the waiting buggy and see Seleste in the back with baby Safia.

"They are dying to see Saffy," she explains. "When Tawny told me she was taking you guys, I had to come along. I love Barbie and Fitz."

"*Everyone* loves Barbie and Fitz," Tawny grins.

Safia gurgles when I climb in beside her mom. "She's gorgeous," I coo.

"Looks can be deceiving," Seleste says in her thick Cuban accent. "She is not so cute when she's screaming for milk at three-thirty in the morning, or refusing to sleep unless one of us is holding her."

I tickle the baby's head and she gurgles again. "It won't last," I say, speaking from some experience having lived with baby twin sisters the last two years. "Enjoy the cuddles while you can."

"I will," Seleste smiles, pulling faces at her daughter.

"Ok, you ready?" Tawny asks, looking over her shoulder.

"You bet," I grin, and the buggy begin ambling along the drive towards Reef Street. It's only when I glance back towards the Hemingway villa and see Paris Navitsky watching us out of the window that I'm reminded just how big a boulder I've thrown into Isaac D'Amico's life.

CHAPTER ELEVEN

saac

THE SECOND WEEK of Aurelia's shows has gone even better than the first, if that's possible. She's still buzzing from the meet and greets as we walk back into the villa.

"Did you hear that six-year-old girl, Melanie? Her voice! Oh my word. She sang *Crazy Baby* perfectly, note for note. And with so much passion and feeling. She's going to be a star one day."

"She was only six? I thought she was at least ten."

"I know, right? It's astonishing. It makes me want to go work on one of those TV talent shows so I can mentor people like her."

"Why do you have to go on a show? Can't you just mentor people anyway?" I say, locking the door behind us.

"I guess I could. I don't know how I'd go about it though. That's the kind of thing Chuck would set up for me, but I don't think he'd go for it. I know what he'd say."

"And what would that be?" I ask, knowing the answer already and hoping she doesn't catch my eye roll.

"I need to focus on my own career and not anyone else's."

"And do you agree?" I follow her into the living area and try not to watch too closely as she kicks off her post-show sneakers and throws herself on the couch.

The past two weeks have been strange. On the one hand, since our confessions on the deck, it's been so easy to be around Aurelia. I find myself not missing my old job or the guys much at all, and I look forward to these evenings when it's just the two of us and we can chat and be ourselves. But, at the same time, I've become aware that my eyes have started taking on a life of their own. I sometimes catch myself watching her while she reads or swims or simply wanders around the villa talking on her phone.

I've started noticing things about her that I wouldn't normally pay any attention to on a women under the age of forty. Like the gentle wobble of her breasts, the slender taper of her legs from the thigh to her ankle, the dip of her waist and the hollow of her throat. Some nights I can even see her pulse beneath the delicate skin of her neck and it makes me shiver. I know what it is. I haven't gotten laid since she arrived. Paris has struck me off her Christmas list and I'm with Aurelia twenty-four-seven.

I can relieve myself, sure, but even that is becoming strange. Until now, whenever I've held my cock in my palm, my mind has been filled with visions of Paris, or the women that came before her. But the last few times I've fisted myself in the shower, all I can see is Aurelia. And stranger still, it fucking helps. It repulses me, the fact I'm masturbating over a teenager, but when I try to put her out of my mind, I can't seem to get anywhere. Then, when I succumb, it's like fucking fireworks. Unbeknown to the popstar sleeping in the next room, I've had her kneeling down in front of me, her mouth stretched open by my girth. I've had her lying beneath me on the couch, on the deck, on my bed, on the damn stage for crying out loud. I've had her bent over the boardwalk gate in the middle of the night, over the kitchen island. Half the time I can't even look at these places in the daylight without getting hard. And now, despite the fact I am only slightly attracted to Aurelia Bird, I'm struggling to handle myself around her.

"No, I don't," she replies, snapping me back to reality. I look away so I don't ogle her while she stretches her limbs out on the couch. "I don't think it's ever too early or too late to help someone else."

"Well, you are a different beast to your stepfather," I say, opening the refrigerator to fix us both drinks.

"Are you saying I'm a beast?" I look over my shoulder and see her head popping up over the back of the couch, a look of mock horror on her face. I can't help but laugh; I love teasing her.

"A friendly one," I wink.

She shakes her head and disappears. I walk around the couch, looking out at the view. Another reason I'm enjoying being Aurelia's round-the-clock security is the chance I get to live as though I'm a damn millionaire.

When Aurelia doesn't take the glass I'm holding out to her, I look round and my pulse quickens. *Fuck.* She's flung off the robe she always wears on the way back to the villa, and stripped out of the stage outfit she'd been wearing beneath it. And she's lying there in a corset and panties, flicking through messages on her phone without a care in the world. As though she isn't giving me a heart attack right now.

"Here," I croak, thrusting the glass towards her, almost angrily. Water sloshes over her legs and she jumps up, yelping from the cold.

"Isaac! What the hell?" She wipes the water off her thighs while I stand there like an idiot, unable to drag my eyes away. "That was freezing!"

"I'm sorry," I splutter, trying hard not to laugh. "It was iced!"

"You're not kidding." Her eyes drop to the glass in my other hand, then she reaches for it.

"You're not having mine," I tease. "You should have been looking out for your own."

"Come on, Isaac," she grins, stepping towards me. I retreat, hitting the coffee table. I twist to stop myself falling, but I lose my balance and grab for Aurelia. The water flies up in the air and we both land sideways on the couch, a little less dry.

"Ha! That's what you get for being mean," she laughs, then she opens her eyes and sees my face inches from hers. Her smell is suddenly everywhere and I drink it in, mentally bottling it for the next time I'm alone.

"I… um," she stutters, pushing herself up.

I follow, heat invading my face. She tries to squeeze past me off the couch but I shift in the wrong direction and she presses a hand down on my cock. After seeing her dressed that way and flicking water from her thighs, I'm hard. Her face jerks up, her expression unreadable, and she withdraws her hand quickly, balling it into a fist.

"God, I'm sorry. I didn't mean… Fuck. Sorry, Isaac."

I'm too flustered to respond so I just watch her rise unsteadily to her feet and pick up the two glasses that, in the process of our fall, had dropped to the floor, thankfully unscathed. I can't believe that just happened. I'm old enough to have conceived her, for God's sake, and she just felt my hard on. A hard on caused by my obvious physical attraction to her.

We'd been getting on just fine. Better than fine. I was enjoying her company, more than I probably should have, and now she's going to think I'm some dirty old guy. I focus on the surface of the table as she shuffles into the kitchen and pours two more glasses. I'm still focused on the table when a fresh glass of iced water appears in front of me.

"Here. I think you might need this," she says. I look up and see her biting her cheek to stop a grin forming. I shake my head and clap my hands over my face.

"Ah fuck. I can't believe that happened. I'm sorry Aurelia, it's not what you think."

"You mean the sight of a young popstar wandering around in a corset and panties didn't turn you on?"

I have no answer so I glare at her instead.

"Frankly, I'd be offended if it hadn't," she continues. "I'm not going to take it personally, Isaac. You're a red-blooded man and there's a reason why women wear this shit. I know I'm not your type, so you can relax."

Am I hearing her correctly? She's really ok with this? She doesn't think I'm some old, dirty pervert for getting turned on by that view?

"Ok, well, thanks," I breathe out. "And I'm really sorry. Please don't read anything into it, ok? Please?"

Her face falls from one of mild amusement to what looks like disappointment, but couldn't possibly be. "It's been a long night," she says, lowering her eyes. "I'll see you in the morning."

"Sure. Night."

I watch her leave, silently kicking the shit out of myself for seeing so damn stupid. Then I retire to my own room, immediately pulling my cock out to finish whatever the hell that corset had started, but I can't do it. I'm too mortified. I go to bed feeling frustrated, embarrassed and full of regret.

CHAPTER TWELVE

Aurelia

I WAKE up with a smile on my face remembering Isaac's hard on the night before. I happily blush recalling the feel of his bulge beneath my hand, knowing no one can witness it. Only I could have caused that. I'd been with him from the moment we left my dressing room, right to the moment he accidentally threw iced water all over me. He hadn't come across any other woman in that time. So, either he has a perpetual hard-on, or he saw me in my corset and liked what he'd seen.

I meant what I said though. There's a reason why girls and women wear this stuff, so really, it could have been anyone parading in front of him wearing sexy lingerie. It was the lingerie that had turned him on, not me. The blush slowly dissipates, along with my smile, and I heave myself out of bed and into the shower.

When I emerge from my suite, I can hear Isaac talking on his cell in hushed tones. It sounds like he's having a difficult, personal conversation. I don't want to loiter conspicuously so I tiptoe past, apologetically, and settle myself on a lounger out on the deck. Unfortunately, the serene quiet the villa affords us means I can still hear everything.

"Mom, you know I don't have that kind of money…" I hear Isaac sigh heavily. "Last time was different. I had to borrow from friends and I can't ask them again."

A pen taps against the kitchen surface where he's hunched over his computer.

"No one needs that amount anyway. What do you need it for?" There's a long pause before he replies in a quiet voice. "I don't believe you."

A longer silence follows and I try my hardest to focus on my book.

"When do you need it by?" Pause. "That's crazy, Mom. A month from now?" He lowers his voice again. "I can get you some of it, ok? But you'll have to go elsewhere for the rest. This is going to wipe me out… No, I'm not borrowing from anyone else, and this is the last time, Mom, I mean it. It seems every time I get back on my feet, you ask me for all my money…"

There's more silence while I try to focus on the words in front of me. I feel terrible to be privy to this conversation. Eventually, Isaac walks out onto the deck and stands at the edge looking out.

"I'm sorry if you heard any of that," he says, finally.

"Of what?" I lie. "Sorry, I was engrossed in my book."

Isaac turns to face me and arches an eyebrow. "It's upside down, Aurelia."

Shit. I slam the book down and sit up. "Ok, you got me. I'm sorry. I really tried hard not to listen, and I only heard bits. I don't want to pry, but are you ok?"

He scrubs at his face and looks back at the sea, his body turned away from me.

"I'm fine, thanks. It's my mother. I don't hear from her for three years and she calls me up wanting money." He sighs and jams his hands into the pockets of his combat shorts. "It's not the first time. There's a pattern. I don't hear from her for years then she calls up apologizing for being out of touch, promising me the world and then, well, asking for obscene amounts of money."

"How much?"

"It's doesn't matter how much, I can't—"

"How much, Isaac?"

He sighs again. "Fifty thousand bucks. The kind of money I don't have. It seems to go up each time. Last time it was thirty grand and I managed to scrape it together using my savings, money from a couple of jobs I did here on the resort and a loan from Connor. That I've only just paid off, mind."

"Are you going to try to give it to her?"

He shakes his head but doesn't reply, so I try a different angle. "Do you have any other family?"

He turns this time and leans back against the railing at the edge of the decking. "No, my father killed himself when I was five."

I can't stop the gasp of shock, even by clamping my hand over my mouth. Isaac, on the other hand, continues unfazed. "My grandma raised me, but then she died ten years ago."

I can hardly breathe. "You were raised by your grandma too."

He nods, a ghost of a smile crossing his face. "Yeah, something we have in common, huh?"

I smile but it's etched in sympathy. My parents might have a funny way of showing their love for me, but at least they've stuck around.

"How did your mom cope?"

He snorts, bitterly. "She didn't. She became a party girl, disappearing for days on end, only returning when she needed more money to pay for her reckless lifestyle."

"It must have been terribly upsetting for her though, losing your father."

He shakes his head. "I guess, but she had a funny way of showing it. After this had gone on for about six months, my grandma intervened and gave her an ultimatum. She told my mom to either seek help and start behaving like a mother again, or to disappear from our lives altogether. My mom barely gave it a thought. She was gone the next day."

I cast my eyes down to my fingers because it's too upsetting to look at Isaac. What he must have been through, having his own mother just reject him like that.

"Have you really not seen your mother since?"

"Once or twice, briefly, to give her money."

"What does she need money for?" I know I'm overstepping the mark by asking these personal questions but I finally feel as though I'm getting to know the real Isaac.

"God knows. She always looks like shit, although never like a junkie. She always seems to be on the verge of becoming homeless. I don't know what she does for a living, if she does anything. She might be turning tricks for all I know."

"Have you ever asked her?"

"I never get a chance. She refuses to say anything until I hand over the money, then she tells me stories that I know are a load of shit."

"I'm so sorry, Isaac." I can't think of anything more appropriate to say.

"It's not your fault," he scoffs. "No one asks for their parents, do they?"

I'm inclined to agree but then a thought occurs to me. "Someone told me once that we do actually choose our parents. Somewhere out there, in the ether, before we're even conceived, our spirits decide on the challenge they want to take on in the next life."

"What a load of BS," Isaac grins.

"Maybe. But think about it. If that was the case, what would your challenge be? If you had indeed chosen your parents, what was the test you wanted them to put you through?"

He shakes his head, as though he's having to humor me and my ridiculous question. Then, his face furrows as he gives it serious contemplation.

"Maybe I needed to know I could survive anything," he says, slowly.

"Well, you've certainly done that," I reply. "I mean, you've lost pretty much all your family. That's a lot to survive. But you also worked for the CIA for over a decade and survived that too. Is that why you joined? Because you wanted to prove you could survive?"

He continues to stare out to sea. "Maybe. I never really thought of it this way before." He turns to face me, finally. "How about you? Why did you choose your parents?" He grins. "Now *this* should be interesting."

I laugh, then take a moment to think. I've considered the question before but my answer changes every time. I hope with age and experience, it will become clearer. I take a deep breath and give him the answer that comes to mind now. "I think I chose my parents so I could learn how to be independent, how to do things my own way. They haven't made it easy for me, that's for sure."

I feel him watching me. "I'd say you're doing a pretty good job," he says, finally.

"We'll see," I say, quietly. "So, what are you going to do? About the money?"

"Well, I can't give it to her," he sighs. "I don't have it. And she doesn't deserve it. The thing that's difficult is living with that. I'm not like her—I can't take, take, take, without giving anything back. She's my mom, I feel like I owe her, or she's my responsibility or something."

"But she isn't," I say. "It was her choice to bring you into the world, and it's her responsibility to look after herself."

"Yeah. But it's one thing to know that, and another thing to be ok with it."

I don't have an answer for him because he's right. "That's the thing about families. You're tied to them, no matter what."

"And on that subject," he says, pushing himself off of the railing. "I got something for you."

I watch him walk back inside the villa, trying my best not to lose my breath again at the sight of him stalking about, all muscle and handsomeness, when I should be thinking a hundred other things. I try to swallow but my throat suddenly feels dry; I need water. I get up to go to the kitchen. The glare of the sun against the glass sliding door is almost blinding so I don't see Isaac as I walk through it. I crash into him, just as he's walking back out to the deck, with so much force I bounce backwards and hit the door. I gasp in shock, and immediately, his hands are around my waist stopping me from toppling over altogether. I regain my footing and look up to see his eyes, dark and questioning, lasering into mine.

A few seconds pass before I realize we're staring at each other, our chests pressed together so close I'm sweating from the heat. "Sorry," I whisper.

He opens his mouth to speak but nothing comes out. His expression is intense, his gaze unyielding. Without thinking, my lips part and his eyes drop to them, his jaw clenching. I'm confused. Isaac is closer to Chuck's age than mine, yet I feel real things for this man. It can't be right, to be attracted to someone close to my parents' age than mine. Can it?

He takes a breath, breaking the spell. "Bank statements going back five years." He hands me an envelope, his eyes not leaving mine. "Let me know if you need more."

I swallow and look up at him as I take them. "Thanks," I say, quietly.

His hand on my shoulder makes me jump. "And Aurelia," he says, softly. "Let me know if there's anything else I can do."

"Have you looked through them?" I ask. "I won't mind if you have."

He shakes his head. "There'd be no point. I don't know what you're looking for." He gives me a small smile that makes my knees weak and walks back into the villa, leaving me alone holding everything I want to know and everything I'm scared to discover. And confused as hell.

CHAPTER THIRTEEN

Isaac

I CHECK the monitors to make sure Jax is ok. He's standing at the main doors to the concert hall, his eyes scanning the room while Aurelia runs through some dance routine changes with her choreographer. I'm pleased she's doing it—those moves have been on her mind all week. The choreographer needed some convincing, but after Aurelia showed us both the changes she wanted to make, and we saw how they could work, she was convinced, as was I.

I've never been a fan of pop music but the last few weeks have taught me there's a lot more to it than a cheesy tune and a sickly sweet singer. The attention to detail is extraordinary, from the fastenings on the stage outfits to the exact key in which one small part of a particular song is sung. The thought that goes into each scene, each move, each exchange with the audience is, frankly, mind-blowing. And, Aurelia Bird is far from sickly sweet. As young and as seemingly innocent as she is, there's a steely resolve behind those hazel eyes. She knows what she wants and she knows how to persuade others so she can get it. The only person she doesn't seem to have any sway over is her stepfather.

I turn back to the email on my screen. He's coming here now. Has something to discuss with me, in private. I told Aurelia I had some accounting business to take care of, and I feel guilty for lying to her. Little do I know, that excuse is not so far from the truth.

"Come in," I call, when the knock comes at the door. "Mr. Bird." I stand to greet him, rising about four inches taller than him. We shake hands and I gesture to the chair opposite.

"Isaac. Call me Chuck, please."

"Chuck," I smile. "What can I do for you?"

"Well, here it is. You've been working with my daughter for four weeks now. I wanted to ask how it was all going? She's not giving you any trouble?"

"None at all, sir. It's a pleasure to work with Aurelia."

"Good to hear, good to hear." He sits away from the edge of the desk, leaning forward with his elbows on his knees, linking and unlinking his fingers. "I suppose you've had to sacrifice other work to take her on full-time, am I correct? You seemed to have a lot on your plate when we last met."

"We've redistributed a lot of the work. There are no issues."

He grinds his teeth. "Listen, I know my daughter is paying you herself." I don't blink, even when he releases an obvious, irritable breath. "Is it an appropriate amount?"

"Yes, it is, sir," I reply, wondering where this is going.

"I can supplement that and make it even more worth your while."

A heaviness appears in my stomach. I was hoping it

wouldn't be true, that Aurelia's father wouldn't try to buy me in some way.

"Go on," I press, hoping I appear interested enough that he'll be brutally honest with me. I need to know what I'm dealing with.

"Now that she's staying here on the island, I don't get to see her as often as I'd like."

You didn't see her anyway, I think.

"I'm sure you understand that, as a teenager, there are things she doesn't like to discuss with her mother and father. We usually pick up on that if we're close by, so we can look out for her safety. We took our eye off the ball when we first arrived in Miami. Her best friend, Ana, persuaded her to leave the hotel, without security. This put Aurelia at great risk and we had to deploy our entire security detail to bring her back safely. If we had seen the signs sooner, we'd have given Aurelia some kind of outlet, a break, anything to satisfy her need for a bit of independence and prevent a stupid incident like that happening."

"I see."

"What I'm saying is, this is the first time we haven't had eyes on our daughter and, naturally, it makes her mother and me a little… anxious."

"I can understand that."

"We usually brief whoever is providing her security to update us on her movements, keep us up to date with her relationships, inform us of any uncharacteristic behaviors. And, of course, because of the additional reporting required, we compensate her security handsomely."

"Right." I lean back, stretch my arms overhead and place my hands at the back of my head. "So, you're saying, you want me to update you on your daughter's movements, friendships and behavior, how often?"

"Daily."

"Without her knowing?"

"Absolutely."

"You want me to *spy* on your daughter?" I say the words slowly, hoping it drives home the ridiculousness of it. It doesn't.

"That's not how I like to think of it, but, yes."

"What do you get out of it?" I ask, annoyance clawing at my throat.

"The knowledge that she's ok and she's safe."

"That's my job," I say, sternly. "She *is* safe. Why do you need to know who she's friends with and how she's behaving?"

He straightens and his frustration becomes evident in his features. "She is the face of a billion dollar empire, Isaac, which I have to manage. We have sponsorship agreements, investments, a sales plan, record company commitments. If her behavior goes off course just once, we could lose all that. She put me in charge of her assets. I am simply protecting them."

"Don't you trust your own daughter?" I fire at him.

"Of course I do," he snaps. "But she's a teenager for God's sake. Don't you remember what you were like as a teenager, Isaac?"

"I do actually. I was holding down a respectable job with a local bank before I was accepted into the CIA."

"But you weren't rolling around in mountains of money, were you? You don't know what money can do to people."

"Oh, I have a pretty good idea," I say, looking him up and down, but the irony is lost on him.

"Look, I do trust my daughter; I just don't trust the people around her," he appeals.

"There is no one around her," I frown. "Only her team. I

don't even see her mother here. She misses her sisters, you know."

"Are you criticizing my family?" He seems to have cottoned on to the fact I'm reluctant to do his dirty work.

"No. I'm simply saying that, as her father, perhaps you should be focusing on ensuring she has stronger support from her family, instead of paying people to spy on her."

"I'm *not* her father," he hisses. "Her father left before she was even born. He was a damn low-life who couldn't face up to his responsibilities. He left Aurelia and her mother with nothing. And they continued to have nothing until I came along."

I rub my chin and cock my head. "Hadn't she already scored a number one hit before you met her mother?"

"One number one record doesn't give you riches, or security," he sneers. "Aurelia is lucky to have me."

I beg to differ but I don't say anything. Despite what I'd told Aurelia, I did go through those bank statements and there's a lot in them that seems untoward, that warrants explanation. But I'm not the one to demand that. Aurelia is.

"If that's true, you would trust her. Aurelia is a grown woman and she can look after herself. I suggest you allow her to do just that." I stand, my narrowed eyes instructing him to do the same. I don't want this snake in my office a minute longer. He scowls at me as he rises to his feet, various chains around his neck glinting in the sunlight coming through the window.

"Just to warn you, I'm cutting her allowance. She won't be able to afford you for much longer," he threatens.

"I'm sure we'll be able to work something out." I have no idea how I'd manage to work for Aurelia for free but showing doubt now would be showing weakness, and I am definitely the stronger one here. "It was good to see you, Mr. Bird. Will we be seeing you at tonight's show?" I know that previous to this meeting, his answer would have been no, but now he has a point to prove.

"Yes. You will."

"Excellent. And when can I tell Aurelia her mother will be bringing her sisters to visit?"

His teeth grind again. "Tuesday. She'll bring them Tuesday."

"That's great," I say, giving him a genuine smile. "I'm so pleased we could talk."

I walk him out of my office and watch as he stomps away, finally unclenching my fists. My eyes follow him as he walks in the direction of the café.

It's then that I see her.

A woman with ice blonde hair to her waist wearing grey linen trousers and a white tank, is hovering by the golf buggies in the parking lot. She's partly concealed by palms and foliage and her jerky movements tell me she's attempting to remain hidden. Her eyes follow Chuck then scan the area until they land on me. I pretend not to notice when she moves shiftily towards a brown Toyota and climbs inside. But I turn to watch as she reverses out of the lot and back along the main drive. My thoughts process her quickly. She isn't a guest and she sure isn't a member of staff. She seems to know who Chuck is. She's something to do with Aurelia. I retreat and close the door, then head straight for the CCTV suite.

I WAIT outside Aurelia's dressing room. It's a Sunday night so there are no post-show meet and greets this evening. She changes in double quick time and bursts onto the corridor with a wide smile. "I'm ready!"

"You're way too excited about this," I laugh, shaking my head. "Don't get your hopes up, ok? It's a just a staff bar."

"Are you kidding me? This is the most exciting thing to happen to me all week!"

"You've just performed on stage for eight thousand people, and *this* is the most exciting part of your week?"

"Yes, it is! Isaac, you still don't get it. I haven't had any sort of young adult life. I've been cooped up since I was fifteen-years-old. I've never snuck out to a bar, or even a coffee shop, with other people my age. I've mostly hung out with people who work for my stepfather—who've been paid to be there."

"You know, whenever you say that, it makes me feel complicit. You pay me too."

"It's different with you," she says, walking ahead of me out of the exit. The concert goers pile straight out onto the main drive, so we're taking a back route past Reef Street and up the staff beach.

"Different, how?"

"I consider you more of a friend. I know that's a little ridiculous because we would probably never hang out if you weren't my security, but I feel like you're on my side, you know? Not my stepfather's."

"Why do you think we wouldn't hang out?" I ask, slightly offended.

"Come on Isaac, all your friends are guys, maybe with the exception of Tawny and Seleste, but that's because they're your friends' girlfriends. I'm just a teenage girl who likes to prance about on a stage."

"No you're not," I retort. "You're more than that."

We're walking close together along a narrow path and, try as I might, I can't help the back of my hand brushing against hers. At first she jerks her arm away and pretends to adjust her top, but then she lowers it again and we resume the occasional contact quite comfortably.

"In what way?" she asks, fixing her eyes straight ahead.

I don't answer immediately. It feels as though we're on the precipice of something and my words could topple us one of two ways. It could either keep us on the right track, or it could push us past the professional marker into more personal territory. The truth is, I've never had such a close bond with a client before. I've never had so much fun or felt so at ease with another woman before. I realize this is probably because she's off limits so I can relax around her. But, for some reason, I feel I still need to be cautious with how I tread.

"You're interesting," I say. "You've had experiences that most guys my age have never, and will never, get to have. You're wise too, beyond your years I'd say. You have a more sensible head on your shoulders than most people I've met."

"That's so hot," she laughs. "Sensible. Great."

"And you're funny. You make me laugh. You never take anything too seriously, least of all yourself, and you'd be amazed at how rare that is. You're kind and loving; you only ever treat your fans and your employees with care and respect. And, yeah, the fact you are pretty as fuck doesn't make it any harder to be around you."

Even in the dark I can see the blush flood her face.

"I'm pretty?"

I stop and turn her to face me. "Your face is plastered on the posters of about a million bedrooms across the United States of America. What do you think?"

The redness in her cheeks deepens. "Thanks for the compliment."

I take a breath and feel the need to change the subject. This seems to be happening more and more when I talk to Aurelia. Encroaching on intimate territory and feeling the need to change the subject. "Chuck came to see me yesterday."

Her smile falls and she chews the side of her cheek. "What did he want?"

"I think you know."

Her chest rises and falls as though she's containing something. "How much did he offer you?"

"We didn't get that far. I made it pretty clear I wasn't going to entertain any sort of arrangement that required me to spy on his daughter."

"Right," she nods. "And… how did he react?"

"He wasn't happy, but he let it go."

"Is that why he came to the concert last night? I was surprised to him there."

"I may have guilted him a little."

Her lips twist into a small smile. "My mom called too," she says. "She's bringing Coralie and Noémie here on Tuesday. Did you have something to do with that also?"

"No, no. That wasn't me." I don't want her to think I've had to force her entire family to behave like that's exactly what they are. "But that's great. I know you've been missing the twins."

"Thank you Isaac," she whispers and I wonder if she can see through me.

The air around us feels warm, as though it's wrapping around us both. I take a step backwards, instinctively. "No problem. Now, let's go. We have an exceptionally dull staff party to get to."

CHAPTER FOURTEEN

Aurelia

THE 'STAFF PARTY' is anything but dull. I can hear raucous laughter, loud music and the clinking of bottles as we approach the security gate in the northeast wall. I remember seeing the wall when I first arrived on Starling Key. It looked prison-like and as though nothing of any interest at all resided on the other side. The noise I hear now blows that perception out the water.

"Ok, I apologize now if you get mobbed," Isaac says as he presses a number into the keypad.

"Hey!" I admonish, playfully slapping him on the arm. "You're supposed to protect me."

"Oh no. I warned you Aurelia. You enter these walls at your own risk. You knew that."

"Ok, fine," I grin, practically pushing him through the opening. I can't wait. At first, I can't see anything but dark walls and windows. A few are lit up from the inside. "Are those the dorms?"

"Yeah," Isaac says, leading me between buildings. "Some of the staff live off the Key, like Carter and Seleste for example, and Arnaud, our head chef. But most people live here. It's easier, especially if you don't have family."

The music fades out and a whoop sounds as a Jimi Hendrix song starts up, louder than the last. "Oh my God, I love this song," I gasp.

"It's a little antique for you, isn't it?" Isaac says.

I spin around, my hands on my hips, defiant. "Maybe I like antiques."

He looks momentarily stunned. "Really?"

"Yeah," I shrug, maintaining eye contact, willing him to read through the lines. "The classics are the best. So, is there a dance floor or what?"

Isaac looks relieved then scrunches his face up in thought. "Um, of sorts."

We finally round a corner and all I can see before us is a mass of scantily clad bodies bouncing up and down in time with the music. There are guys in board shorts and combats, not many wearing shirts, and there are girls wearing flimsy dresses, tiny shorts and bikini tops. Sweat glistens on all of them as they move, carefree and unchoreographed, to the heavy guitar. I am engulfed with the need to join them. Without thinking, I push past Isaac and straight into the crowd. I recognize Tawny and Esme, and make a beeline for them. They cheer as I arrive, and throw their arms around me, before losing themselves again in the music. I close my eyes and move my hips, swinging my freshly-washed, still-damp hair from side-to-side. No one is bombarding me, no one is fighting to get a selfie, no one is scrutinizing my movements.

I'm being totally left alone to move to the music, free and uninhibited.

When I finally open my eyes, Tawny has paused and someone is shouting in her ear. When the person straightens, I see it's Isaac. He stands and fixes his eyes on me. There's something burning behind them. It's intense and I don't know whether to like it or be afraid of it. I keep moving, running my hands up through my hair, then flicking it to the side while swinging my hips to the bass. He watches me, unwavering. I notice his Adam's apple bob up and down. I decide I like it. I like having him watch me, and I suddenly wish there was no one else here, that I were dancing only for him. I hold his eyes as I move my ass to the music, until he suddenly breaks the contact and turns away. When I turn back to Tawny, she has her eyes diverted. When she looks up, she gives me a timid smile and arches an eyebrow.

I dance out the Hendrix song then follow Tawny through the crowd. A few people do a double take but don't attempt to stop me. We emerge out of the dancing mass and I take a deep breath. The air is thick with alcohol, sweat and, thankfully, incense. A string of fairy lights hangs on a far wall and we make our way towards it. As we approach, a makeshift table comes into view and two guys stand behind it, fixing drinks for a small crowd gathered around.

"That's Ché and Camiro," Esme explains. "They work some of the bars here, and on Sundays they work this one. Unofficially," she winks.

"Do you drink?" Tawny asks.

"Um, maybe, a little," I say, hesitantly.

"Don't worry, I'll ask him to make you a weak one," she smiles.

"A weak what?" I look up at Esme.

"Mojito. Ché makes the best. You'll love it."

"How long does this go on for?" I ask her, gesturing around us.

"It varies. Sometimes to one a.m., other nights longer. If we have a full day on the Monday, it doesn't go on too long because staff need to sleep here too." She glances up at the windows, and I follow her gaze to one in particular that seems to hang right over the courtyard we're standing in.

"I don't envy whoever lives in that one."

"Ha! No one lives there anymore," Esme explains. "Only people who've pissed off the boss." She nudges Tawny.

"Don't remind me," Tawny says, shaking her head. "He's still paying for it."

"What happened?" I ask.

"It's a long story," Esme starts. "But briefly, when Tawny arrived here to start a new job she crashed her car into the wall around the resort. Connor was not happy, and decided to punish her by making her stay in there—8A."

"Connor? The head of the security team? Your boyfriend?" The shock must be evident on my face.

"Yeah," Tawny laughs. "Like Esme said, it's a long story."

"But it has a happy ending," Esme adds.

"How about you?" I ask Esme. "Do you have a boyfriend?"

"I'm working on it," Tawny says. "She's a little picky is our Esme."

"Hey!" Esme says. "I love my life as it is. It's going to take someone very special to improve on it."

"That's such a good attitude to have," I say, taking the glass Tawny is passing back to me.

"Go easy with that," Esme says. "We may have asked for it to be made weak, but Che's definition of weak is very different to ours." She grins and takes a long sip of her own.

"And you? Are you seeing anyone Aurelia?" Tawny asks.

I shake my head, acclimating to the zingy bubbles hitting my throat. "Not since Nate."

"Who's that?" Esme frowns.

Tawny shrugs.

"I take it you don't read *People Magazine*, then?"

"No, I'm afraid not," Tawny says, apologetically.

"Don't worry. It's a relief actually. I dated another singer for a few years. He was a member of a boyband called Jinxed."

"What happened?" Esme asks, taking another long sip.

"He cheated on me with Amber Mayhew, a famous model. I found out about it through *Us Weekly*. I was completely humiliated and couldn't get out of bed for about a week. It's one thing to be cheated on, but to have it done to in public is a whole other level of humiliation. What's weird is, it didn't stop my parents loving him." I frown slightly. It still hurts.

"So, um, what about now?" Tawny asks, keeping her eyes on her glass. "Anyone here caught your attention?"

I feel myself flush. "Not really. Why?"

"No reason. It's just, you and Isaac seem to be getting along really well."

I smile, nervously. "We are. But as colleagues. He's a lot older than I am."

"Age is just a number," Esme says.

"Yeah." I look past them to where Isaac is standing with Luca, Connor and Jax. Just as my eyes find him, he looks up, and for a moment we just stare at each other. Can he hear us? I break the eye contact feeling suddenly out of my depth. "Anyway, I'm not his type. I'm nothing like Paris Navitsky."

Esme does a double take. "You know about that?"

I nod and take another sip, enjoying the way the alcohol

relaxes me. I feel like I need it, just to cope with the burning sensation of Isaac's eyes whenever he looks up. "We bumped into her once, the day after I moved here. It was really awkward so I asked him about it."

Esme and Tawny look at each other then back at me. I feel like I have to emphasize the point. "Anyway, I have to focus on the shows while I'm here. I can't really afford to be distracted."

They spend the next hour telling me about how they each ended up on Starling Key, and I'm amazed at how people find such joy after facing such horrific circumstances. I feel utterly privileged in comparison, even though my family life feels far from perfect at the moment. At one point I look up and Isaac is not there. As my eyes scour the area, nervously, I notice Jax is watching me instead. I feel a sharp sense of relief knowing that whether he's there or not, Isaac has my back. Just before it's time for me to head back to the villa, my favorite Stevie Nicks song, Edge of Seventeen, starts playing over the speakers.

"I have to dance to this," I announce. My limbs are already moving. "I can't not."

"I'll come with you," Esme laughs. Tawny hugs me goodbye before heading out of the bar with Connor.

I follow Esme into the crowd feeling instantly lifted with all the other bodies. I'm surrounded by people who are smiling and losing themselves in the music. I don't think I've ever had the chance to dance with other people in this way, without every move being closely choreographed, and backup dancers tracking every step. I feel hands on my hips and I move with them. I watch a couple a few feet away, joined together at the mouth and pelvis, slow-dancing to the rock music. Esme jumps to the music with an arm above her head. I'm spun around and passed to another pair of hands that lift me up then lower me gracefully. I don't feel at all afraid or unsafe; I feel so incredibly protected by all these people around me. And I'm so happy I can hardly breathe.

As the song comes to an end, I turn around to face whoever is softly guiding my hips from behind, and see a tall, heavily tattooed, strong-jawed beast of a man staring me down, not unkindly. He bows his head slightly and takes my hand. I let him lead me out of the crowd, to the edge of the courtyard where I search for Isaac. My eyes scan the walls looking for familiar faces, then I feel it. The searing hot sensation of eyes boring into my face. I turn slowly and my breath sticks in my throat. Isaac is staring at me and the giant man, with a look that says he wants to kill someone. This is my cue to leave.

I turn to the man who is still holding my hand. "Thanks," I say. "I'm Aurelia, by the way."

The man breaks a small smile and it looks strange, as though he was designed to look forever serious, menacing even. "Axel," he replies, before kissing my hand and letting it go.

Isaac turns his back before I reach him and I follow his footsteps back through the buildings to the gate. He doesn't say a word as he holds it open for me to walk through and he doesn't say a word the whole way past Reef Street to the boardwalk.

"What's wrong?" I ask, eventually. It's a question born more of annoyance than curiosity. I feel as though I've done something wrong, but I can't think for the life of me what it is.

"Nothing," he says, fixing his eyes on the wooden slats.

"Have I done something wrong?"

He whips his head round. "No, of course not."

"You've gone awfully quiet."

"I just want to get you back to the villa, that's all."

"Why? Am I in danger?"

"No more than usual," he replies, cryptically.

We arrive at the villa and Isaac lets us inside. I really need another shower. I showered after the show but dancing in the middle of a sweaty mass of people reversed the good that had done. But, I need to hear what Isaac's problem is.

"Now are you going to tell me what's put you in a shitty mood?"

He spins to face me and, for the first time, he looks angry. "You know, you really shouldn't just let any old stranger feel you up like that."

"What? The guy dancing? Axel?"

"Doesn't matter who he is. You don't know him. He could be anyone."

"But you thought the northeast wall was safe enough for you to take me there. I figured I was ok to dance with whoever."

"It is safe," he snaps, taking a step towards me.

"So, what's your issue?" I crane my neck to look up at him.

"I don't know him and I don't trust him."

"But he's part of your team," I argue.

"Doesn't matter. I trust the others with my life. Not him."

"Everyone was there. Nothing would have happened." I shake my head and look down. The way he's staring at me is making me feel things I shouldn't.

"That's not how it looked from where I was standing." His voice is barely recognizable and I realize with a jolt, he's jealous. My insides turn to liquid.

"I didn't do anything to lead him on," I say, quietly. "I won't do it again if… if it bothers you." And I mean it. On the rare occasion I've thought about Isaac with Paris Navitsky, I haven't liked the way it made me feel. I've never known what jealousy is until now. If Isaac is feeling it too, I need to be kind. I care about him, too much.

After an eternity, he steps backwards. "It's not me I'm bothered about, it's you."

He disappears into his suite while I walk unsteadily towards the kitchen and perch on one of the kitchen bar stools. When he returns, he places a series of photographs in front of me.

"Do you know this person?"

I'm staring at some grainy black and white CCTV photos of a woman, about eight years older than me, slender, pretty, completely unfamiliar.

"No, I've never seen her before."

"Are you sure?" Isaac's eyes are burrowing into me, as though he's trying to see my soul.

"Absolutely. Never seen her before in my life."

"So, you've no idea why she would be hanging around the parking lot while your stepfather was here on the island?"

"No." I look up at him. "You think she's something to do with Chuck?"

"I thought that was one explanation, but then Hudson caught her on the monitors this evening, while we were behind the north east wall. Chuck, as far as I know, had left to go back to Miami. That's why I disappeared and left Jax watching you. I went to see what she was doing."

"And what was she doing?"

"She was hanging around the marina, according to Hud. By the time I got to the suite, she'd made her way back to the parking lot. She drives a brown Toyota. This really isn't ringing any bells?"

I shake my head. "None at all. Maybe she's nothing to do with me."

"Maybe," Isaac says, sounding skeptical. "But I don't want to take any chances. I've doubled security on the gate overnight. Whoever she is, she doesn't appear to be a paying guest, and nor has she been invited. We're closely monitoring the route in and out for the concerts. It could be that she got in that way, so we're going to be extra careful.

"Ok," I say, feeling completely calm. "I trust you, Isaac. You make me feel safe."

He looks like he's about to say something else, then he stops himself and shuffles the photographs into an envelope.

"Did you find what you wanted from the bank statements?"

"I'm not sure," I shrug. It's the truth. I don't know what I'm looking for either, but what I do know is there are payment streams set up to funnel money out of the Bird Holdings accounts to other accounts I'm unfamiliar with, but they could be anything, they could be completely innocent. "Could you do something else for me?" I ask, forcing myself to look him in the eye.

"Anything." One look into the dark pools beneath his brow and I believe him.

"Thank you. I need passwords."

"For what?"

"Everything connected to Chuck Bird and Bird Holdings."

He straightens, picks up the envelope and looks at me with a seriousness that makes my chest swell.

"Consider it done."

CHAPTER FIFTEEN

saac

"HAVE you been checking the monitors again?" Luca asks as I rejoin the team in the meeting room for Connor's weekly huddle. I haven't attended one of these since I took on Aurelia's detail, but I'm curious to figure out this Axel guy.

"Yeah. So?"

"Dude, Hudson's with her. Not even a Mossberg 930 shotgun will get past him. She's safe."

"It's not shotguns I'm worried about right now." It's a strange blonde woman who has an uncanny ability to sneak past our perimeter to get onto the island without our knowledge.

Luca knows this. "No one's seen her for a few days, and we're all on it. Relax."

I sit down and look around the room. Carter has his forehead on the desk; he's either asleep or dead. Luca has returned to typing out a message on his phone while maintaining a separate conversation with Jax. Connor is bashing something out on his laptop and Axel has yet to appear.

"How's everything going?" I ask no one in particular.

"Yeah, good," Connor says, snapping the laptop closed. "Axel's taken over the cleaning business…"

"For Bianchi?"

"Yeah. It's going well. Bianchi's given us more, but I've made it clear we're almost at capacity. We still have our legit work to do and I don't want anything getting in the way of that."

"Good to hear."

"How are things with the residency?" Connor asks.

"Great. I can't believe we're almost halfway through."

"It has gone super-fast," Jax agrees.

"Aurelia happy?"

I nod, not trusting myself to say anything further about her. It's getting harder and harder to not let my hands wander when I catch her from falling, or when I argue with her about dancing with men she doesn't know. Her lips are starting to taunt me. And when she does that thing where she licks them or she chews the flesh of her bottom one, I can barely hold myself together. The idea of keeping all of this in for another two months is excruciating. But I can't act on it. I can't.

First, it would be a complete violation of our agreement, our contract. Second, I really am old enough to be her dad. Hell, I might even be her dad. God knows what I was getting up to at the age of fifteen. I may have donated sperm for cash, who knows? But, then again, I would have remembered. I was no ordinary fifteen-year-old. With a high IQ, a photographic memory and a weird obsession with math, I was never too interested in underage drinking and debauchery. Too boring. Plus, Aurelia is as fair as a sea breeze, while I have the standard issue jet black hair and deep olive skin bestowed by Italian descent.

"Her manager happy too?"

"As far as I know," I say, holding back a disdainful grunt. "He doesn't have much involvement."

"That's probably a good thing," Connor, says, one eyebrow raised. I'm about to agree when the door opens and in walks Axel, my temporary replacement, and currently, my fucking nemesis.

"Gentlemen," he greets, in an impossibly deep, low voice. The man towers over all of us at seven feet tall. He is built like a house too.

"Hey, man," Connor says. "How's it going?"

"Good," Axel rumbles. "I just came from the marina. One of the dive boats got stuck in the mangroves so I just helped them tow it out."

"That would explain the river that just followed you in here," Jax said, staring at the sodden floor.

"Yeah, sorry about that. Didn't have time to go change my boots."

"We were just talking about the residency," Connor continues.

"Aurelia Bird," Axel says. "I heard it's going down well. Met her the other night at the bar. She's a firecracker."

I narrow my eyes at him. Luca catches it and kicks me under the table.

"Does she hang there a lot?"

"At the bar?" Connor asks.

"Yeah. I wouldn't mind slow-dancing with her again. She can move, that one."

"No," I snap. "It was a one-time thing."

Axel slowly drags his eyes from Connor to me and they're doing a damn slow dance of their own. "Is that right?"

"Yes. I shouldn't have brought her there. She really needed her rest."

Luca is glaring at me, I can sense it.

"She seemed to be unwinding just fine," Axel says, gloating.

"Dancing always relaxes her," I growl in reply. "That's just how she is."

"Are you two… together?" He asks, not-so-innocently.

"No, not at all," I reply. Luca, who's been watching us nervously, drops his eyes back to his phone.

"He wishes," Jax says, and in a way I'm thankful because it lightens the mood.

"You know that's not true."

"He just hasn't got laid in a while, since Paris left," Luca adds.

"Ah yes," Axel says, rubbing his hands together. "I heard about that. Beautiful lady."

"Yes, she is," I say, the dark cloud returning. *And you can keep your hands off her too.* I decide in those few minutes I'm not ever going to warm to this heathen.

"Well, you never know, Caroline might be back this season," Jax says. "Doesn't this room bring back memories?" He nods towards the storage room and I can't stop a grin spreading across my face.

"Those were the days."

"They weren't that long ago," Carter says, surprising us all by simply being awake.

"They feel like it. I need to get back in the game," I jest.

"What happened in this room?" Axel asks.

"Oh, just Isaac engaging in some unorthodox guest relations in the store room, *during a staff meeting*," Luca fires at me, accusingly.

Axel roars with laughter. "Man…" He stands and fist pumps me. "Kudos to you, that's awesome."

I laugh back and decide I might get along with him, after all.

"Right then," Connor says, commanding our attention. "The schedule this week…"

He goes through everyone's duties and, strangely, I don't envy Axel his. He might be doing my old job but I'm surprisingly quite happy being Aurelia's bodyguard. I'll miss this job when it's over.

"There is one thing I could use your help with, Isaac," Connor says, breaking into my thoughts.

"Sure. What is it?"

"Bianchi is starting up the shipments again next week. Has a big one coming in from Mexico. Middle of the night job. I have to do some stuff for Starling, keep him away from the marina. Can you take the delivery?"

"Absolutely." I know what's in it for us. A little bit of extra pocket money for the whole team. Not just the security guys but the entire resort. If I can do my bit to help, I will.

"It won't tire you out?"

"Nah," I wave my hand, dismissively. "But what about Aurelia?"

"We can have one of the agency guys cover her. Will she be ok with that?"

"She'll be asleep."

"Great. That's settled."

I FOLLOW Aurelia and her mother, each holding a twin toddler, back up the beach where they load their bags and the two girls into the golf buggy. I sit quietly in the buggy behind, maintaining a respectable distance. I like my clients to feel safe, not crowded. As Aurelia starts the buggy, her mother turns and fires another glare at me. It's one I've become quite familiar with in the last three hours.

I'd stayed at the top of the beach, discreetly hidden beneath a cluster of palms, watching as Aurelia and the girls in her family enjoyed a picnic courtesy of Arnaud, our resort chef, on the fine, white sand. The sound of the waves caressing the shoreline was soft but loud enough to mask any hint of the conversation Aurelia and her mother were having. For the most part it looked pleasant, but occasionally they would both look back towards me and Aurelia would put her hand on her mother's arm as if to reassure her. It annoyed me. I wasn't the one Aurelia needed to be cautious of.

The bored and resigned look on her mother's face as she stepped out of the sedan made it clear she'd shown up to meet her eldest daughter under duress. Two nannies bundled the twin girls out of the back seat, preened their sundresses and pushed them lightly towards their mother. To Mrs. Bird's obvious relief, Aurelia was there in an instant, scooping the girls up into a smothering embrace which, as evidenced by their squeals and squirms, they obviously loved.

Mrs. Bird watched for a few seconds as Aurelia took the girls to the water's edge, letting them paddle in the surf, then she laid back on the luxury lounger and worshipped the sun. Occasionally, a light gust of wind would blow a little sand onto her oiled skin and she would push herself up, tut loudly and make a show of wiping away the invisible grains before liberally applying more oil to which sand would inevitably stick after the next gust of wind.

The twin girls were immaculately behaved and, frankly, adorable. It was obvious Aurelia doted on them and they on her. I felt something like my heart twisting when I thought of the time Aurelia spent away from her little sisters. She must miss them dreadfully.

I stand back as Aurelia gives her little sisters sloppy, tickly kisses, then bends to receive a chaste peck on the cheek from her mother, before waving them off as the sedan disappears down the drive towards the exit. When she finally turns to me, her face is alive with joy. I'm not prepared for what happens next. Aurelia runs to me, slamming the wind out of my lungs and wrapping her small arms around me, trapping my own to my sides.

"Thank you Isaac," she says, her words muffled against the fabric of my shirt.

I laugh, trying to prize my arms out of her grip. "I didn't do anything."

She stands back, her eyes wet with unshed tears. "Well, accept my gratitude anyway."

I take hold of her hands and wrap them around me again, before wrapping mine around her neck. She rests a cheek against my chest. It feels completely natural.

"Did you have a nice afternoon?" I ask her, softly.

"It was amazing. They've grown so big." She pauses and I know there's more she wants to say, so I wait. "I hate that I'm missing so much. They're both talking and Coralie has the most beautiful singing voice..." She stops again and my chest suddenly feels wet with tears. I kiss the top of her head without thinking. Neither of us speak and I, for one, don't want to pull away. But, the longer we stand like this, the more questionable it becomes. And I'm a professional. I'm also her bodyguard. I'm also fifteen years older than her.

I unwrap her arms and step backwards. "How was your mom?"

She sighs and rubs her neck, a gesture I've come to recognize as a sign of stress. "The same as ever. Keen to get back to Miami. She's going out with some friends in the morning for brunch and shopping. It's great that she's seeing people and living her life and not just Chuck's."

Yeah, on your money, I add, silently.

"Is she ok with you being here? Full time I mean? She didn't seem to be too happy with me."

She shrugs, dismissively. "She would prefer I was in Miami but she understands. I think she just wants me to hang out more with people my own age."

I gasp in mock offense and she looks up at me, sharply.

"She doesn't know what she's talking about. It's not as though you're, like, my parent's age."

"It makes me feel better you think that, but I am actually old enough to be your dad," I remind her.

"Don't be ridiculous. You'd have to be having sex at fifteen," she frowns up at me.

I arch an eyebrow in reply.

"You were having sex at fifteen?"

"I've always been innately curious. All my teachers thought it was a gift," I say in my defense.

She shakes her head. "Anyway, you know what I mean. It's not like you're a friend like that—"

I narrow my eyes.

"You know what I mean," she says again, fumbling. I don't help her. I genuinely want to know what she thinks this is, this relationship we have. It's more than professional, I'm reluctant to admit, but I still haven't been able to define it for myself. "We're friends, yeah, but it's different, isn't it?"

I hold her eyes. "How is it different?"

"Well, um, you're my bodyguard, aren't you?" She pauses, searching my face. There's a thread of sadness in her next words and crooked smile. "You're paid to hang out with me."

I can't argue with that, but I also can't let those words hang as though that's the sole truth. "And I care about you. That has nothing to do with my age."

She stares at the ground but I can't miss the flush in her cheeks. I feel instantly warm again, at once hating and relishing this hot, cold, up, down tempo of emotions that seem to pass between us.

"Come on, let's head back." I climb back into the golf buggy. "I thought you wanted to spend your rare night off watching scary movies and stuffing your face with popcorn."

"Oh yeah," she grins, climbing in beside me. I allow myself a smug smile at the knowledge I have another surprise lined up for her tomorrow and I can't wait to see her face. Seeing Aurelia happy is one of my new favorite things.

CHAPTER SIXTEEN

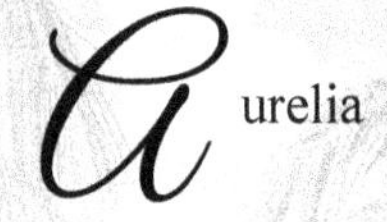

urelia

I SHOWER and change into shorts and a tank, then I do what I hardly ever do when I'm planning to spend a night in watching crappy movies and stuffing my face with bad food. I check myself out in the mirror. Without makeup, I look even younger than I am. Maybe sixteen, seventeen. I pull out my makeup bag and apply some concealer, blush and mascara. I still look too young. I layer on some shadow and run a kohl pencil along my eyelids. Marginally better. I could pass for twenty-one, twenty-two maybe.

I stand back and stare at my reflection. What am I trying to achieve? Do I want Isaac to simply notice me? Something tells me he already has, so what is it? Do I want him to make a move? Just the thought makes me blush and I feel like a damn adolescent, not a strong female performer who has no qualms about forcing my sex appeal onto hundreds of thousands of fans. As my eyes roam my face, my large brown eyes, my carefully mussed-up hair, my lightly glossed lips, a thought occurs to me. I want to affect him and I want to see it. I want to be reassured that this isn't all in my head. I know he feels something for me, despite the difference in our age, and the responsibility he has towards me. I want him to show me, in some small way, that he's attracted to me—beyond that one time when he saw me in a corset and very little else—so I know I'm not going insane.

I walk out of my suite and head straight for the kitchen. I'm nervous, and my shaking hands make opening the popcorn wrapper a lot more challenging than it should be. Isaac is standing in front of the giant TV screen with the remote in his hand, scanning through potential movies.

"Did you have anything in mind?" he asks, without looking round.

"Something scary," I reply, focusing on the task of finding a bowl to pour the popcorn into.

"Yeah, you already said that, but are you into blood and guts? Or freak the shit out of yourself scary? Or ghosts and ghouls?"

"Um…" I locate a bowl and place it on the counter. "I don't mind. I liked *Get Out*…" I turn the bag upside down.

"Psycho thriller, huh? I'm seeing you in a different light, Aurelia."

I turn too quickly and popcorn rains down on the counter. "Shit."

I sense Isaac coming towards me. "Ah man, you know this means I'm gonna have to let you share my bag, and Isaac doesn't usually share food."

He bends down to where I'm crouched on the floor scooping up pieces of popcorn. My hands are still shaking.

"Hey." I feel his finger under my chin and I look up, nervously. "You ok? You're shaking."

"Yeah, I'm fine, bit cold, that's all."

"Come here, sit on the couch and I'll fetch a blanket."

He pulls me to my feet then looks at me again, narrowing his eyes as they roam my face. I suddenly feel uncomfortable about the makeup I've applied. He sees me covered in it every night on stage, but as soon as we're back in the villa, I always wash it off.

"Wh—what?" I stammer.

"Nothing." He leads me to the sofa and sits me down carefully, like I'm eighty years old. Then he goes to his suite and returns with a beautifully soft, grey cashmere blanket. I cuddle it to me, to give him the impression I really am cold and not just shivering with lust-sick nerves. Even though we spend every night in the villa together, tonight feels as though we're on a date. I wonder if he feels it too.

"Soda?" he asks.

"Can I get a hot chocolate?" Might as well keep this pretense up.

He looks at me, amused. "Sure. Coming right up."

Once Isaac has cleared the kitchen, he brings over the bowl of popcorn and places it on the table. "You can share mine," he winks. Then he hands me a giant mug of hot chocolate and sits down beside me with a bottle of alcohol-free beer.

"How about *The Purge*?" he says, crossing an ankle over his knee.

"The what?" I take the opportunity to look at his profile. He has a look of mischief in his eye and I notice the corner of his lips twitch as though he's holding back a smile. Sometimes he seems a lot younger than he is. Other times, like when he first moved me into the villa, he appears older. Either way, I can't imagine anyone wanting to mess with him. He's not built as large as some of the other members of the security team, but with his firm Italian features and the tastefully placed tattoos sneaking out from beneath his shirts and t-shirts, he can look just as menacing.

"*The Purge*," he grins. "It's a personal favorite." He twists to face me and pulls up one knee to rest between us. "Imagine the United States government sanctioned one night a year when all crime was permitted. The film is basically about what happens on the night—how people vent their pent-up anger..."

I arch an eyebrow, suspiciously. "And you like this movie because the idea of killing people without any consequence appeals to you?"

He doesn't answer straight away but allows his eyes to roam my face. I wish I knew what he was thinking, but I can't tell if he's confirming my summary or feeling insulted by it. "No, I like this movie because I'm interested in the lengths people will go to, to protect themselves."

I look away, feeling slightly foolish. "Right. Sounds good. Let's do it."

Just before he turns back to the screen, I shiver, involuntarily. I'm feeling more and more small and vulnerable in his presence, as though he knows my secret—that I feel something for him—and he wants to make me sweat.

"Are you still cold?"

I can't think of another plausible alternative so I nod.

"Come here." He pulls me towards him and nestles me between his thick thighs, so I'm leaning back against his chest. He crosses his right arm in front of me, pinning me to him, and rubs my left, lightly, enough to give me goosebumps. "I don't want you catching a cold."

My heart sinks slightly. "Yeah, you don't want the star of your residency having to cancel shows because they caught a bug."

His hand stops moving and I feel his chest expand with a breath. "That's not what I meant," he says, his voice quiet.

"I know. I'm joking," I say, weakly.

"Is that what you really think? That your performances are more important to me than you are?"

"Well, yes. I don't mind, Isaac. I know what my shows are worth to the resort."

"Aurelia." He sighs and grips me tighter. "You have no idea, do you? You've become more to me than just a resident artist."

"Really?" My insides are blooming and something is doing a dance inside my chest.

"Of course. You're a friend. Someone I care about."

And just like that, my heart sinks with a thud. A friend. He doesn't see me as anything more, because I'm nothing like Paris. I'm not mature, or refined, or experienced. I might bring in the dollars, but to him I'm childish and naïve, and certainly not someone to have a relationship with. I don't know what I was thinking, putting on makeup and getting nervous about watching a freaking movie. It's all in my head.

"Thanks Isaac." I force out a whisper, then reluctantly sink into his chest, feeling every ridge and muscle against my back.

I DON'T REMEMBER HALF of the film, the one simple reason being I fell asleep. The warmth of Isaac's chest and the blanket and the feeling of pure and utter safety wrapped me up into a cocoon, and I drifted. I wake up just as the credits start rolling. It takes only seconds before it hits me again: the realization I'm nothing more to Isaac than a friend and client, and I never will be.

I can feel from the looser grip of his arm around my body and the soft rise and fall of his chest that Isaac is asleep too. I slowly extract myself from beneath his arm and twist to face him. I was already battling with the fact Isaac is good-looking, in a kind of efficient, domineering kind of way, but seeing his features deep in sleep, he looks beautiful. I can't tear my eyes away. Even as the credits stop rolling and the screen turns black, casting the room in darkness, I can't drag my open eyes from his closed ones.

Then, I do it. I can't stop myself. It happens in slow motion. I close my eyes and press my lips to his. A warmth creeps through my skin, my veins and my bones, and shocks my eyes open. I gently move my top lip from side-to-side across his, the thrill of doing something so elicit, so forbidden, firing up my insides. He twitches slightly, deep in sleep, and it jolts me back to reality. I'm suddenly disgusted with myself. I just kissed my bodyguard without him knowing. My bodyguard who has made it abundantly clear he doesn't see me in that way. I'm sure in some state or other, that's illegal—advancing on someone without their permission. I slowly curl myself back around and pull his arm around me tightly. Thankfully, it doesn't take long before his embrace, even in slumber, lulls me again into sleep of my own.

CHAPTER SEVENTEEN

Isaac

As much as I want to tense up, I don't. I need her to believe I'm asleep. But the truth is, I can't sleep. I'm relaxed but very much awake, soaking up every second I can of Aurelia sleeping like a baby against my chest. It's taken all my willpower to keep from getting hard. If I did that again and she felt it, I would feel so ashamed. I was happily lying here with my arms wrapped around her, her head turned slightly to the side so I could see her beautiful face whenever I opened my eyes. Then she woke up. I was curious to know what she'd do when she thought I was sleeping too. But I did not expect *that*.

I felt her breath on my face, sweet and warm, as she peered over me. Then I felt her lips against mine, and fuck if she didn't feel my heart pounding out of my chest. I laid there, soft and still, while she brushed her top lip against mine. It tickled, but the sensation of every single nerve ending firing up stopped me from laughing. Because it wasn't funny. It was the most gorgeous thing I've ever felt. But I couldn't open my eyes. I couldn't break the spell. I couldn't make it real, because we can't go there. As well as all the other very valid reasons why we wouldn't work, Aurelia hasn't even lived. She may have traveled and experienced things most people never will, but she's had only one boyfriend—one. She's got no idea what she wants from a guy, or what she needs. But I do, and it's not me. She needs to have fun with guys her own age, who are probably in the industry too and understand her life.

I waited until she settled back into my arms before I finally breathed out. Then when I was sure she was fast asleep, I gently carried her to her suite, laid her down on the bed and covered her with the comforter and blanket. Then I left the villa, nodding to Jax on the way out.

I CAN SEE the boat already approaching, it's distant lights looming large, until they are switched off, revealing on the surface of the sea only the glittering reflection of the stars. A truck has already been parked up, a tarp pulled taut across the back. As I get closer, I see Luca in the driver's seat.

"Is Connor with Starling?" I ask as he rolls down the window.

"Yeah. They're staying up in Miami. It's just me and you, kid."

I snort sarcastically. I'm ten years older than Luca and hardly a 'kid'. Aurelia would be better off with Luca than me—he's bound to be more on her wave-length. I push the thought away because it makes my stomach cave.

"So, what's the drill? We just take the boxes and drive them straight up to the city?"

"Not this time. Bianchi's getting nervous. We're to take them as far as Islamorada, then change vehicle, you head back here and I continue up to Key Largo and we switch hands there."

"Got it." I look out to the deck and the boat is almost here. "Let's get it over with."

The two guys give us a cursory nod as we unload the boxes of ammo into the back of the truck. Bianchi is taking a risk letting us transport the goods in what is effectively an open top vehicle, but his view is the less suspicious it looks, the better. I pull the tarp across and climb in beside Luca who keeps the lights dead as we drive back through the resort and up onto the Highway.

"Does Aurelia know you've gone?" Luca says, glancing across at me.

"No, she's asleep. If I told her anything, she'd ask too many questions."

I get another feeling in my gut I've never felt before, and I suddenly realize, I'm lying to Aurelia and I don't like it. Well, not lying exactly, but concealing the truth from her. She's not the first woman I've kept the Bianchi stuff from—Paris is a case in point—but she is the first woman I wish I could share it with. Everyone on the Key knows we do this, and they each benefit from the extra money we make. Our wages for working on the Key are so poor, the additional 'bonuses' we get from the Bianchi work allow us to pay for stuff that helps our people and their families. But, we can't let an outsider know what we do to support our Starling Key family. And as deep inside my head as Aurelia is, she's still an outsider.

For the rest of the journey, Luca fills me in on what the

rest of the team have been up to, while I feign interest, my mind still reeling from the sensation of Aurelia's lips on mine. Two hours later, I take the steering wheel of the truck and watch Luca drive away in a non-descript car. Then, I put my foot down, my need to get back to Aurelia overriding everything else.

CHAPTER EIGHTEEN

Aurelia

I HUG Ana so tightly my arms ache. "I miss you so much," I breathe into her hair. It smells of Ana, all clean and fresh, of watermelon and lime, her favorite soap.

"I miss you too, Ray," she says. "Promise me you'll come home as soon as the residency ends?"

"I promise. And I'll call you, ok? Now I have your new number."

"Yes, you must."

I pull away reluctantly and wrap my arms around Billy.

"And you," I whisper into his ear. "I want you to kill it at Yale, ok? You are the brightest guy I know; you deserve to be there."

"Thanks Ray. You take care of yourself, ok?"

"I will. I'll be fine."

He pulls back and puts his hands to my cheeks. "I think you will be too. Isaac is a good guy. He didn't need to do this

—track us down and fly us here. It makes me feel a hell of a lot better knowing you have him."

My smile is bittersweet. "Yeah, for a couple more months anyway."

"I think he'd like it to be for longer than that," Billy says, narrowing his eyes.

I shake my head. They don't know Isaac like I do. "No, it's not like that. We've gotten close, but…"

"Ray," he stops me. "I'm a guy, right? I don't know if you've noticed. We're not all good, but I know a good guy when I see one. He's as good as they come. And I think you mean more to him than just a job."

"Maybe. We've just become really good friends, that's all. But I know I'm lucky to have him. I really am."

"Come on, that guy Luca is waiting for us," Ana says, tugging at Billy's sleeve.

"Yeah, I can see he means a lot to you."

"He does." I smile, weakly.

"It's a shame he isn't just a little bit younger," Billy winks.

"What's that supposed to mean?"

"Well, you could mean way more to him then, couldn't you?"

I wish that were true, but even if he were younger or I were older, I'm pretty sure I still wouldn't measure up. Not when are the likes of Paris Navitsky parading their impeccably manicured, sexually experienced selves around the resort every day.

"It isn't like that," I frown, pushing Billy away with a smile. "Now, go. Enjoy that helicopter ride."

Billy rubs his hands together. "Oh, I will. This is one more item I can tick off my bucket list."

Not another word is said as Ana plants a giant kiss on my

cheek and drags Billy away down the boardwalk. They both turn back and wave, and I watch them reach the gate then climb into a golf buggy bound for the helipad.

I wipe a hand across my face and it's wet. I didn't even know I'd been crying, but it would make sense. I've missed my best friends more than I'd admitted to myself. The only person who'd stood up and done something about it, was Isaac.

Luca doesn't drive the buggy away until he's seen me turn around and let myself inside the villa. I expect to see Isaac hunched over his computer at the kitchen counter like usual, but he isn't there. I walk through the villa but he's not there either. I look out to the deck, but still there's no sign of Isaac. I go to his suite and knock tentatively on the door. There's no answer. I carefully open the door and peer round the corner.

I've never before stepped foot in Isaac's suite but it's pretty much the same as mine. White, pristine, airy. But his suite smells of him—a mixture of woody spice and freshly washed clothes. Out of all the security guys, Isaac is by far the most fastidious about his appearance. Connor is not far behind but his floppy dark blonde hair and the obvious prey bird tattoo across his back betray a certain rebelliousness. Carter looks disheveled at best, barely functioning at worst, probably the result of being a new dad. Luca is the epitome of a laidback surfer with the requisite beach-tousled, sun-kissed hair and boyish tan. Jaxon is quietly tidy, but a scar across his scalp gives him an obvious edge. Hudson, well, he's a barbarian if ever I saw one. All long hair, muscles, tats and tight tanks. Isaac, in comparison, is neat, slick and understated. Even his tattoos are tidy. Everything about him is well-groomed, everything except his eyes. His eyes are like

Wuthering Heights. Dark and stormy, raging even. Whatever secrets lie behind them, he works hard to conceal.

I crane my neck, not wanting to venture too far; Isaac deserves his privacy too. Then I see him, sprawled across the bed, sleeping deeply. I gaze at him for a few moments, allowing my eyes to roam his entire form, voyeuristically. Eventually, I tiptoe into the room, pull a blanket from the box at the foot of the bed and cover him from the chill of the conditioned air. Then I tiptoe out of his suite, closing the door quietly behind me. I walk out onto the deck and immediately pull out my phone. I don't wait for the person at the other end to speak.

"It's me. Can you get here in the next ten minutes?" I pause to listen, then hang up. I run on tiptoes to my suite and pull out a bag I haven't opened since I left Miami. I tug on the dark wig Ana had bought for our ill-fated escape from the Ritz Carlton. It's too hot for the trench coat so instead I drape myself in a kaftan I wouldn't normally be seen dead in. Finally perching giant sunglasses on my nose, I gather the pile of papers I've carefully marked, slide them into a bag and head out of the villa.

I half walk, half run down the boardwalk to the beach. Keeping my head down, I pace along the sandy pathways, up towards the main building. A couple passes me on their way to the beach bar and I nod, briefly, thankful they haven't recognized me. Despite the intense, on-stage workouts I do every night, I'm out of breath by the time I reach the loading bay. I turn east and weave my way through the foliage lining the perimeter wall, to a secret entrance I overheard Isaac talking about with Connor. As planned, a nondescript grey car with shaded windows is parked up just behind the wall, it's engine cut.

I walk up to it, just as the front passenger door pops open.

I slide in without needing to look at the people seated inside. As soon as the door closes I turn to face the man in the front seat.

"How long do we have?" he asks.

"About ten minutes. I can't risk any longer."

Another man's voice comes from the back seat. "Do you have the papers?"

"It's all here," I say, turning to hand the pile of papers over. "How long will you need?"

The man in the back speaks first. "I can look over these right away."

"And you?" I turn to the driver.

"I'm probably going to need a few days. I'll let you know the second I find something."

"Thank you," I say. "Before we go into details. There's one other thing I need you to help me with." I look pointedly at the driver again. "There's someone I need you to find."

CHAPTER NINETEEN

Isaac

It's the sound of silence that wakes me up. The first thing I do is look at my wristwatch. It's twenty after four. Ana and Billy left an hour ago. I leap up, almost knocking the side table off the wall in the process. *Fuck, fuck, fuck. I slept on the job.*

I wrench open the door to my suite, barely noticing the blanket that has slipped to the floor. I don't call out for her, even though every part of me wants to. I can't let her know that even a second of daytime has passed where I haven't had eyes on her and her safety. I walk hastily though the villa, my eyes scanning every corner, every surface. There's no sign of life anywhere. I'm on the deck in an instant. Nothing. No empty glass or coffee cup, no indent on the lounger where her weight has been lightly pressed. I turn on my heel and scoot to her suite. I press my ear to the door and knock.

"Aurelia, you in there?"

When there's no reply I push open the door and walk straight in. The room is in slight disarray, like any teenager's room would be, I guess. Drawers are open, pens are scattered, the contents of a bag are strewn across the bed—a beige trench coat I've never seen her wear, various sunglasses and pairs of shoes that don't look like anything she would put on her feet. *She been playing dress-up in here, or what?*

"Aurelia?" I shout, loudly. "You here?"

My pulse vibrates in my ears and I silently curse it. I can hear even less with the throbbing of blood against my temples. It quickly dawns on me she isn't in the villa. I run to the main entrance and fling open the door, my head whipping left to right, up and down the boardwalk. Seeing nothing, I narrow my eyes and scan the shoreline. No sign of Luca, Ana or Billy. No sign of any golf buggies. No sign of any helicopter. No sign of Aurelia.

Years of working as a CIA operative have conditioned me to remain calm under this kind of pressure but, for the first time in my career, my heartrate is through the roof and my limbs are stunned. They want to move but they don't know where to. I know the resort is secure. I know we have eyes on every possible access and exit point. I know the guys are the best in the business. But I also knows there's a strange woman loitering around. If she can find a way to get onto the island undetected, there must be a way off it. I want to break my own bones for not addressing this sooner. I've got complacent. I've got carried away with simply being around Aurelia. My vision's been blurred; my professional integrity compromised. And now, the one person I need to put every ounce of my focus into protecting, is missing.

I whip my phone out of my shorts. "Luca," I pant. "Aurelia's gone. She's not in the villa."

"What are you talking about? She was right there when I left. I watched her go inside."

"Fuck!" I rush out, tugging my hair. I can't believe what I've done. "I fell asleep, Luca. I don't know where she's gone. I've looked all over the villa."

Luca speaks slowly. "When did you fall asleep?"

"Not sure. Just before Ana and Billy left, I guess."

"What were you thinking, Isaac?" Luca's words smack with disappointment but there's no malice or judgement behind them. He's too good a friend for that.

"I wasn't thinking. I was too tired to think. Damn Bianchi and his midnight delivery from Mexico. I can't juggle this stuff. I thought I could…"

"Don't beat yourself up, Isaac. We'll find her. I'm on my way to the CCTVs now. Stay where you are in case she comes back to the villa. I'll call Hud at the marina. If she went down there, he'll find her."

I nod, even though he can't see me, then I say the words that are turning my stomach as I think them. "What about the woman?"

"We haven't seen her in a while, and Jax is on the monitors. He's got eyes like a hawk. We'd know if she was back on the island. Relax, Isaac. We'll find Aurelia."

I hang up and scan the coastline again. It's calm and empty but for a few wandering guests in bathing suits.

My breathing is short and shallow.

Where the fuck are you, Aurelia?

CHAPTER TWENTY

urelia

I CLOSE the door behind me as quietly as I can and tiptoe into the villa. I can't hear Isaac and I breathe a quiet sigh of relief. I round the corner into his suite and see the blanket on the floor. He's gone. Shit. My heartrate picks up. *When did he wake up? Does he know I left? Is he going to kill me?*

I walk towards the sliding doors, planning to set myself up out there as though I've been bathing all morning. I don't get that far. Wind whips my face as a large, powerful hand presses on my chest and rams me back against the wall. My eyes are still getting accustomed to being out of the direct sun, so all I can see is a shadow looming over me, almost crushing my collarbone. His voice is unmistakable, as is his rage.

"Where the FUCK have you been?" The growl burrows into my core and I'm so shocked I want to throw up. In close range, at several decibels higher than I've ever heard him, he's terrifying. "Aurelia, ANSWER ME. Where in hell have you been?"

His eyes come into focus and in them I see weakness—my weakness. It dawns on me, slowly but surely, he thinks I can't survive without him. A little part of my heart breaks. I thought Isaac was different but maybe he's just another man in my life who thinks I'll be nothing if he isn't around. I feel suddenly, irrepressibly angry.

"It's none of your DAMN business," I shout back. Fear has morphed into anger.

"It is absolutely my business," he growls. I've never heard this sound come out of his mouth before. It's like I've unleashed something in him he wanted to keep concealed. "It's my job to protect you. I can't do that if I don't know where the fuck you are."

I try to reason. "I was FINE. I'm not a child."

"You PAY me to make sure you're safe, Aurelia. What the hell?" His hand is anchored against the wall and his chest lowers towards me.

"Do you speak to all your clients this way?" I ask, ducking out of his way and stomping into the kitchen. He follows.

"None of my clients fuck off somewhere without telling me. They're more mature than that."

Now, that hurts and I don't give any thought to what I say next. "Are you kidding me, Isaac? You don't know what mature is."

"Oh I do," he replies, bearing down on me again. "You know I do." He raises an eyebrow, taunting me. I don't feel like we're talking about my safety anymore, and my young, inexperienced heart feels way out of its depth.

"Fucking fifty-year-old women does not make you mature," I spit, not knowing where those words even came from.

He steps closer, backing me up against the counter, bringing his chest to mine. "And neither does scurrying off alone without telling your security."

My chest rises and falls at the proximity. "My security fell *asleep.*"

He pauses and glares at me, and I realize what I've just done. He's never going to sleep again. I mentally kick myself, hard.

He lowers his voice, controlling every word. I still feel every consonant as it lands on my face with force. "You need. To grow. Up."

"And you need to stop comparing me to your old ladies," I say, slowly, and with venom.

He steps back, a look of shock on his beautiful features. "I do not compare you to them."

The widened gap between us emboldens me. "You just did." I take a step towards him, closing it again. "Your old ladies would never do something so stupid as walk out of this villa onto a tightly secured island for all of twenty minutes, to do something extremely important to them. Only I would do something like that, because I'm just a little girl to you, aren't I? A ridiculous little girl who can't think for herself, and needs to have a man around her at all times in case she —*shock horror*—does something meaningful and important on her own? A burden you only care about because I bring money and publicity to your resort, right?"

All I've ever known for the last five years is how to be polite and courteous, never to say what I really think in case I offend someone who buys my records or who influences the air play on the local radio. I feel liberated, and I can't stop.

My head cocks to one side, of its own accord. "Not for you my real breasts and ass, my buck teeth, my unhighlighted hair, my youth, my virginal image, right? You only want women who are part plastic, whose hair doesn't move when the wind blows, whose tits don't bounce when you fuck them over your office desk, right?"

I can't believe these vile words are coming out of my mouth, but I feel as though I'm purging. I'm angry. Not just because he doesn't trust me to be out of his sight for ten minutes, but because he doesn't want me the way I want him. Ana is constantly telling me I could have any man I want, but it's not true. I can't have this one standing in front of me balling his hands into fists as I stand my ground.

"You only want women you can't have. And that's why you would never want me. Not because I'm younger, not because I'm your client, not because I pay you to keep me safe. It's because you're so scared of someone else abandoning you, you can't get close to someone who has the freedom to leave." The words are out of my mouth before I realize I've seriously overstepped the mark. That was cruel and uncalled for.

Isaac's eyes narrow. "That's not true," he says, quietly.

"That you only want what you can't have? Bullshit," I spit.

"No." He shakes his head. "That I could never want you."

I blink, unsure if I heard right. It feels as though the air around us is burning and my world has shrunk to just two people locked in a battle of wills. I'm panting from the exertion of letting all that out. I shake my head lightly. I don't believe him. He nods once, then an eternity passes between us.

We launch for each other at the same time, our lips crashing together like waves against rocks. I can feel his broad hands gripping the back of my head, grazing my neck, and his lips consume mine in an aggressive, ravenous onslaught. I open my lips to let in his tongue and he plunges into me, holding me so tight I think I might stop breathing. His hands are everywhere, holding me to him. A thigh is lifted, a pelvis is drawn closer, a heart pounds against my own. One fleeting thought passes through my mind. No one needs experience for this. My response to him is completely innate, instinctive… Written.

He pulls back for second and his eyes are glazed. "Fuck. You are infuriating," he says, his voice low and dry. Then his mouth is on mine again and I circle my arms around his neck. When I think my lips are about to bruise, he frees them, sliding his wet mouth across to my cheek. He nibbles and kisses the curve of my jaw and I let my head drop backwards from sheer pleasure. He moves to my neck and licks softly at the hollow of my throat, then along the length of my collar-bone. Then I'm lifted and placed on the counter.

He keeps kissing me, making me feel things with his lips and tongue that need a censorship all of their own. I'm almost sweating from the intensity of our hands roaming each other like they've been held hostage for a century. One of his reaches up and tugs my top and bra down over my right breast in one swift motion and his lips are suddenly surround my nipple. It's a sensation I've never felt before and I gasp, instinctively pushing myself into him. He sucks at it hungrily, moaning a vibration through my skin.

"Jesus, Aurelia," he murmurs. His voice sounds far away. "Stop me. Please, stop me."

He's got to be kidding me. I'm capable of stopping him. I need more. I need everything. "I want this Isaac," I whimper. "Please don't stop."

As if that permission is all he needs, Isaac's hand is between my thighs and he tugs my shorts to one side. I pull back, gasping. He looks up at me, his eyes faraway. "Are you sure, baby girl?"

"I'm no baby," I reply, thrusting myself towards him. His fingers don't move when I press against them. He doesn't drag them back and forth like I expected him to. He simply watches me, fascinated, as I gyrate my hips, feeling the tips of his fingers against the fabric of my underwear. My clit beneath it is straining for connection, and driving me wild.

"Aurelia," he whispers. "Look at you."

"What?" I gasp.

"You're insatiable, baby girl. I like you this way."

I rub myself against his fingers, feeling more and more confident knowing my raw need for him is on full display and it's too late to do anything about it now.

"Oh God, Isaac," I choke. I'm right on the edge and my vision is spinning. "What do you mean?"

"I like that, in this moment, you really need me. Even if it's just for my fingers."

I feel delirious. "It isn't just for…" I gyrate again and his thumb presses against my clit. The first vibration rocks through my insides. The force of the sensation is strange, but not unwelcome. A groan comes out of my throat, without my permission.

"You're so beautiful, Aurelia," he says, his breath labored and heavy on my face. "How in hell was I ever meant to resist you?"

"Please, Isaac," I choke.

"You feel it too," he whispers.

I don't know what he's asking but I nod anyway. Right now I will agree with this man on anything. I can't believe what he's doing to me, the intense feeling it's drawing out of my core. Before I can comprehend what's happening, my body seems to ball itself up into a knot of tightness. I look into Isaac's eyes and he nods once, pushing his finger beneath the cotton and into me, all the while rubbing circles around my hardened clit.

"Gah," I splutter, then the shaking starts, and I grip onto Isaac for dear life. He wraps one arm around me while plunging his fingers so far into me, it almost hurts. I hang onto his shoulders, shuddering with each convulsion.

Completely disoriented by what just happened, I rest against him, breathing heavily, as though I've just run a marathon. Barely a minute later, I hear the snap of a belt. Isaac lifts his head to face me and his eyes are blacker than ever.

"Aurelia," he pants. "We might just be able to get past that. But this… You have to stop me." His voice is a whisper as he slowly unbuttons his fly.

I shake my head and lick my lips. Whatever he's planning on doing next, I want it. The man just made me feel everything and he expects me to stop him, now? I wriggle out of my shorts and kick them onto the floor. He shoves his combats down his thighs and frees his cock. I don't even have a chance to swallow and he has my thighs in his grip. He steps closer and I can see his jaw tick.

"God, you are everything," he says, dipping his lips to my collarbone. Just that small contact sends a current right across my skin and I shudder again. He laps at the dip with his tongue and I drop my hand to his cock, eager to know what he feels like. This all feels so alien, but at the same time completely natural. And inevitable.

As soon as my hand wraps around him, his head drops

and he groans, then curses softly. Another wave of lust ripples through me. I'm high on the realization of what I can do to him, without even trying. I'm half-expecting to wake up from a dream. This kind of thing doesn't happen to me.

He whispers something else, inaudible. Then my brain catches up. He's begging me to stop.

"I… I don't want to," I reply, but my heart is falling already.

"Please," he says, not looking up.

I slowly withdraw my hand, feeling the warmth of his cock evaporate into the cold atmosphere.

"Why?"

He doesn't even look up. "We can't."

"Why not?"

"We just can't."

The next full minute happens in slow motion. He pushes his head into my stomach and breathes in deeply. Then, he bends to pull his combats back up his legs, fastening them. Then, he raises his head finally, and looks at me.

"I can't do it," he breathes out. "It's not right."

What? I close my legs and inch to the side, recoiling.

He turns away and rubs a hand over his face. I watch him, fearful of what has just happened and what's about to happen next. The villa is eerily quiet now, the sound of our actions a mere echo. So, when he puts his hands over his face, bends at the knees and screams, "Fuuuuucckkk!" I shoot about a mile off the counter.

Not even a second later, I'm livid. And mortified. And humiliated. I leap off the counter, ram my shorts back over my ass and run into my suite slamming the door behind me. I storm into the shower and turn the water on full blast, hoping the hammering droplets drown out the sound of my crying.

I put my heart on the line out there and he just shot right through it. I opened myself up to him, I came under the briefest of touches. He inhaled my breath and fed me his. Then he shut down. Just like that.

I thought I'd finally found someone I could trust. He was supposed to protect me, but he just broke me in two.

CHAPTER TWENTY-ONE

saac

I HEAR the door slam and seconds later, her shower is turned on and I hate myself more than I've hated anyone in my life. I stare at the marble counter she just leapt off and fantasize about breaking my fist on it. The urge is overwhelming but it would jeopardize my ability to do my job. Like I hadn't already just jeopardized it to hell and back.

Isaac, you fucking idiot. My head is shot to pieces. I just kissed my client, and not just any client, an international superstar—a *child* star—who relies on me to protect her. I was in a position of trust and I just abused it, without a thought for anyone other than myself. Of course she thinks she's attracted to me. I'm her bodyguard for crying out loud, and I look after myself. I'm not being arrogant when I say it's entirely conceivable she might have developed a crush on me. It was my responsibility to not fucking act on it. Not only that, she is NOT MY TYPE. I still want Paris. I still want no strings, I still want what I can't have. I don't want some nineteen-year-old following me around like some puppy dog, not when it's my job to keep her alive.

I stop pacing, anchor my hands on the back of the couch and stare out at the same view we admired in comfortable silence when she first arrived. Who the fuck am I kidding? I haven't thought about Paris for weeks. And my client is not just any nineteen-year-old popstar, she's Aurelia. My Aurelia. Who just came hard for me when I brushed my fingertip across her clit. Fuck her Grammy award-winning, chart-topping voice. The gasp of shock she released as her breast shook against my lips was the most beautiful sound I've ever heard. And those few minutes of exploring her body with my lips and fingers were deliriously hot.

I don't move from my spot behind the couch for a whole hour. Eventually, I hear the door to her suite open and close, and her footsteps as she enters the living area. She walks straight past me onto the deck, carrying a book. Tentatively, I follow her out and sit in a chair opposite the lounger she's laid herself down on. She's wearing a sheer sundress with a turquoise bikini underneath. I mentally curse her choice of outfit as my hard-on has only just subsided.

"I'm sorry," I whisper.

Her head snaps to the side and she plasters a fake smile to her face. "Whatever for, Isaac? Nothing happened, you'll be relieved to hear…"

"That's not true—"

"…and if you don't mind, I'd like to finish my book before tonight's show."

She turns back to the open pages, signaling the end to our conversation. At least this time her book's the right way up. I sigh, resigned. Maybe now isn't the best time to talk. I stand and walk back inside to give her space. I'll try again later.

"How's Aurelia?" Luca asks as we stand outside Aurelia's dressing room. "Did you find out where she'd been?"

"No." I stare straight ahead at the wall, still trying to shake the feeling of heavy gloom that has taken up residence in my chest. "She won't tell me. But she's alive. That's the main thing."

"You shouldn't be too hard on yourself, Isaac. You took on too much, that's all. Sometimes we need to be reminded of our limits before we stretch them to breaking point."

"I know," I sigh. "Doesn't make it any easier."

"Is Aurelia ok with it? With you not knowing where she was?"

"Yeah, annoyingly ok with it. She actually chose it as her moment to go do something she won't fucking tell me about."

"Well, maybe it was a private matter."

I turn to face him, trying hard to disguise my burgeoning fury. "I don't care what it was. If I don't know where she is, I can't do the job she's paying me to do."

"But if anything had happened to her, she'd breached the contract so you wouldn't have been to blame anyway."

I disguise the horror in my chest. "That's not the point, Luca. The point is, something could have happened to her."

Luca frowns. "I know you're worried about that weird woman, but I've seen a lot of CCTV images of her, and Isaac, she doesn't look like a killer, or some unhinged stalker. She may not even have anything to do with Aurelia."

I face the wall again. "She does. You have to trust me."

"Fine." Luca holds up his hands. "We're not going to take our eyes off her, man."

I continue to seethe silently.

"There's something else, isn't there?" Luca knows me well. Too well sometimes.

"What do you mean?"

"I mean, there's more to this than the fact she went off somewhere without telling you."

"No," I lie. "That's enough to be getting on with."

"Did something else happen?"

"I don't know what you're suggesting, Luca."

"Is there something going on between the two of you?"

I grind my teeth.

"That's a yes," Luca states. "So, what? You guys had a fight?"

"Something like that."

"What did you fight about?"

"It wasn't exactly a fight," I reply.

"So, what was it?"

"We kissed."

Luca whistles through his teeth. "That's the total opposite of a fight, man. Unless you're a terrible kisser, but I doubt that. I've seen you in action too many times."

I don't answer.

"Did she not want it?" He asks, arching an eyebrow that says he'd find that hard to believe.

"She started it."

"Ok. Look, I'm not following. Was there a fight or not?"

I push my back off the wall and lean my shoulder against it, facing him. "We went too far…"

Luca's eyebrows shoot up.

"Not *that* far, but too far for a client and her bodyguard, ok?"

"You're not going to be her bodyguard forever, and it's clear she really likes you… What happened?"

"I stopped it."

"And she didn't want you to stop?"

I shake my head. "No."

"Did you want to stop?"

"No," I reply, without needing to put thought into it. "I haven't wanted anything so bad in… forever."

"Have you talked to her about it?"

"No," I sigh. "She won't. She's just kind of shut me out."

"Give her time. She's probably embarrassed."

I narrow my eyes at him. "You know, for someone so young yourself, you're actually pretty seasoned."

"Generously," he winks. "But, seriously, is that it? She's young. You're worried about the age gap between the two of you?"

My back thuds against the wall again and I rub my hands over my face. "That's one of many reasons why this would never work."

"What else is there? You're a bit older and you're her bodyguard? Well, here's a revelation: girls like older men, and it's not like you're old enough to have conceived her."

I visibly cringe. "But I am, Luca. And it's not just that. I don't want to hurt her. I've never had a relationship where there hasn't been, you know, a third party."

"You've never been monogamous?"

"No, I have been, but the woman is usually married. You know that."

"So, that doesn't mean you can't have a relationship with someone who's single."

I sigh and close my eyes. "But, there's the thing. I don't know if I can."

"There's only one way to find out."

I shake my head. "Aurelia is too good to be a fucking guinea pig. I'm not testing any theories on her. She deserves better than that."

Luca goes to object, but doesn't get a chance, as Aurelia's door opens and the object of our discussion stands in the frame. I don't know if it's just me but her shorts seem shorter, her tank tighter, her lips darker, her heels higher. She notices my eyes popping out of my head and shoots me a glare that is way, way sexier than she intends it to be. She walks straight past, while Luca and I trail closely behind. She sings a few bars of the opening song, warming up her vocal chords. It's beautiful, and disarming, as ever. But all I can hear is the sound of her cry as she came against my fingers.

CHAPTER TWENTY-TWO

Aurelia

I STARE at my mom across the table. "Say that again?"

"Nate wants to come visit you. He sounded really sincere over the phone, genuinely sorry for the way it all ended."

"Genuinely sorry for the way he just happened to stumble into the arms of supermodel Amber Mayhew behind my back? Genuinely sorry for not extracting himself for two whole months before I found out about them? Genuinely sorry for the fact I found out via *Us Weekly*?"

Mom waves her hand as though all of that was simply a mere misunderstanding. I hate that this is what she's become. Someone who cares more about the surface image than the scars underneath. "He loved you so much, Aurelia. And I think he still does. You two were so happy together, and the press just loved you both as a couple…"

She pushes back her shoulders, she way she always does

when she wants to stand her ground on something. "I told him he could come here and stay for a couple of weeks—"

"Here? On the island?"

"Yes, of course. You have two spare suites in the villa; he could stay in one of those."

"What? You can't do that, Mom. I don't want to see him. He broke my heart!"

"But he's sorry, honey. He really is. He was almost in tears over the phone—"

Almost.

"And he was begging me to speak to you to give him another chance."

"Mom—"

"Honey, I was as surprised as you are, but think about it. Your father has forbidden Ana and Billy from coming here, and you spend all your time around that security guard. You need to be with at least one other person your own age."

"Tawny isn't much older than me."

Her sneer is contemptuous. "Tawny works behind the reception desk at a holiday resort. She's hardly the sort of person you should be hanging out with. Nate is in the business. He knows the kind of life you live. You need more people around you who really understand, and more importantly, will still be around after this residency has finished."

"I don't want to see Nate."

"Well," she straightens again. "You have to."

"Why?" I demand.

"He's arriving tomorrow."

"What?" I would be fuming if I wasn't so stunned. "Mom, how could you do this? I cried over Nate Hannigan for months. I was in love with him and he cheated on me, in front of the damn world!"

"Yesterday's news," she says, dismissively. "And besides,

it isn't *me*. This was his idea. I'm just the person in the middle. Whatever issues you might still have with him, you need to work through them between you. Anyway, I would bet my life the rest of the world has forgotten and forgiven what Nate did as a young, impressionable young man."

I slump down in my chair, remembering exactly why things between Mom and I had become so strained before Isaac had insisted she visit. "But I haven't," I whisper.

"I HAVE A GUEST ARRIVING TOMORROW," I announce as I open the door to my dressing room, leaving Isaac outside in the corridor. I flick my eyes to his briefly.

"I know," he says, looking past me.

I'm about to close the door but I stop and glare at him. "How do you know?"

He grinds his jaw, his face betraying nothing. "I received a memo," he replies. "From your manager."

I can't see anything in Isaac's face that suggests he might feel annoyed at this new development, so I drive the point home. "He's my ex."

He doesn't respond.

His face is set like concrete.

I close the door.

That night's show goes by in a blur. Fortunately, I know every step, every beat and every bar so intimately I could do it all my sleep, but my heart isn't in it. It's flailing around in my chest, all at sea, no anchor in sight. It's not my ex's impending visit that has made my mood plummet. That, in fact, I have given barely any thought. It's the relationship I have with Isaac, and how Nate being here will affect it. I'd finally admitted to myself there was something between us.

Then, he not only reciprocated, raising my hopes, he then smashed them back in my face and refused to lay another finger on me.

Quite simply, I can't compete with a woman like Paris Navitsky, and I get it. She's beautiful, she takes care of herself in ways I cannot fathom. She has curves to die for, and no doubt a collection of undergarments that cost the same as my house in West Hollywood. She has so much more experience with men than I do. She knows what they want, when they want it, and crucially, when they don't. She's worldly, well-travelled, well-read. She's probably been to every museum and art gallery in the world. And what do I do? I prance about on stage singing bubble-gum pop to hordes of tweenagers. The only experience I have with the opposite sex is a brief and very public relationship with a boyband member who cheated on me in front of the world. I have zero experience with grown men, and because I've worked in showbusiness all my adult life, I haven't lived like normal young women my age. There is literally nothing Isaac could see in me.

He's waiting outside my door again as I emerge from my dressing room and we walk in silence back to the path leading to the sea villas. As we near the boardwalk, my mood turns.

"Is this how it's gonna be from now on?" I snap. "We don't speak to each other? You just follow me around like a shadow?"

He leans past me to open the gate and waits for me to walk through. "It's for the best. It's the only way I can protect you."

I look up at him and see nothing. No regret, no sadness, no resignation, nothing. "So, you think kissing me was a huge mistake?"

He stares straight ahead when he answers. "Yes."

I WAKE up with a strange feeling in my stomach and zero appetite. I spend longer than usual showering. I don't know what it is I'm trying to clean off my skin, but there will never be enough soap in the world. I dress in a short playsuit and resist tying my hair in pigtails. Nate used to love that, but it's certainly not how I want him to see me now. I don't really know how I want him to see me. I want him to feel guilt and regret for treating me the way he did. I want him to realize what he lost and to want me back. But I don't know if I want him. I thought about it all night and barely slept. Had I ever loved Nate? He was my first and only boyfriend. We had some cute moments and he took my virginity, but he also went behind my back and he broke my heart in front of millions of people. Sure, the public sentiment was decidedly #teamAurelia but that didn't stop the humiliation seeping into my pores.

And then there's Isaac. He's made it abundantly clear nothing more will ever happen between us, and to be honest, I was foolish to ever think it would. But I live with him. He's around me twenty-four-seven. I can't get any respite from the way he makes my heart pound whenever he's close, whenever he so much as breathes in my direction. Before we arrived at the concert hall last night, we heard a sound from behind some of the foliage in the grounds and Isaac held my arm. It burned where his skin touched mine and, for a moment, I was glued to the spot. It's almost as though the fact he won't come near me anymore has intensified everything. Or perhaps it's because I know what his lips taste like against mine, and how it feels to have him lose himself on me, just for a second. I shudder, thinking about it. Nate was always slight and fumbling with his touch, whereas Isaac was aggressive and decisive. He knew exactly where to grip my hair, exactly how far to tilt my head, exactly where to press his tongue, exactly how to caress my jaw with his lips. His experience was clear and domineering, and I wanted to drown in it.

A knock at the door surprises me. "Who is it?"

Isaac's voice comes from the other side. "Tawny's here to see you."

"Ok, I'll come out."

Tawny envelopes me in a warm hug and we walk out onto the deck, leaving Isaac inside watching us.

"Connor told me about your ex-boyfriend coming here today," Tawny says. "I just wanted to check you were ok."

"That's so thoughtful. You didn't have to come here."

"Yeah, I know, but, well… I read up on the two of you last night after I heard he was coming. You went through a lot back then, so I just wanted to say I'm here if you ever want to talk about anything."

"You're so kind, Tawny. I really appreciate it." My eyes flick to the villa. Isaac is sitting at the kitchen island, turning his head to look at us every so often. I'm relieved he's far enough away that he won't hear our conversation. "I'm not overjoyed about it, to be honest, Nate coming here."

"Yeah, I thought as much. Why is he coming?" Tawny asks.

"He spoke to my mom apparently. Said he misses me and wants another chance."

"Don't you think that's strange? I mean, have you guys been in touch lately?"

I shake my head. "Well, Nate works in strange ways. He's usually super busy with the band but I guess they're taking a break or something. He's single right now, I know that much. I don't know why I'm suddenly on his mind though."

"You have switched up your image a lot over the last year or so," Tawny suggests. "Maybe he's seeing you in a different light or something. I mean, you're gorgeous anyway, but with the skimpier outfits and the raunchier lyrics, I wouldn't be surprised if you've caught his eye again." She raises a cynical eyebrow. "How is his band doing at the moment?"

"Not well," I say, toying with the hem of my playsuit. "I think their fans have kinda grown out of them a little. It's harder for them to grow with the fan base, you know?"

"Right," Tawny muses. "And I guess if you two got back together, the press would go crazy?"

I roll my eyes. "God, yes. If they even get wind that he's staying here, they'll jump to conclusions and go crazy anyway, if we were together or not."

Tawny looks around at the spacious villa. "Is he staying here? With you?"

"I guess," I sigh.

"And Isaac too?" Tawny tips her head towards the villa.

I can't help the frown clouding my brow. "Yeah."

"Hmm," Tawny says, laying back on the lounger she'd been perched on. "I guess someone has to be a third wheel, right?"

"What do you mean?" I watch her stretching out on the lounger and for a moment I envy everything about her life. I know my mom thinks Tawny and I have nothing in common, and right now I agree. Tawny is free to come and go as she pleases, she's found the love of her life and he loves her back, she can do a job she loves without people trying to make more money out of her.

"Well, I mean, you and Isaac… you know? You guys seem to get on so well. Is Nate going to be ok with that?"

I glance back at the villa and see Isaac turn his head back

to his laptop on the counter. "I don't think that's going to be a problem," I mutter.

Tawny's head flips to the side.

"Why? Has something happened?"

"Isaac and I had a, um, disagreement. I don't think our working relationship is going to come between anything I have with Nate."

"But you guys get along so well," Tawny frowns. "I mean, it's like you're the same person sometimes."

I suddenly feel cold all over. "How?"

Tawny sits up and looks over her shoulder to check Isaac is oblivious to our conversation, then leans towards me and lowers her voice. "It's just that you seem so comfortable in each other's company. You're always laughing together at the weirdest things. It's like he's your big brother or something."

My heart sinks. "Yeah, I guess maybe that's how it feels sometimes. I mean, he's paid to protect me, isn't he?"

Tawny narrows her eyes. "It's more than that though, right? I think he really cares about you, and it looks to me that the feeling is mutual."

I sigh inwardly. "Yeah, I suppose so."

"Do you think Nate will be jealous of that?"

I shrug. I honestly have no idea. I'm still having a hard time believing he genuinely cares for me at all. "There's nothing to be jealous of." I lower my voice to a whisper. "Isaac and I are not that close anymore. He's hardly spoken to me since, well, since we had that disagreement."

"Isaac? Not speaking to you? That doesn't sound like him."

"He does a little, but only when it's about work, you know? My security."

Tawny turns to look at Isaac. He's glued to his laptop.

"What did you disagree about? If you don't mind me asking," she says, quietly.

"Um, well..." I really don't know if I should tell her, but the words are burning my throat. I need to confide in someone. "It's ironic, really. It was about how, um, close we are."

Tawny cocks her head. "I don't understand."

I lean towards her and fix my eyes on the floor. "I kissed him," I whisper.

Tawny puts a hand over her mouth, biting back a smile. "You're kidding, really?"

I feel a little mortified by her reaction. "Why would I be kidding?"

"No reason," she says, forcing a serious look onto her face. "I think it's great, actually. You two are super cute together." Suddenly, her face falls. "Wait. What did he do? Did he kiss you back?"

Blood rushes into my cheeks and I nod. Tawny sucks in a breath, her face lighting up.

"Oh my God, Aurelia! You two kissed!"

"Shh," I say, my eyes wide. "He will be mortified that I've told anyone."

"Why? You're Aurelia Bird! Every grown man in the western world wants to kiss you!"

"I doubt it. And Isaac certainly isn't proud of it. He thinks it will stop him from being able to protect me properly."

Tawny's face straightens. "If you and Isaac have some sort of a thing, it will only make him more effective at protecting you, if you ask me."

"It doesn't matter," I sigh. "He's been pretty clear about the fact it was a huge mistake. And I'm not his type anyway. I'm way too young for him. And I don't just mean that I'm *younger* than him. He likes older women like Paris Navitsky.

I'll never be that to Isaac, so it's pointless even thinking about it."

Tawny sits back and lets out a long, even breath. "Maybe," she says.

I hear a shuffle inside the villa and I look up to see Isaac walking towards the door to the boardwalk. His shoulders are set back, his gait smooth and defiant. He has one of those physiques where his shoulders are unfeasibly broad, and his muscular back tapers down to a solid waist. I can barely take my eyes off him.

Tawny and I watch as Isaac opens the door and steps backwards. I can hear several different voices out on the boardwalk but only one person walks in. It's Nate. For a few seconds, he and Isaac stare at each other. Nate is still a boy in my eyes. His abundant fair hair is stylishly mussed up, his black jeans snug around his slim legs, an oversized fishnet sweater pulled over a thin black vest. He looks every inch the boyband singer. Meanwhile, Isaac towers over him in both height and width. His clean-shaven face and close-cropped hair seem to mock Nate's disheveled look, and his thick combats, heavy boots and SKS branded tee—the outfit I insisted he wear when he first moved me here—could quite literally stomp all over my comparatively weak-looking ex-boyfriend. My heart lurches seeing them both eyeing each other up, communicating silently in the way guys sometimes do.

"Where is she?" I hear Nate ask.

Isaac doesn't reply. Instead, he simply nods our way and watches as Nate heads in our direction. Tawny and I stand and Nate saunters towards us, far too cool to show true enthusiasm. It reminds me of the side of him I was never comfortable with. He didn't like to go to people; he liked people to come to him. He was always bigger and more famous in his head than in reality, and he hated the fact my popularity was greater than his. I plaster on a smile. "Hey."

"Hey you," he says, a genuine smile brightening his face. He steps up to me and holds out his arms, surprisingly not presumptuous enough to assume I would want to hug him just yet. But, in that moment, the familiarity of his face and the warmth I also remember from our time together, come surging back through my veins and I throw my arms around him. There's relief in his laugh and he wraps his arms tight around me. Despite everything Nate put me through, it's good to see him again. "You look amazing," he says, and my chest floods with emotion.

"So do you," I reply, pulling back to have a good look at him. We stare at each other for a few seconds, then I hear Tawny cough behind me.

"Oh, God, I'm sorry," Nate says. "I'm Nate. Pleased to meet you."

"Hey," Tawny says, shaking his hand. "I'm Tawny. I work here."

"Right," Nate replies, and his eyes flicker over her uniform.

"I'll leave you two to it," she says. "I'll come by later Aurelia, before the show?"

"Sure," I reply, watching her leave. "And, um, thanks Tawny," I call after her.

She gives me a small wave before stepping back inside the villa. I hear her exchange a few words with Isaac, then the door goes again and she's gone.

CHAPTER TWENTY-THREE

Isaac

I GO BACK to my place at the kitchen counter, applying all my focus to the conversation on the deck.

"Let's sit over here," Aurelia says, leading Nate around the outside of the deck, out of view of the kitchen. I curse under my breath.

"I hear the residency is going really well," Nate says. I relax a little, relieved I can still hear them.

"Yeah, I think so. The concert hall's full every night so I must be doing something right."

"You're getting great reviews," Nate says. *Of course she is, what do you expect?*

"Why are you here, Nate? Couldn't you have just called?" *That's it, my girl,* I think. *Cut to the chase.*

"Would you have taken my call?"

There's a pause. "If you'd persisted, maybe."

"It doesn't matter though. I didn't call your mom; she called me."

"What? Why would she do that?" I can hear the hurt and disbelief in Aurelia's voice.

"She's concerned about you, Aurelia. She thinks you're lonely out here and could use a friend—someone who, you know, is part of the business and understands a little of what you're going through every night."

"She is not concerned," Aurelia says, the bitterness clear in her voice. "She barely cares at all."

"Hey, don't be hard on her. It's not easy being the parent of someone as famous as you or me." I almost vomit at his arrogance. I don't know whole lot about Nate or Jinxed, but I do know Aurelia is far out of his league when it comes to level of talent and fame.

"I not being hard on her. I can't believe she contacted you, of all people."

"Oh come on, Ray. Your mom loves me, always did. You know, she even wrote me after we broke up, inviting me to stay."

"She did what? I would never have allowed you to stay. Not after Amber."

"I know," he replies. "I had cheated on you, for God's sake. That's why I was so surprised to hear from your mom."

"Did you reply to her?"

"Yeah, 'course I did. I told her it probably wasn't appropriate. I asked after you. I guess she didn't say."

There's another pause and I lean to the left—anything to ensure I don't miss a thing. "I'm really sorry I did that, Ray. I was a fucking idiot and I didn't ever want to hurt you."

"Please don't call me Ray, Nate. Only Ana calls me Ray." *You tell him, my girl.*

"Oh, yeah, right. Ana. Where is she anyway? Isn't she

normally stuck to your side like a limpet?" *Who the hell are you? Ana's her best friend.* I bunch my fists, fighting every urge to stomp out onto the deck and kick him over the edge.

"If you've come here to be a dick, Nate, you can just leave, ok?"

"Ok, ok, I'm sorry. Did something happen?"

"It's a long story. I got into a bit of trouble up in Miami. My parents blamed Ana and stopped me from seeing her until after the world tour."

"Ouch," he says. "That's a little mean." *Ok,* I concede. *There's one thing we agree on.*

"Yeah." I can practically hear her shrug. "But, thanks for apologizing for, you know, about the cheating."

"I should have done it a long time ago."

I hope she's nodding in agreement.

"So, who's the angry guy in there?" I cock my head at the mention.

"Isaac? He's my security while I'm here."

"Around the clock?" *Yes, dude.*

"Mostly. He has breaks and some of the other guys fill in. There's a great team here. They're really nice." *Nice.* I wince.

"He looks far from *nice*." *Damn right, kiddo.*

"Yeah, well, he's protective of me. That's his job."

"Whatever you say."

Silence follows before Nate speaks again.

"So, you're ok with me being here?"

"I guess. I mean, I only found out you were coming yesterday and I haven't seen you for three years. It's still a bit of a shock."

"I really wish all that hadn't happened, you know. I hope I can make you forgive me."

There's a pause before Aurelia speaks. "Why is it even important to you?"

Nate mutters something and I crane my neck further, unable to hear.

"What?" Aurelia asks and something about her tone makes me think she doesn't believe what she just heard.

"I miss you," he says, and this time I hear him loud and clear and it makes me want to hurl. "I miss you, Aurelia."

More silence follows and I hope she's communicating in glares alone.

"You don't have to respond to that. I know it's a lot. Let's just have fun the next few days, ok? If you decide you want me to stick around for longer, I will."

When she speaks again, her voice is low. "Do any of the press know you're here?" *Good question.*

"No. I was careful to cover my tracks. And it's pretty secluded here, isn't it?"

"Yeah, it is. Listen, Nate. I have to go." I hear her getting to her feet.

"Where to?"

"I have rehearsals. Come to the show tonight. I'll catch up with you after, ok?"

"Of course! Yes! I can't wait to see the show." His enthusiasm is sickening.

"Good. I'll see you then."

Her footsteps sound on the deck, then he speaks up again.

"And Aurelia?"

"Yeah?"

"Thanks for being so understanding. It really is great to see you again."

"You too." Her footsteps resume and I spin back to my laptop faking unwavering concentration as I sense her movements behind me, then the door to her suite closing softly.

For the next few days, I play the role of third wheel. I watch Aurelia's every move, I watch everything around her. I watch Nate's every move too. And I watch him move in on Aurelia. And I allow myself to feel utterly shit about it too, because it's what I deserve.

I've tagged along for sunset walks along the beach where Nate has tried to hold Aurelia's hand, but she's yet to give him the satisfaction. I've stood by and watched them play crazy golf, old-time fondness creeping through the cracks of tension that still linger between them. And I've sat in the corner of our restaurant while they've laughed over sharing plates and champagne, forgetting I was even there.

Tonight, we're at the casino. Aurelia has never wanted to come in here but Nate insisted. He appears to have an overly enthusiastic penchant for the slots, and the poker snob in me can't help but snicker at his choice of gambling poison. There aren't many shadows inside the casino but I stand back trying to be as invisible as possible. Occasionally, Aurelia catches my eye and nods her acknowledgment. Despite the fact she's pissed at me, she's sensitive enough to know how uncomfortable this is, having Nate around. Plus, it makes my job just that little bit harder, watching two people instead of one. I don't have to watch Nate but if someone really wanted to get to Aurelia, they could use Nate to do it.

He downs another glass of bourbon. It turns out slots aren't his only poison. Without looking around from the machine, he starts clicking his fingers above his head. I grit my teeth and grip the floor with my feet. I have a strong urge to stride over there and break those damn fingers because the staff here deserve more respect than that, but I stay rigidly put. Aurelia clasps a hand over Nate's. "Hey," she whispers, "I'll get it."

Luckily, right then, a waiter walks by and she gets his attention, then turns back to Nate.

"Maybe you should make this your last one, huh? You've had, like, eight already."

"Relax Aurelia," Nate replies, lazily. "The night is young. I'm on a streak here."

"Really? You've hardly won a thing and you've easily put four thousand into those machines."

Finally, he turns to face her. "Aurelia, I can't stop now. They have to come through sooner or later. The key to winning is to be patient. I'm going to get all that money back, and more. Just you wait and see."

Aurelia steps backwards, presumably in an attempt to conceal herself between two of the slot machines. It's my bet she doesn't feel like this represents her image too well. Her eyes flick to me and I detect some embarrassment in them. I pretend I'm not even looking her way; I don't want to make her feel even worse.

Thirty minutes go by and Aurelia is still standing at his side while he inserts coin after coin into those greedy machines. Nothing has come through yet, and the frustration he's feeling is evident. He's had three more bourbons and is barely balancing on his stool. Finally, Aurelia looks over to me as though admitting she needs some help.

I take a deep breath. Ordinarily, I wouldn't step in; I'm supposed to be totally invisible. But this is no ordinary situation and Aurelia is no ordinary girl.

"Aurelia has a show tomorrow," I say, monotone and mechanically. "It's time we left."

He turns to face me, probably for the first time since he arrived. "Who the fuck are you to tell me what to do? If Aurelia needs to leave, she can fucking leave."

I don't look at Aurelia; I know that's going to hurt, even if it's only the alcohol talking.

"Come on, Nate," I say, my tone a fraction more friendly and accommodating. "The slots are not giving up, and you've had a lot to drink. We're going. I suggest you come too."

He twists his head and fixes his thin eyes on me. "Oh, *you're* going? You and who's girlfriend?"

I straighten. Are they back together? I feel Aurelia wringing her hands next to me.

"Nate, it's really late. I need to get back. Isaac has to come with me." I watch her visibly cringe. "I pay him to." She's not denying they're back together and that sticks in my throat.

"Fine. I'll see you later," he says, dismissing her. He turns back to the slots, simultaneously feeding the machine and clicking his fingers for another drink. Suddenly, lights flash and sirens blare. The fucker's won. Aurelia and I fix our gaze to the neon windows Nate has been fawning over for the last couple of hours. Coins come pouring out of the dispenser and Nate practically shrieks in glee, like a heroin addict who just got a lifetime fix.

Aurelia swallows. "How much?"

"Wait, wait…" Nate holds up his hand, trying to comprehend on double figure bourbons what he's actually made. "A couple grand."

"Is that all?" Aurelia looks appalled. "You spent double that."

"So?" He throws her a vicious look. "Who's keeping score, huh?"

Aurelia steps back as though he's physically slapped her. "Let's get back," she sighs. "We can talk about it in the morning."

"Talk about what?" he seethes, half-lunging off the stool.

He's got way too much alcohol in his system and gravity plays its hand, drawing his forehead to the floor. "Fuuuck," he groans, pushing himself up by the hands.

"Nate," Aurelia repeats, firmer this time. "We're going. You're embarrassing me."

"What?" He looks up, not computing her words.

She turns on her heel and I have no choice but to follow.

"Aurelia…" he calls after her.

It's not my business, but I know if we don't help him, despite the fact he really doesn't deserve help, she won't forgive herself in the morning.

"Wait here," I say, pushing her gently into a corner. I look up at a camera and nod, knowing Jax will be at the other end of it. It's my code for, don't let her out of your sight.

I stride back to where the drunk idiot is still in a pool on the floor.

"Get up," I say, sharply.

"Fuck you," he slurs.

"Get the fuck up or you'll feel the surface of the Atlantic Highway on your ass first thing. Trust me."

He groans and moves, slowly. Too slowly. I hoist him up with one hand and he sways as though the sensation of being upright is completely new to him.

"Walk." I push him in front of me, keeping one hand to his back in case he forgets what his fucking objective is. He has one, and one alone. Get back to the fucking villa, fall asleep, then apologize like hell to Aurelia in the morning.

Aurelia's eyes are wide as we pass, but I'm taking no prisoners. When we reach a buggy I push Nate into the back seat and shoot a look at Aurelia. She knows better than to ask questions. She slips in beside me and, teeth clenched, muscles engaged, I pull that thing out of the lot and towards the villas. This whole situation is painful enough, without a nineteen-year-old sexpot and her juvenile popstar boyfriend making it even harder. Like some world-weary parent, I've lost all my patience. If either of them try to argue right now, I'm going to snap, spectacularly. Fortunately, they sense this, and the children behave, all the way home.

CHAPTER TWENTY-FOUR

Aurelia

"THANK YOU SO MUCH AUTUMN," I gush as we sail slowly back to the dive center. We've just finished up the snorkel trip to the reef that Isaac had arranged. He sits at the front of the boat with Clark, who's driving, both of them deep in conversation. "I've never seen anything so incredible."

"It's pretty mind-blowing, isn't it? I see it almost every day and it never gets boring."

I look over at her sorting through the equipment we just used, at the back of the boat. I envy how effortlessly beautiful she is. Long blonde hair hanging in perfect waves just like the ocean she lives on, tan skin and bright blue eyes. Isaac told me she's the sister of a small screen actress in Hollywood and I can now see the resemblance.

"When did you start doing all this? Diving and stuff?"

She finishes up putting items in bags and straightens. "Oh, I don't know, I was thirteen maybe? I used to go down to Sunset Point after school with the guys in my class. We'd ride the waves until the sun went down."

"Wow, I wouldn't have been allowed to do anything like that at thirteen. Your parents must be pretty cool."

She laughs and her face lights up. "Yeah, pretty cool or just pretty preoccupied with my sister's career. I used to get away with a lot. Thankfully I was too surf-obsessed to get into any real trouble, and the guys were a little older and always looked out for me."

"So, when did you start diving?"

"It wasn't long after I started surfing. I got PADI certified when I was fifteen and started entering competitions soon afterwards. I held a world record for a while."

"Really? That's so cool."

"Yeah, I thought it was too." Her smile softens and I sense some sadness behind her words, so I change the subject.

"When did you come to this resort?" I hold a hand up to my face to shield my eyes from the sun. It's late afternoon but the rays are still intense here at this hour.

"About three years ago. Best decision I ever made." She sits down opposite me.

"Why did you choose Starling Key?"

"I didn't really. I think it chose me," she laughs. "I traveled east for a fresh start, to find some independence I suppose. I traveled to most of the Keys, spent some time in Miami, just bummed around for a while. I decided to settle on Key West but as I drove past Starling Key I got curious. It was the only Key I hadn't spent time on, because it's privately owned, of course. I just wandered into the reception and saw Connor there. I asked if there were any jobs going. He asked what I could do. I told him water sports mainly but I would have been happy waiting tables or housekeeping. I just wanted a change—to make a living somewhere near the ocean. He offered me a job on the spot, arranging dive trips. Then when Antonio, the dive master at the time, decided to move on—dive masters tend not to stay in one place for very long—I took over his job."

"Do you think you'll move on soon, too?" I find myself hoping not, even though I'll be moving on myself in a matter of weeks.

"Probably..." She looks down at the long strands of hair she's untangling. "I've been seeing this guy, Jesse. He's a vice president at Office Heaven up in Miami. It's been going pretty well and I think he might be about to propose."

"Wow, that's huge!"

She grins, embarrassed. "Yeah, I know. If he does, I'll probably go live with him in the city."

"The city? Won't that be quite a change for you?"

"Maybe. But Miami Beach is right there—I'll be near the water—and I should be able to find work easily. I need to get serious about settling down eventually."

I'm surprised—Autumn doesn't look that much older than me. "How old are you? If you don't mind me asking?"

"Twenty-six," she replies, looking slightly embarrassed again.

"You've got plenty of time to settle down yet."

"Yeah, but when you have a twenty-two-year-old sister who not only achieved every single career goal she set herself by age twenty, but has also met the love of her life and is planning the Hollywood wedding of the decade, the pressure is on."

"That's pretty unusual though, to find 'the one', so early, right? Your sister sounds like she's very lucky, but you have your whole life stretched out in front of you. I wouldn't rush it if I were you."

Autumn focuses her eyes on mine, pausing mid-thought. "You are so sweet, Aurelia. For someone so young yourself, you have a very mature head on your shoulders."

"I guess I had to grow up quickly." I smile and look down the front of the boat. Beyond Isaac, I can see Nate waiting on the deck in the distance. I'd asked him to join us but he's afraid of the water, and actually, it's been nice to have some space from him especially after that night in the casino. The last few days have been a little claustrophobic. He has no idea what to do with himself, even though there's so much here on the Key, and has spent most of his time hanging around the villa, and around me. It's been nice to get some breathing space. Especially as the atmosphere with Isaac around too feels like an unexploded device. One spark is all it will take to blow up this superficial sense of calmness I've managed to surround myself with.

Autumn smiles, sympathetically. "You had good reason to. My reason is my parents, mainly. They don't want their eldest daughter to be a spinster. They're worried I'm falling too far behind Skye and no one will want me in a couple years."

"Well, it's nice that they want the best for you, but you shouldn't feel rushed into marriage if you don't feel ready."

She shakes her shoulders lightly, as if to throw off some thought or other. "I am ready," she says, firmly, more to herself than to me. "And they love Jesse. They think he's perfect, and they have more experience with this whole love and relationship stuff than I do." She laughs and it's infectious.

"I'm glad I'm not the only who's clueless about this stuff," I chuckle.

"Well, you seem to be doing something right," she smiles, nodding towards the deck where Nate's form is looming larger as we sail closer. "Your little puppy dog over there is quite attached to you."

"Hmm." *Attached is a good word for it.* I keep my voice down so Isaac can't hear me. "I'm not sure it's for the right reasons."

"What do you mean?" Autumn asks, then stops herself. "Sorry, I don't mean to pry."

"No, it's fine. We used to have a thing a few years ago, but he cheated and we broke up. He wants another chance."

Autumn narrows her eyes. "And do you want to give him one?"

"I don't know," I sigh. "I'm fond of him, despite everything."

"Fond?" Autumn winces and I laugh.

"Maybe 'fond' isn't the right word. We went through a lot together, growing up and dating with the world watching. We have history, and that will always mean something to me. But, I don't know if I feel *that* way for him, if you know what I mean?"

She cocks her head to one side. "I do. I think… when you know, you know."

"Hmm," I nod. *I think that's the problem.*

We reach the deck and Clark pulls the boat alongside and ties it up with rope. Nate moves in front of Isaac and extends his arm to gallantly help me onto the deck. I turn back to Autumn one more time. "Thanks so much again. For the dive and for the chat."

"Anytime," she smiles, then winks. "Good luck."

Nate keeps hold of my hand as we walk out of the dive center to the main pathway. Isaac follows close behind.

"Where to?" He asks. I try not to feel too irritated but it would be nice if he came up with some ideas of things to do himself, without having to look to me all the time.

"I'm pretty tired after that," I say. "And I should get some rest before tonight's show."

"Ok," he replies, chirpily. "Back to the villa it is."

We walk hand-in-hand all the way and it's kind of nice, despite Isaac's eyes burning into my back. But I know Nate's hand is not the one I want to be holding. Talking with Autumn has clarified a few things for me.

I already know what I want. I want him. And he's already told me I can't have that. But he's only given me one reason —an excuse, really—and I think there's another, bigger one that he isn't telling me. I need to prove it, if only so I can move past these feelings which are getting stronger and more intense with every day that passes, and with every jealous look he's unwittingly flinging my way every time he sees me with Nate.

We get back to the villa and I lead Nate straight into my suite, for the first time since he arrived a week ago.

"I thought you needed to rest," he grins cheekily as I lean past him to close the door. I catch Isaac's eyes as I shut them out. They are burning.

"I can still rest with you," I smile. I walk across to my bed and lie down, propping my head on one arm. I tap the comforter. "You coming or what?"

He seems to come to his senses and practically runs to the bed, throwing himself down next to me. "Are you sure about this?" he asks.

I nod and bring my lips down to his before he can say anything else. I don't want to talk, I just want to get this over with. The taste of Nate is familiar but it doesn't do anything for me. His lips move just fine, but they don't set mine on fire. His tongue is soft enough, but it has no urgency, no life of its own. I run my fingers along Nate's shoulders and along his biceps to his hands. They are smaller than Isaac's, not as firm, and they don't pin me down while I'm devoured by his mouth. I push my fingertips through his hair but I don't pull him deeper onto me as he feels almost like he might break, or at least be offended or put off by the force.

His fingers work their way, clumsily, into my shorts. He doesn't think to unbutton the fly and struggles to squeeze his whole hand inside. The pressure against my pelvic bone is almost painful. Isaac would have ripped it open by now, I'm sure of it. I don't really want Nate's hand down there but there needs to be a good reason for the noise I'm about to make.

I squirm slightly to ease the way for his fingers. The tip of one finally makes it to my clit, but only just. It brushes against me, lightly, like air, and I feel nothing. If anything, I want to laugh, because it tickles. I pull my lips away, feeling the effects of his stubble against the delicate skin. I moan, hoping it reaches through the wall. "Oh God."

Nate jumps slightly, unused to me making any noise during our fumbling. Then he returns his mouth to mine, renewing the scratchiness against my skin. I let his tongue flick at mine a few times then I pull away, kissing along his jaw and his neck, anything to lighten the assault of short, blunt hairs against my raw lips. Nate continues to barely graze me with his finger and I continue to make encouraging, slightly delirious noises—mm's and ahh's—in all the right places. Nate joins in, loving the effect he thinks he's having on me.

After a few minutes, I want to stop. I don't like what I'm doing but I've come this far. "Nate!" I call out. "Right there, oh God, yes." I thrust myself forward as though I really am chasing his fingers, and fake a jerk or two, all the while moaning into higher and higher octaves. I pant from the exertion of faking an orgasm and press my lips to Nate's. "Thank you," I murmur, lazily.

"You're very welcome," he replies, the surprise on his face almost comical. He goes to kiss me, probably hoping I'm going to return the favor, but my work is done. I roll onto my side and close my eyes, about to fake a sleep that I will no doubt fall into anyway. I've played my part, I've set the stakes. Now I just have to wait and see where the chips fall.

CHAPTER TWENTY-FIVE

Isaac

I CAN'T UNHEAR THAT. It's been twenty-four hours since I heard that dick Nate fucking Aurelia in her suite and I can't get the sounds out of my ears. Her little moans and gasps, his grunts and groans. The gentle creak of the floorboards. Even when I sat out on the deck, as far from Aurelia's suite as I could get without actually leaving the villa, I could still hear them. At one point I think I heard Aurelia shush Nate and whisper something I couldn't make out. But it did nothing to quiet him down. It was almost like he knew it was killing me, and he wanted to enforce upon me a slow, agonizing death. I thought I hated the boy before, but now I loathe him with every fiber of my being. I honestly think that if I saw someone about to mow him down with a rifle, I wouldn't stop them.

Thank God Luca was around this morning to follow them

both as they took a lover's stroll along the beach. I don't know if I would have been able to handle that. In fact, I know I wouldn't.

I sit at the kitchen counter and run through some figures Axel sent me. My eyes scan the numbers but nothing is going in. My phone buzzes and I pick up, grateful for the distraction. It's Mom. The slight spike in my mood is immediately dashed as I swipe open the message. I have no idea how I'm going to find the kind of money she's asking for, and I still hate that I feel I have to. That woman has done nothing for me my entire life, yet I've given her whatever she's needed, whenever she's come crawling. I wish I could just cut her off and forget about her, but I can't. She's my mother. She gave me life. There is still something of my beloved grandmother in her, somewhere. I would never forgive myself if I didn't step up when she needed help.

I read the words, then I read them again.

And again.

This can't be right.

Thanks for the money sweetheart. I know it was you and I want you to know, I'm forever grateful. It breaks my heart to agree to this, but, whatever you need Isaac. You won't hear from me again.

I read the message a fourth time but it doesn't matter how often I consume the words, I still can't seem to digest them. They're crawling back up my throat like vomit. *Someone* has given my mother the money and made her think it was me. *Someone* has treated me like a charity case, as though I wouldn't be able to find that money myself. *Someone* is going to get a fucking earful the second she walks through that door.

First she's getting hot and heavy with her ex in the villa

she's sharing with me, and now she's paying off my mother like it's anything to do with her. Who does she think she is?

An hour later and I think I've worn the floorboards down by a couple inches with my pacing. Luca texted to say they're on their way back. I give myself another pep talk. *Do not lash out while dick boy is here. Make her take the money back and do not take no for an answer. Order her to leave you and your family the fuck alone. Do not let your eyes drop below her jawline, or you'll be fucked all over again.*

I hear the key card being swiped and I clench my jaw. Without realizing it, my posture has grown; I feel like a bear standing it's ground ready for a fight. Every muscle in my body is engaged. I know this has nothing to do with Nate but I am ready to throw that kid to hell and back if he gets up in my space. I can't remember ever feeling so angry.

Aurelia steps inside and takes one look at my face.

"Hey," she turns to Nate behind her. "Why don't you go straight to the gym and I'll meet you afterwards."

I don't hear him answer but I assume he's done as she's suggested because he doesn't follow her inside. Luca's head appears instead.

"All good, Isaac?" he calls.

"Yeah, thanks man." He's far enough away that he can't see my murderous expression. "I'll catch you later."

The door closes and it's just me and her. She straightens and anchors her feet on the floor. She knows she's in for a verbal hammering and her defenses are up.

"Why did you do that?" I cut straight to the chase.

"Do what?"

I expected this. For her to think she'd got away with it. But the guilty look on her face tells me my suspicion is right on.

"You gave my mother the money."

"That wasn't me."

"Oh, it wasn't?" I half-laugh. "You were the ONLY person who knew she wanted that money. That *exact* amount of money. And out of the two of us, you are the only one who has that kind of money lying around." I can't help the sneer on my face. I'm not bitter that Aurelia has more than me, just that she felt she had to step in when I can handle my mother perfectly well myself.

"I don't have it *lying around*," she bites back. "I had to go behind my fa—*manager*'s—back to get it moved to your mother's account."

"No one asked you to do that. I want you to take it back. She doesn't deserve your money. You earned that. My mother has hardly worked a fucking day in her life."

"I'm not taking it back. I want her to have it."

"Why?"

"So that she'll never ask you for money again. That was part of the deal."

I narrow my eyes. "Does she know it came from you?"

"No. It was anonymous."

"So, how is she going to know anything about a deal?"

"I had someone deliver the message."

"Oh, right. The same 'someone' you met with without telling me where you were going?"

She chews her lip instead of answering and my gaze hovers around her mouth. *No lower, Isaac.*

"I'll take that as a yes," I snap. "And I insist you take that money back."

"No." She folds her arms defensively.

I claw my fingers down my face, barely concealing a frustrated growl. This *woman*. "Why are you so fucking infuriating?

She shifts from one foot to the other, her chest rising and

falling. She puts up a good front but I can practically see the nervous adrenaline coursing beneath her skin.

"Look," she says, her voice high-pitched. "There isn't a lot I can do for you, Isaac, but I can do this. You've gone above and beyond for me. Consider it compensation."

The taste of fury is quickly dissipating, to be replaced by the sour tang of disappointment. "Is that all it is? You just want to repay me?"

She chews her lip. "No."

"Then why?"

"Because I care about you."

"You care about me?" I scoff. "And that's how you show it? By giving money to my mother like we're both charity cases?" I grit my teeth, my gaze traveling to her jaw, threatening to slide down to her collarbone, the very same one I've fantasized about licking until she squirms. The words are out before I can stop them. "And by fucking your ex in the room right next to mine?"

A smile tugs at the corner of her mouth and her eyes are triumphant. "Oh, that bothered you did it?"

My fists clench at my sides. I feel like I'm going to combust with anger. "Of course it did."

"Why?" Her arms unfold and she plants her hands on her hips, drawing my eyes to the subtle curves beneath her fingers.

"You know why," I reply, my voice scratchy. My eyes are now roaming her whole body, hungrily.

"I need to hear you say it."

I take in every limb, every bone, every muscle, then slide my eyes back up to hers. They are defiant and blazing. "Because…" *Fuck it.* "I want you."

"I thought you couldn't want me. Because I'm your client. Because I'm *too young.*"

"I don't care anymore."

"What's changed?"

"Nothing. Except that, through that fucking wall I heard everything I needed to, to know you've never been given what you truly deserve. You've never been made to feel the way should, like you're the most beautiful, delicious, sexy woman who ever stepped foot on this island. You've never had someone put their tongue on you and really taste you." She swallows, her chest heaving with the effort of holding herself together. "You've never had someone caress every part of you making you feel things you never thought possible. You've never had anyone die inside you at the feel of your heat around their cock. Have you? You've only ever had *that*." I jerk my head towards the wall of her suite, not concealing the disgust I feel at the thought.

She takes two steps towards me, then gives me an antagonizing glare.

"So what are you gonna do about it?"

I step forward too, closing the gap between us, bearing over her, enjoying the decision I've just made, against every principle and every rule I've ever set myself. I lower my lips to hers, being careful not to let them touch. "I'm gonna fuck you better."

I continue to hover over her as a whimper leaves her throat. "It's about time," she whispers.

I slowly reach a hand up to her neck and take a firm grasp of it, before racing her backward several paces to the wall. We both slam against it, then we're clawing at each other. Her nails rip my shirt and my teeth bite into her shoulder like some feral animal. My hands reach behind her back pulling her forward and her head drops back against the wall exposing her neck. I feast on it, not caring if I leave a mark. My mark.

Her fingers work my fly, yanking at the buttons, ripping the last few before shoving my shorts over my hips. I join my lips to hers and kick the combats away, holding her head fast to mine. Her hands find me and wrap around my girth and I can't help it, I cry out from the relief. I've needed this. God, I've needed *her*. My own hands pull up her dress and shove her panties roughly to one side. A finger brushes against her velvety clit and she comes, falling apart in my arms. It takes barely anything.

"More," she gasps, breathless, against my lips. "Fuck me better."

"Oh, I will baby girl," I reply, pulling her bottom lip between my teeth and flicking my tongue over the sore.

I press both hands to her chest, pushing her forcibly against the wall, then straighten out my arms taking a long, hard look at her. We both stand still, out of breath, panting hard. She's beautiful. Everything about her is raw, fresh, completely authentic. I drop to my knees, her panties still bunched to one side, and bring my lips to her warm, soft flesh. She jumps from the contact and I press her chest harder. I've always loved going down on women, but this time it feels like less of an indulgence for me and more of a necessity for her. The girl is boiling over. She moans as I suck on her tenderly, the sounds nothing like the ones I heard through the wall. They are spontaneous, untethered, beautiful. And she tastes gorgeous. Her moans pick up pace and her body stiffens. Her hands come down to my head and draw my mouth deeper until I'm one with her as she shudders against my face.

I give her a few seconds to come down before dragging my tongue along her clit then standing to give her a taste of her high. She moans into my mouth, delirious, and reaches again for my cock.

"Now," she breathes. "Fuck me better. Now."

I pull back. Her eyes are swimming with lust and my cock thickens at the sight of her. "You fucking bet," I say, hooking my hands beneath her arms and lifting her to my eye level. She wraps her legs around my waist and lowers her lips to mine, kissing me slow and deep. I walk at a decadent pace out through the sliding doors, then I bend at the knees and lower her slowly to the deck. The sound of the sea lapping at the struts only adds to the fucking serenity I'm feeling right now. I'm high on her. She doesn't take her eyes off me as I kneel up above her and reach for my wallet on the table. I pull out a condom and meet her eyes as I slowly roll it down the length of my cock. She bites her bottom lip and a pulse of lust floods through me. I brace my hands either side of her shoulders.

My tip brushes her entrance and she shivers.

"Are you cold baby?" I whisper.

She shakes her head, her eyes hungry.

I dip my mouth to her collarbone and suck gently at the damp skin. She shivers again.

"Are you ticklish?" I murmur, pushing the delicate tank up her stomach and dragging my tongue lazily between the mounds of her breasts.

She shakes her head again, watching me.

I anchor one arm into the deck and run my fingers of the other from the crook of her knee to the top of her inside thigh and she trembles.

I lift my head and lock her eyes. "Are you nervous?"

For a few seconds she does nothing but lick her sweet pink tongue across her dry lips. Then she nods.

"So am I," I whisper, brushing my lips across her mouth while pushing myself into her warmth, inch by inch. It isn't a lie. I'm shitting myself. As much as I want this, and as much as it's all I've been able to think about in weeks, I'm terrified of what this will do to us. I push my worry the side. I may only get this chance once. I need to relish every second. I don't tear my eyes from hers as I slowly bury myself inside her. Inside Aurelia Bird. I know this is every grown and ungrown man's wet dream come true, but for me it's something else. She lets out a long breath, a faint cry, a gorgeous sound. I reach her edge and stop, not for her but for me. I won't last a fucking second if I don't take this slow. She grips me with her entire body, and her bright, set eyes confirm she's the one in control, not me. My eyelids slide shut as I try to capture everything about this moment. I feel her wrapped around me, urging me to move, to feel even more.

I open my eyes and see her smiling, blissful. I'm moving now, the sensations throbbing outwards from my groin to my skin, which is prickling hot and cold. I'm fucking her. I'm fucking her, and I'm not stopping. I'm going to take every slow, agonizing thrust I can get, before she comes to her senses, before she realizes I'm past my prime, before she has no choice but to fire me for taking advantage of her. As I look deep into her eyes I know this is the happiest I've ever felt inside a woman, and if I never get the chance to be inside her again, I'll still die a happy man.

"Isaac," she chokes, suddenly. Her face takes on a pained, stunned expression and I'm fixed by a tight grip around my cock that challenges every urge I have to fire myself into her. Her spine arches and her head rolls back as her cry of release sails across the deck into the wind. Oh, but Jeezus, the feeling of her coming all over me is incredible. I graze a hand across her forehead and she turns her face to kiss the dampness on the pads of my fingers.

I move again into a deeper place and slant my mouth across hers. "God, Aurelia," I moan into her. My hand roams her breasts and I subconsciously marvel at how they bounce softly as I push into her again and again. Her tight body beneath me holds me close, her small muscular legs wrapped around my hips coaxing me as far as I can go. I bury my face into the taut, silky skin of her neck and breathe her in, while her fingers snake through my hair. Our tongues entangle, our moans combine. And I'm floating up and up. I'm so close but I don't want it to end. As if reading my mind, her lips detach. "Roll me over," she gasps.

I fall to my side, pulling her with me, the momentum taking us all the way until she's straddling me, her baby soft hair forming a veil around our faces. It frames the sense that it's just us. Us against the world. Us in our little bubble, the way it's been since I moved her here. I crane my neck to join our lips again, groaning as she pushes herself onto me with torturous decadence.

"It feels even better than I dreamed," she whispers between each slow thrust.

"You dreamed of this?" Normally, the thought of a woman dreaming about me would have me running for the hills, but hearing Aurelia say it makes me soar.

"You must know I have," she pants, sitting back and pulling off her tank, giving me a game-over view of her naked torso. I bring my hands down to her hips and feel her as she pushes them back and forth. So close. She moves faster, trailing a finger along my jaw. When she removes it, a pearl of sweat runs a track from the tip to her knuckle. We're both wet with the exertion of holding back.

"Ride me, Aurelia," I say, pulling her lips back down onto mine, swiping my tongue across hers.

"With pleasure." I catch her breath in my mouth as she pumps my cock faster, her small hands gripping my shoulders for dear life. "Oh, God," she groans. "Oh God, Oh God…"

"That's it baby, let it go."

Her groans freeze as her climax overtakes her, then she's crying out, again, gripping my cock fiercely. I push myself up, wrapping an arm around her waist. She falls across my chest, limp, as I pump upwards into her. I'm right on the edge and it's so good. My thigh muscles are burning, my lips bleeding as she bites into them. Her arms circle my neck in a vise as she holds on, her breathless cry returning.

"Fuck, Aurelia. Fuck, *fuck*..." It has never felt like this. A white heat engulfs me and I fuck us both over the line. Her lips move blindly to my ear, filling it with a throaty whimper, as though it's all she has left.

"Don't stop, Isaac."

I grind everything I have into her as the orgasm shoots through my veins, obliterating all that's around us. She closes in again, one final decadent grip, and I'm gone.

I float down to the deck, rolling her onto her back, my lips molded to her throat. As we still lay still, I can feel her heart racing beneath mine, as though they're galloping together like wild horses. Our breath slows in tandem, our chests settling into a steady rhythm. I don't know what the hell just happened but that was like nothing I've ever experienced. I've had lots of great sex, with lots of very experienced women, but none of it has ever come close to this. I'm half in love with this girl, and instead of the thought petrifying me to the bone, it heats me up.

After several minutes of us lying together in post-coital bliss, I feel her take a deep breath. "We should move. I need to meet Nate," she whispers.

This is not the first time a woman has voiced the name of another man while I'm still inside her, but it is the first time it's ever felt like a punch to the stomach. I pull out, straightening my arms, and look down at her face. She feels guilty, I can tell. That's another big difference between Aurelia and the other women I've slept with. Either she's far more human than the rest, and lets her feelings show, or it's simply because she hasn't botoxed all emotion from her face. Then, in a split second, it all changes. There's triumph in her eyes and a confident smile that remains only on her lips.

CHAPTER TWENTY-SIX

Aurelia

Isaac really does wear his heart on his sleeve. I can see a multitude of emotions and questions flit across his brow. I feel bad about what I've just done, not because it's going to hurt Nate, but because I've stooped to his level.

"So, what now?" Isaac rolls off the condom and busies his eyes with it, avoiding mine.

I arch an eyebrow. "What do you mean, what now?"

"You gonna end things with Nate?" Still no eye contact.

I pause for effect. "Why would I do that?" Part of me hates this. That was the single best experience of my life, feeling Isaac's pure and raw need for me override his better judgement, and I'm giving up any chance of it happening again.

Isaac looks up, rewarding me with another glimpse of those lust-drenched eyes. He's speechless.

"You only did this because I'm unavailable," I say, shrugging as best I can with my back on the floor. I push myself up to my elbows and he sits back on his heels, eyeing me suspiciously. "If I break things off with Nate, I'll be available again and you won't want me."

"That's not true," he says, appalled.

"Isaac," I start, pulling my legs from beneath him and getting to my feet. "Name one time you've been with a woman who's been available to you."

He doesn't answer.

"Right? You can't do it. You can't open yourself up to someone who might leave."

"So, your plan was to fuck Nate so you could fuck me too?"

I glare at him. Then I remember this was what I wanted. He's right. I have wanted Isaac for weeks, and I know he's wanted me too. But the only time he's given into his feelings is the only time I've been truly out of his reach. I shrug my shoulders again.

"Do you realize how absurd that sounds?" He stands to face me.

"Yeah, I do." I say, matter-of-factly. "Do YOU realize how absurd this sounds?"

"What's that supposed to mean?"

"Why did it take this, huh? Why did I have to get involved with my ex-boyfriend for you to admit your feelings for me? And for you to do something about them?"

His frown deepens and I can't tell if he's more mad with me or himself. "I admitted my feelings for you before."

"And you shut me down."

"Because you're my client."

"So, what's changed?" I look up at him. He clenches his jaw and doesn't respond. "I was no longer available," I conclude.

I pull a hairband from my wrist and scrape my hair back into a ponytail. His throat constricts as he watches. When he still doesn't say anything, I feel the weight of what I'm doing sticking in my throat like a fishbone.

"So, it won't be happening again," I say, with finality. Then I walk back inside the villa before he can see me cry.

I CAN STILL FEEL Isaac inside me as I follow Luca and Alana to the back of the stage. Just five minutes to go and I'll be back in my own world, surrounded by my music, my dancers and my fans. Normally, this is the moment I try to keep Isaac at the front of my mind. Over the last few weeks, every performance has become more and more about him. Every note I've sung has had his name on its tip, and every twist of my hips has had his invisible touch on them. But, this time, I have to push him back. And this is how it has to be. As earth-shaking as it was to feel him all over me, inside my body, my mind and my heart, I proved to both of us today that this can never be real.

I broke up with Nate straight after, knowing what I'd done was wrong, and also knowing it would render me completely undesirable to Isaac. Sure, in the heat of some moment Isaac might want to kiss me, like he did the first time, but ultimately, I'm not worth more. I'm only worth something if he can't have me.

I'm not proud that I used Nate to get to Isaac, but I guess we're even now. I simply can't be with my boyband ex after the way he treated me in the past, and when I'm clearly in love with someone else. He took it surprisingly well, making me believe his heart hadn't exactly been in it either. If I had the headspace, I'd be wondering why Nate had traveled so far to be with me if he wasn't as invested in the idea after all. I resolve to interrogate my mother about it as soon as tonight is over.

I smile back at Alana as a runner counts down my entrance, then I inch onto the platform, take a deep breath and step into Aurelia Bird. The show must go on.

I glance at the set list one more time as the platform starts to move, slowly carrying me upwards to a plinth on which I perform my opening song, *Feel Me*, a new raunchy number that signals my transition from girl to woman. It seems pretty apt right now.

Tonight's show is going to go a little differently. My second costume change has been brought forward to coincide with a very special announcement. I have to push aside the sadness of my own love life, to help two wonderful people celebrate their own.

When I walk back onto the stage, second outfit in place, instead of launching straight into *Crazy Baby* as usual, I walk to the front of the stage and wait until the audience quietens. No matter how hard I try to stop them, my eyes search the crowd for Isaac. He's not standing in his usual place at the side of the stage. Luca is there tonight instead. I know for a fact the rest of the security team is here too. I spot Carter, Hud and Jax in the security bay at the front. Tawny, Seleste and Maisie are standing to the side, watching, and waiting to hear what I'm about to say. Isaac is nowhere to be seen, but he *must* be here somewhere. He knows what's about to happen, it was his idea. A part of me irrationally wonders if I've pissed him off so much he's stayed away on this important night to avoid me. I shove the thought away and launch into my planned script.

"You know, it's usually around this point in the evening I invite someone up onto the stage."

Another roar goes up from the crowd and a few kids are hoisted onto parents' shoulders to catch my eye.

"Tonight is going to be a *little* different," I say, walking along the front edge of the stage, enjoying myself. A few shouts of "How?" "Tell us!" and "I love you, Aurelia!" rise up from the mass of bodies.

"A certain person will be joining me on stage in a moment. But, I want you to be gentle with them. I know this person suffers terribly from stage fright." I stop and scan the audience, slowly, dramatically.

"So," I continue, resuming my strut along the stage, "here's what we're going to do." I wait for complete silence. "We're going to be super welcoming and super supportive to this person. We need to coax him up here, ok?"

A voice comes through my headset—one of the runners. "He's ready. He's shaking like a fucking leaf but I've gotta hold of him." Good. The last thing I need is for Connor to bail.

"Are you ready, guys?" I say, standing at the center of the stage, my arms open. "After three, we're going to chant 'Connor', ok?"

I see Tawny's head flip to Seleste in the corner of my eye, and can't help but smile at what's about to happen.

"One, two, three. *Connor, Connor, Connor…*"

The voice comes through my headset again. "Ten seconds and he's coming on."

Connor, Connor, Connor…

"That's it, guys, perfect! Keep it going! *Connor, Connor…*"

I look to my right and see a pale, sweating Connor walk tentatively onto the stage. He gets a few feet and looks out at the audience. For a second I think he might be about to turn around and bail, but to his credit, he keeps moving towards me. I extend my arm. *Connor, Connor…* He takes my hand and I thrust it aloft both of us and the crowd cheers like they're trying to bring the house down.

When the applause gradually dies down, I lower our hands but keep hold of him. He really is shaking like a leaf.

"I would like you to meet my very good friend, Connor Johnson. He's the head of security here on Starling Key and he has something very important he wants to say." A runner scurries across the stage and passes me a hand-held mic. Connor is trembling so bad I hold it up in front of him, afraid that if he takes it from me, he'll drop it.

"Um," he starts, then swallows and coughs. "Um…"

I drop his hand briefly to close my fingers around my mic. "Look at me," I whisper, then I grab his hand again. He turns to face me and I nod encouragingly.

"I, er… I would like to invite my girlfriend onto the stage," he says. I glance at the sound guy so he knows to up the levels on Connor's mic as he's so quiet I suspect no one heard that.

"Can you say that again?" I press.

He coughs again and this time it reverberates around the concert hall. It seems to shock him into action. He takes hold of the mic. "I'd like to invite my girlfriend up to the stage," he says, more resolutely this time. The crowd hears that and there's uproar. Everyone knows now what's about to happen. Carter and Hud lift Tawny up as though she's made of cloud particles and she lands red-faced and trembling on the stage. I extend my now-free arm and beckon her over.

"What the fuck?" she mouths at me. Another runner

sprints over with a second mic and hands it to Tawny. I glance at them both to check they're going to be ok. It's nerve-wracking as hell being up on a stage in front of eight thousand people all hanging onto your every word. Connor nods, his expression a chaotic combination of fear and conviction, and I step backwards giving them the stage.

When almost-total silence finally descends, Connor looks lovingly into Tawny's eyes and I feel another wave of sadness flood my stomach, only for it to be quickly replaced by joyful anticipation. It's like being on a rollercoaster of emotions.

"Tawny," he begins. "You know there's only one person in the world I would stand up here on a stage for."

She presses a hand to her mouth and nods, sending a stream of tears running over her fingers.

"I've wanted to do this for as long as I've known you; it's just taken me a while to translate the feeling into words."

He holds her eyes as he swallows and takes another sobering breath. My gaze drifts to his pants to make sure he isn't actually peeing. He's nervous enough.

"You have changed my life, Tawny Graham. You are the finest, loveliest, tenderest, and most beautiful person I know. And even that is an understatement."

I haven't had the same education as most people but even I recognize those words by the famous F. Scott Fitzgerald.

"I truly don't believe anyone can deserve you as a wife, but I am prepared to spend the rest of my life trying to become worthy."

Tawny's shoulders are heaving and the audience is still and silent, except for the occasional sniff and wipe of an eye. I grit my teeth to hold back emotion. If I'm the slightest bit choked up, I can't sing. And there's not a lot that won't tip me over the edge tonight.

"Tawny Graham, love of all my lives. Will you marry me?"

The audience collectively holds its breath as Tawny removes the hand covering her mouth. She drops to her knees and takes Connor's face in her hands. A tear rolls down my cheek and I quickly wipe it away.

"Yes."

The crowd is in uproar again as Connor scoops Tawny up into his arms, hugs her tightly and spins her around. The band spontaneously bursts into a raucous jam and I clasp my hands together, grinning like a proud mother. I let them have their moment and laugh when Connor gently places Tawny back to the ground, turns to the audience and whoops. The crowd goes crazy for it. Eventually, the two of them turn to me and it's clear they now want to share this moment together alone.

I step forward and hug them both, then I nod to a runner who sprints over to us and escorts my two friends backstage. As they reach the left exit I see him. Isaac. The man who had made me feel that special for a few minutes. He must have been waiting for them both all along. Our eyes connect and he sends me a timid smile before wrapping his arms around Connor and Tawny, giving his own congratulations. Suddenly choked, I turn back to my band and nod, signaling them to launch straight into *Crazy Baby*. I need to focus on something else. The bass kicks in and the crowd erupts. The dancers bounce into action with renewed energy. Connor's proposal seems to have lifted everyone but me. And no matter how high I jump, or how fast I spin, I can't escape the feeling of a lead weight sinking to the pit of my stomach.

Somehow, I manage to get through the rest of the show without faltering. The hours and hours of relentless rehearsing is being truly put to the test. As I bring the show to a close, dancing out the last bars of *Break His Heart*, I see something that breaks mine. I thought Isaac's silent admission that I was right, that he won't ever commit to someone who's free to be his, would be the thing that causes me the ultimate pain, but I was wrong.

I hold my final stance at the front of the stage and sing out the final note, elongating it with the last remaining ounces of oxygen left in my lungs, and I see her. In the front row, of course.

Paris Navitsky.

Looking every inch the woman for Isaac that I will never be.

CHAPTER TWENTY-SEVEN

Isaac

I PLASTER a broad smile to my face as I lead Connor and Tawny off the stage, even though my heart is far from smiling. Try as I might to be happy for two of my closest friends, I can't get past the feeling I will never have this for myself, and for the first time in my life, I want it. Watching Aurelia do everything we'd planned together, talked through, and giggled about had brought everything back. The beautiful friendship we had, the easy comfort we felt in each other's company, the mutual respect and admiration we had for each other. Although, for the life of me, I couldn't understand what she'd have to admire me for. I'm just a beefed up security guard at the end of the day. Sure, I helped her get a few bank statements and passwords using connections from my CIA days, but she's mentioned no more about the information so I figure it wasn't as useful as she'd hoped.

I lead the newly engaged pair down the corridor, knowing

the agency guys are watching Aurelia, and let them into the Dolphin suite where I know Carter, Luca, Jax and Hud are waiting with Esme, Maisie, and Seleste. I still don't know what Carter was thinking leaving baby Safia with former petty thief Maggie 'from the hole' but he clearly trusts her, so who am I to argue? A loud cheer that could only emanate from the mouths of overbearing security guards can be heard the second the door is opened, and I follow them inside, almost being crushed myself by group hugs.

As far as celebrations go, it's perfect. Everyone close to Connor and Tawny is here, apart from perhaps Barbie and Fitz, but this is way past their bedtime and I'm sure they'll have their own ideas for celebrating the happy couple. As infectious as the smiles are, for me, there's something missing. There's someone else who should be here. I try to ignore the gaping hole in my chest as best I can, but it's hard. It feels like nothing I've ever experienced, as though my heart itself has been physically kicked and is limping along, bruised and battered.

When the door opens, it shoots into my mouth and I hold my breath waiting to see who's standing at the other side. It would make sense for her to come here. She couldn't express her true feelings, or give genuine, heartfelt congratulations while up on stage with a few thousand fans watching her every move. But here, in the privacy of the backstage area, she can be free with her support for two people who've become her friends too.

The door opens further and the breath leaves my throat. My heart doesn't do the flip I expected it to. I don't feel it hammering against my ribcage. My cock doesn't even budge at the sight of her. Because it's not who I hope it's going to be.

"Paris."

We sit on the beach opposite the marina. I chose this spot because I don't want Aurelia to see us when she makes her way back to the villa.

"You left without saying goodbye," I say, looking out to the blackened sea.

"I know, I'm sorry." Her voice is quiet and full of genuine regret. "I thought you might have had other things on your mind."

"It's just my job." I sigh, feeling suddenly tired.

"I know that now. I'm sorry for behaving like a child."

"You didn't behave like a child, Paris. I understand it now. I know how it must have looked. Aurelia is an attractive girl…" I force the words, "but nothing's changed. She isn't, and never will be, the girl for me." Not because I don't want her, I don't say, but because she's right. I can't commit to someone who's available. I'm petrified of being left. I've been left too many times in my life and I can't bear the thought of the protective wall I've built around myself being knocked to the ground all over again.

I sense Paris breathing out slowly.

"I missed you, Isaac."

"I missed you too." As I say this, I know it's a lie.

"I realized something while I was away." I turn to face her but she still looks out to sea. "I don't want to be shared."

My chest stills. "What do you mean?"

"I mean, I don't want to be with both you and Roman…"

I swallow as discreetly as I can, pushing down the horrible feeling I have that I know what she's about to say.

"I just want to be with you."

There it is. The sentence I really don't want to hear, and not for the reason Aurelia would assume—that I can't bring myself to be with someone who isn't available—but because of who Paris is. Or, more importantly, who she isn't. I take in Paris's profile and for the first time it's clear to me what is real and what is not real. There's very little of the former. Her exterior has been toughened with fillers and fats and fancy sculpting. There's very little evidence of who Paris used to be. It used to appeal to me. I now realize I liked having the wall of disguise between me and the women I slept with. I never got to really know them, and they never got to know me. There was always a veil of fakeness in the way. With Aurelia, no such veil existed. She was truly, effortlessly and unashamedly herself. And with it, she saw me, my failings and all.

I don't reply. I can't. So I reach an arm around her shoulders and pull her close. It probably took a lot for Paris to say that. The least I can do is make it worth her while.

CHAPTER TWENTY-EIGHT

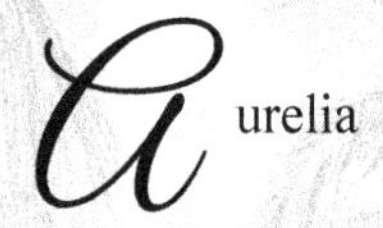

urelia

"Thanks for doing this Luca, I appreciate it." We step out of the sedan and make our way to the golf buggies. We're returning from the fifth and final private gig in Miami that Chuck had scheduled, and I'm pretty beat.

"No problem. Your management's security took over at the venue anyway. I was able to watch the show and actually enjoy it. It was pretty intimate. Do you prefer the smaller venues?"

I throw a bag into the back and hop onto the passenger seat next to him. "Usually, yes. These corporate gigs, not so much. They're full of drunk salespeople who didn't need to buy themselves a ticket. Not all of them are fans. I love performing but it's much more rewarding when it's for people who've saved up their money to see me, or they've bought all my records and it means something to see them performed live, you know?"

"I hadn't thought of it like that," Luca admits, backing out of the parking lot and ambling the golf buggy towards the south shore. "Gotta pay the bills though, I guess."

"Exactly," I grin. This was the only gig Isaac hasn't accompanied me to, and as much as I enjoy Luca's company—he's closer to my age for a start, and at least knows who Billie Eilish is—I missed Isaac. I've missed him for days. Goading him into sleeping with me was both the best and worst thing I could have done. Best, because I now know what everyone's talking about. Sex is better than anything else—if you're doing it right—and Isaac knows everything about doing it right. But worse because I've simply shown myself what I can't have. I will never be enough for Isaac. I'm not old enough, wise enough or otherwise attached, and I'm certainly not going to make myself unavailable again just so he'll look seriously at me.

Isaac didn't argue with me when I confronted him with that truth, which only confirmed what I had figured out. He can't bring himself to get involved with someone who might leave him, like his father did when he killed himself, and like his mother did when she left him with his grandmother. I wouldn't blame him for going back to Paris. She's beautiful, refined, mature and, crucially, unattainable—everything he wants in a woman. When I finally reached the Dolphin suite after Connor's proposal, Isaac had already left, and the rest of them were cagey about his departure. They are nothing if not loyal. Even now, when I press Luca for any information at all about Isaac, he remains resolutely neutral.

"How many more shows before the residency ends?" Luca asks, pulling me from my thoughts.

"Just three."

"Oh yeah, of course. Your birthday is on Thursday, right? The night of your last show?"

"Yup. I'll be twenty-years-old. Officially an adult, according to Grams."

"Grams?" Luca glances at me before pulling the golf buggy round a corner onto the road alongside Reef Street, or the 'retirement village' as the staff fondly call it.

"My grandmother. She set up a trust for the rights to all my music. It's all transfers to my business the day I turn twenty."

"Will that change anything? I mean, will you suddenly have more money than you know what to do with?" He smirks then throws me a wink. "Asking for a friend."

I chuckle. "Not money exactly, but I could sell the rights to my music if I wanted to. It could be worth a lot."

"Wouldn't you miss out on future royalties? I'm not sure how it works."

I would have said the same a few weeks ago, but since Isaac gave me the bank statements and passwords, I've learned a lot. I've had to. "I'd no longer receive the royalties for the songs I sell the rights to, but I'll continue to earn royalties on new material and live performances. The benefit in selling the rights now would be a large cash injection. Probably a few hundred million."

"What?" Luca accidentally jabs the brake sending us both slamming into the front of the buggy. "Shit. Sorry. I mean, are you kidding? That's huge!"

"Yeah, it is. But it doesn't make sense for me to do that yet. I don't need that kind of money right now. I'm not sure who does, to be honest. It would make more sense for me to wait until I'm older before I consider selling the rights."

Luca makes a whistling sound through his teeth then turns the golf buggy into a parking space by the beach.

"Will you stay around for a while after the residency ends?" He climbs out and grabs my bag from the back.

"I don't know yet." I already know the answer but I can't tell anyone. There are so many details to iron out and I'm still relying on two people who can help me finalize my plan. It's going to change my life and the lives of everyone around me, so other arrangements are hard to make right now. I follow Luca down the path to the boardwalk and wait as he opens the gate. "I'm going to miss this place."

"This place is going to miss you," he replies, arching an eyebrow as I pass. "Will you sing for us one more time? Maybe behind the wall one night? I'm sure Ché and Camiro will make it worth your while in mojitos."

I laugh. "Now there's an offer I can't refuse."

"Maybe the day after your birthday. We could hold a kind of birthday/end of residency celebration for you."

"That sounds like a plan," I grin.

We walk the rest of the way in comfortable silence, the only noise coming from the quiet sea lapping at the struts holding the boardwalk above sea level. We pass four villas before reaching the Morrison. Then, just as Luca swipes the door unlocked, another one opens. I turn towards the Hemingway villa at the end of the boardwalk and see a familiar figure emerge. His sexy, cheeky smile drops the minute he sees my face. As he steps outside to close the door, I see her. Our eyes meet and she stares back at me, her filled face devoid of everything but a hint of smugness. My insides twist and I want to cry, but I hold it together as I step inside the villa.

"Can I get you a drink?" I ask Luca. My mouth is suddenly as dry as a desert. I head straight for the refrigerator to grab a bottle of water.

"No, I'm good, thanks. I'll leave you to it, shall I?"

Isaac appears in the doorway and nods discreetly to Luca.

"Sure, Thanks for tonight, Luca."

"The pleasure was all mine," he replies with a thin smile before bumping awkwardly past Isaac and out onto the boardwalk. The door closes and the silence inside the villa is excruciating. I walk out onto the deck unable to bring myself to look at Isaac. Out the corner of my eye I can see him move around like a shadow.

After a few minutes, he appears through the sliding doors. "Did you have a good gig?"

"Yes, thanks." I glue my eyes to my phone, reading through my lawyer's latest update.

"Great."

I can feel him hovering, knowing he feels like shit because I saw him exiting Paris's villa—and no doubt bedroom. I take a deep breath. I can't put this off. I need his help so I may as well get it over with.

"Isaac?"

"Yes?" he replies, quickly.

"Can I ask you for one more favor?" I keep my eyes on my phone.

"Of course. What do you need?"

"I need to set up a meeting."

"Ok. Who with?"

"My record company."

The night is so quiet I can hear him swallow. "And how can I help?"

I turn to face him, ignoring the thumping in my ribcage. "It needs to be in secret. My manager can't know about it. And I need to meet with Amy Kissinger, the President. I need to go straight to the top. I don't have enough time to work my way up the chain. Can you get me her direct line? Or, even better, a confidential meeting for tomorrow?"

He watches me carefully. "No problem."

"Thank you." I give him a thin smile, then look back at my emails.

A few minutes pass and he's still standing there.

"Feel free to sit out here." I don't look at him as I speak. "I'm going to bed soon. You can have the deck to yourself."

"Aurelia—"

I get to my feet, quickly. I don't want to talk. I don't want to confront what I just saw. I just want to forget I saw it.

"Night, Isaac."

I go to walk past him but he takes hold of my arm. "Aurelia… I'm sorry."

I fix my eyes dead ahead towards the front of the villa. "What is there to be sorry for? You're helping me."

His voice is a whisper. "You know what I mean. I'm sorry you had to see that. I'd planned to get here before you came back."

"See what, Isaac?" I still can't look at him. "You were off duty until ten minutes ago. You can do whatever the hell you like any other time." I push past, yanking my arm free, and walk straight into my suite, closing the door firmly behind me.

I WALK OUT of the nondescript building and open the door to the SKS truck. Amy was happy to meet somewhere neutral in the city and it was Isaac's idea to forgo a sedan this time, figuring one of the security trucks would be less conspicuous. Still, I donned the wig and trench again just in case.

I catch Isaac's smile as I slide in behind him and pull the itchy, sweaty mass of hair off my head.

"How did that go?" he asks, pulling away from the sidewalk onto the main street.

"Good, thanks." I immediately whip out my phone again and peruse my inbox for any updates. It was better than 'good' actually, but I can't afford for anyone else to know the details. Not even Isaac.

"Straight back to the Key?" His eyes watch me through the rear view mirror but, again, I avoid them. I have trouble thinking straight when they lock with mine.

"Yes please. I just have a few more things to tie up before tomorrow's show."

He's quiet for a few minutes. "The last one. How are you feeling about it?"

I take a breath and look out of the window at the bright sky, the luscious palms and the crystal ocean stretched out around us.

"Nervous," I reply, honestly. "A little sad."

We both fall silent.

After a few minutes he speaks again. "And the last day of your teenage years," he says with a slight smile. "Does it feel significant?"

I laugh inwardly. "Yeah, it does." It will feel significant for a whole lot more than that, I think to myself. Just one more day to finalize the rest of my life.

We travel the remaining way without speaking, and when we pull into the parking lot on the Key, a man is waiting for us. He's young but disheveled, wearing his signature hound-stooth jacket and grey slacks, his dark hair somewhat unruly.

"Who's he?" Isaac asks, immediately.

"Just someone I'm working with," I reply. "I need to speak with him privately."

"Aurelia—" Isaac warns with an exasperated sigh.

I'm about to open the door but I stop and turn to face him, hoping my face convinces him to trust me. "You don't need to worry about this guy. He's the same one I met before and I came back, didn't I?"

He holds my eyes, the memory of that afternoon flashing between us both. The first kiss followed by the first crushing rejection. He's the first to look away and I push the door open. The man nods and walks backwards to a black Silverado. I hear Isaac's feet on the gravel but I don't look back. I slide into the passenger seat and wait for the man to get in the other side. Then the doors close and I block out everything else around me, including Isaac.

CHAPTER TWENTY-NINE

Isaac

The lights burst out, illuminating the audience. They fixate on the crowd for longer than all the nights that came before, then just as our eyes become accustomed to the brightness, they twist round and up to point at the back of the stage. Slowly, she appears, and my breath sticks in my throat, along with my pounding heart and a not-insignificant proportion of yesterday's breakfast. I know it's that meal specifically, because I haven't been able to bring myself to eat anything since then. Aurelia's residency is ending. Tonight.

I take note of everything. The curl of her hair, the cut of her outfit, the sharp point of her boots, the tone of her stance. Her face is soft but her overall look is unapologetically fierce. It feels as though she has grown fully into her new, womanly image over the course of the last four months. She's leaving Starling Key a more fully formed version of herself, and she knows it too. Part of me wonders if that had been her goal all along. To get some space and separation from her suffocating parents so she could find herself on her own terms.

They're all here tonight. Her mom and Chuck have prime seats at the front, while her two sisters are backstage, their nannies ready to sweep them off to bed the minute the show is over.

It is epic. In fact, even epic doesn't do the show justice, or Aurelia's performance. When the final song kicks in, Aurelia is swarmed by her dancers in an impromptu group hug, sending the crowd crazy. She joins in with the cheering and turns the applause over to them: the dancers, her band, her roadies. She refuses to take all of the credit. She dances until the sweat pours off her and belts out the lyrics like her life depends on it. I stand and watch the emotional rollercoaster, my heart soaring and diving with the gut and tempo of each song. Throughout it all, she sheds not one tear. As she reaches the final crescendo, the band cuts out and the light cuts away from everyone but Aurelia. She stands tall and commanding at the front of the stage, singing the chorus for the last time, a cappella. The final bar is long and high. She anchors her feet into the stage and expands her lungs, pulling out note after note. When her voice finally tapers, her eyes open and she drops them to mine.

The crowd erupts again into one collective scream. Around me people are leaping up into the air and bouncing around, arms waving, torches beaming, phone cameras flashing. But I don't move. I'm frozen into place by her gaze and the soft smile tugging at her lips. My heart is beating so hard it's making me dizzy, or it could be the resounding echo of thousands of feet stamping around me.

It feels as though an eternity is passing as I drink in the look she's giving me—and only me. Then she sharply turns away just as I hear a voice in my ear.

"Let's get out of here." I'd clean forgotten Paris was standing next to me. I turn to her and shake my head.

"I can't do this," I say.

She can't hear me above the music but she can read my lips. She blinks once, twice, then she steps backwards and slaps me across the face, hard. I deserve it. I had agreed to go exclusive with her; I'd built up her hopes. Thankfully, she has yet to end things with Roman so at least she has that option if she still wants it, and knowing Paris, the money means too much. But I can't live this lie anymore. I'm in love with someone else, even if that someone is about to leave, convinced I could never want her.

I watch Paris turn around and fight her way through the dancing crowd, then I look back to the stage. Aurelia is striding along the edge, coaxing more cheers from the crowd. If she'd seen the slap, she betrays no evidence of it. I move to the side of the stage and nod to two of the bodyguards we hired through the agency. I lean into the ear of one of them.

"I'll take her upstairs."

He nods and mouths, "We'll follow."

When Aurelia finally comes off stage, instead of going to her dressing room like usual, we make our way along the corridor, followed by more security, her dancers and some of the band, and up the back stairs to the executive suite. This is where Aurelia will have her after-show party.

"Is everything set up?" she asks, all business again, her fond smile from earlier gone without a trace.

I nod. "There is a small podium with a mic, and a connected monitor, as you specified. Your mom and Chuck are being escorted from the hall as we speak. I believe the girls and the two nannies have been taken to one of the villas for the night. We'll have security all over the room. Was there anything else?"

"No." Her smile is business-like but I can tell she's operating firmly outside of her comfort zone. Whatever she has planned, she's planned it on her own. But she won't let me in. I lost that privilege a long time ago.

"Is Paris coming?" Her question almost makes me jump. "You can invite her, you know."

"I think this is the last place she'll want to be," I mumble.

"I'm sorry to hear that."

One of the security guys holds the door to the exec suite open and I follow Aurelia inside. She immediately scans the almost-empty room, verifying that I've fulfilled all her requests correctly.

"It's not because of you," I clarify.

Aurelia whips her head around as if she's already forgotten what we were talking about. "What isn't?"

"The reason Paris doesn't want to be here. It's not because she's jealous of you."

"Well, that's a relief," she says, looking far from it.

"It's because of me," I persist. "I ended it tonight."

Her shoulders drop and finally I see genuine feeling in her face, not just the professional veneer she's been reserving recently, especially for me. "I'm sorry to hear that too." She follows the words with a heavy sigh. "I feel like I played a part. You were perfectly happy before I came along."

I take a step towards her even though we're in the center of the room and no one can hear us. "No I wasn't."

I don't know why I'm telling her this. Aurelia was right. I don't know how to be with a woman who isn't already committed to someone else. The thought of it scares me to death. But I want her to know I wasn't happy before. I was happy when I was with *her*.

The pace of her breathing picks up and her cheeks flush an adorable shade of pink, visible even beneath all the stage makeup. Then her head cocks to one side. "I think you have some soul-searching to do, Isaac. Maybe you and Paris parting ways is for the best."

I grind my teeth to stop any further words erupting, and nod, slowly. Then she turns away, leaving me to resume my duties, exactly as she pays me to.

ONLY FIFTEEN MINUTES LATER, the room is full to capacity with all the people who've played a role in the residency, Aurelia's family, some Starling Key staff who've managed to sneak in, and some exceptionally high paying guests and concert-goers. I search the crowd for Chuck and find him hanging at the back of the room, periodically scrolling through his phone, then exiting the room to talk into it. Aurelia's mother is hovering at the front by the podium, basking in the glow of her daughter's glory. Security personnel, including every single one of my guys, are dotted around the room. We're unmissable in our black tuxedos, pistols discreetly hidden, earpieces fixed, eyes surveying the room. Anyone who's anyone wanted to be inside this room, press and legal teams included, but Aurelia was unequivocal: only teams and family. And of course, the monitor.

I have no idea what she plans to do with the monitor but it is all set up and ready to go, for whatever purpose she has planned for it. Only she holds the password. I could obtain it, of course, but I have no interest in going behind Aurelia's back. If she wants to tell me something, she knows I'm right here. Or, at least, I hope she does.

Sasha, one of Aurelia's dancers taps a wine glass, calling the room to attention. It takes a good five minutes for everyone to pipe down and watch as Aurelia steps up onto the podium. In this moment I find it so hard to believe she's still only nineteen, if only for ten more minutes. I look at my wristwatch. Ten minutes exactly.

"Good evening everyone," she begins. The room replies in a chorus.

"Thank you so much for coming here tonight, I know a lot of you are exhausted and dying to get home to your families and loved ones. She smiles at her dancers and backstage team apologetically. "I won't keep you too long."

I watch every single person in the room. Everyone is smiling back at Aurelia, all ears, except for one person, Chuck, who continues to scroll through his phone at the back of the room. Aurelia leans forward and switches on the monitor in front of her, splitting her attention between the screen and the room.

"I wanted to take this opportunity, while all the people I care about are in this room—apart from my good friends Ana and Billy—" she looks pointedly at Chuck, unfazed by the fact he isn't even listening, "to not only thank you all for making this residency a huge success, but to make an announcement."

I watch her mom shift from foot to foot, obviously keen to move on so she can work the room as the star of the season's mother.

"This was the first residency that I have done, and that Starling Key has hosted." She nods her acknowledgment to Connor. "It was a risk for the resort and for me, but I think you'll all agree, it was one well worth taking." The room claps and murmurs it's whole-hearted agreement. She continues. "As many of you know, I turn twenty years old at the stroke of midnight."

Another cheer goes up in the room. She waits for quiet before going on.

"To most people, this is quite an uneventful birthday. I mean, eighteen was a pretty big deal, right? Nineteen? Not so much. Twenty-one is the next big birthday. The one where we can enjoy an alcoholic drink—legally!" She looks at the monitor and smiles. "But twenty… it's not too special, is it? Well, for me it is."

She pauses for effect and I notice that Chuck, for the first time, looks up from his phone.

"Twenty is the age I get access to the rights to all the music I've recorded so far. That's a pretty big deal. My beloved grandmother—may she rest in peace—made sure the rights were held in trust until exactly five years from the release of my first single. The contract stated that at twelve zero one a.m., exactly, on the day of my twentieth birthday, all rights would transfer to Bird Holdings, Inc., the company currently operated by my manager, Chuck Bird."

My gaze flits to her mother and, as suspected, she looks quite unhappy about Aurelia's deliberate omission of the fact Chuck is not only her manager, he's also her stepfather. I'm not the only one who can sense Aurelia is up to something. Something big. I look at my wristwatch. Three minutes from midnight.

"That…" she says, loudly and pointedly, "is no longer going to happen."

There's an audible gasp from certain sections of the gathering. Not everyone understands the significance of what Aurelia is saying, but those who do—including, I suspect, the people on her screen whom I now have no doubt are from legal and media stock—appreciate the gravitas of what she's saying.

I feel my heart racing as Aurelia continues. I don't know what she's up to but I've never felt more proud of anyone in my life.

"Bird Holdings, Inc., as of ten minutes ago, is no longer operational. All assets, including the rights to my back catalog when they transfer, have been moved to a brand new company, Aurelia Bird, Incorporated, of which I am President, presiding over a brand new board of directors."

My eyes flip to Chuck. He is staring at Aurelia now, pale-skinned and open-mouthed. *What on earth is she up to?*

"You might be wondering why I went to the trouble of creating a new company for all my assets. Well, here it is."

Aurelia takes a deep breath and I can't tell if she's feeling deeply uncomfortable about what's to follow or if she's reveling in it. I suspect both.

"For the last four years, my stepfather and manager, Chuck Bird, has been reappropriating my earnings for his own benefit. He has purchased no fewer than nine properties in *his* name using *my* money."

Her mom's head swivels around, searching for Chuck, as though it's on a stick. This is clearly news to her too.

"He has squandered my profits on luxuries that were hidden from me and the rest of my family. And worse, he had, in principle, sold the rights to all my music before they had even transferred."

In the corner of my eye, I see a couple of Aurelia's backing dancers rush to Aurelia's mother who appears to have collapsed.

"Chuck Bird, I'm afraid to say, has behaved immorally, unethically and fraudulently, and is no longer a part of my business, my career, or my personal life."

The room is completely silent, then a voice pipes up from the monitor, confirming there are reporters on the screen after all.

"Aurelia, why do you think Mr. Bird would do something like that?"

"I regret saying this with my mother in the room but I believe this is the sole reason for Chuck Bird's deception of my family, a deception that has run for no fewer than five years…" She takes a deep breath and I try to telepathically reach out to her with every ounce of support I can muster. "He has another family. A wife and children—two boys—he has kept secret from us for all this time."

The room gasps, and all eyes are suddenly on Chuck. He pales even further, if that's possible, and darts to the back of the room, yanking open a door to Starling's office. Starling's *super private* office. I mean, not even Connor goes in there. I glance across at Luca who raises his eyebrows at me. We both know there's no other way out of that room. The man is cornered.

"We need some help here," someone calls from below the podium. Aurelia's mother is lying limp on the floor, the latest revelation having finished her off.

Aurelia looks back to the monitor and out to the room. "That's all I wanted to say." She looks at her wristwatch, then up at all the people who have genuinely supported her, and grins. "Happy birthday to me."

I don't know if I want to spin her around, drop to the floor and worship at her feet, or bend her over and screw even more joy into her for the fucking awesome, game-changing announcement she just made. Instead, she jumps off the podium, plants a small kiss on her mother's cheek then strides through the room of shocked faces towards me. She doesn't stop in front of me like I expect her to. She walks straight past, wrapping her palm around the handle of the door to Starling's office and turns her face sideways.

"Come, Isaac. I want you to hear this."

CHAPTER THIRTY

Aurelia

Isaac is right behind me as I step into the office my ex-manager just ran to like a petrified dog with its tail on fire.

Chuck has made himself temporarily at home, bent over one of Eric Starling's expensive computers with his phone tacked to his ear. He looks up as we enter and positively snarls.

"Get out," I say, evenly. I can't put into words the elation I feel at finally being able to tell this guy to go run and jump.

"It's a load of crap," he seethes. "You can't move anything at this time of night."

"Then keep staring at those numbers. They're not gonna get any bigger, believe me."

I feel Isaac's chest filling up behind me, either from pride or from readying himself to pounce on a man he's made no secret of disliking since the first day we met. I wanted to do this on my own, and I did, but I couldn't have done it all without Isaac. I want him to share this moment with me. I owe him that much.

"It was all legitimate, Aurelia," Chuck says, rising from Starling's chair. "The houses, the vacations. I did nothing behind your back. It was all there in the accounts for you to see, in black and white, in broad daylight."

"You knew I trusted you with the accounts, Chuck," I hiss. "The first house purchase was four years ago. I was sixteen. You don't honestly think I was capable of staying on top of my business's finances at that age while also performing a world tour and camping out in studios, recording not one but two new albums, do you? I guarantee the lawyers don't see it that way."

"Lawyers," he sneers. "You had to get the lawyers, Aurelia. Always one for the drama weren't you?"

Instead of defending myself, or recoiling from the accusations, as I would have done previously, I step towards him and cock my head. "Drama is underrated. How on earth do you think I was going to make all that money, Chuck? I wasn't going to do it being a wallflower, was I?" I step backwards again, my eyelids heavy. I feel drunk. "Even this announcement… I couldn't waste an opportunity to get some serious column inches. But isn't that what you always drilled into me? Get the column inches where you can. Because I only have another couple of years, and then no one will be interested in me anymore." My smile widens. "Good thing I still have the rights to all my music though, huh? I can cash that in as soon as people stop caring. And don't worry, I'll make sure my mom and sisters have everything they could possibly need. That wasn't your intention though, was it?"

He's dumbfounded.

"You were going to take the money and disappear with that woman, weren't you?"

I can sense Isaac's brain working overtime, picturing the blonde from the CCTV. I turn to him. "The very one," I confirm.

Isaac's jaw drops. Chuck, to his credit, stands his ground and stops lying. "Yes. I was."

"What about the girls? You were just going to leave them?"

"They're not mine."

I fix my face firmly, even though this is the first I've heard of it. "Can you prove that?"

"Yes," he laughs bitterly. "I'm incapable of having more children. After Joan had the boys, I wasn't interested in adding more to the family. We couldn't afford it. I had the operation. I can show you all the damn paperwork."

"Does my mother know?"

"Well, she got those girls from somewhere, didn't she?" Chuck snarls.

Did Mom go to another sperm bank? She must have tried to trick Chuck into believing the girls were his. Chuck starts walking to the door, his face twisted up and pointed like a rat's.

"Do you have anything to say to my mother?" I say as I watch him go, probably for the last time.

He shrugs his shoulders. "Like what? You've said it all for me."

He goes to open the door but I'm not finished and Isaac knows it. He pushes his hand against it, slamming the door shut.

"You're not even going to say sorry?"

He laughs, bitterly. "I'm the one who deserves an apology," he snaps, deluded. "If you think that woman ever loved me, you're more naïve than I thought."

I feel Isaac's eyes on me, waiting for my next instruction.

I close my eyes and jerk my head away. Isaac releases the door and growls low as Chuck yanks it open and storms out. Isaac pushes it closed again and faces me.

"Jesus H Christ," he breathes out.

"Yeah," I say, simply.

"What can I do?" he asks, after a minute of intense silence has passed. I'm pretty sure there is commotion outside but Starling has had state-of-the-art sound-proofing built into the walls of this office so it is deathly quiet inside.

"It's all done," I reply.

"Well, yeah, I can see that. I mean, is there anything I can do for you? Do you have people helping you?"

"Yes. My grandmother's lawyer and Randy, the private detective you met briefly."

"The guy in the jacket? Who hadn't washed for a week? He was a private detective?"

I can't stop a grin forming. "Yeah, that was him."

A minute passes.

"That was phenomenal," he says, quietly. "You're phenomenal."

"Thanks." My voice is a whisper.

"How did you…? When did you…? How?"

I sigh heavily and pull out one of the chairs, sinking into it. I've been on my feet for hours and the soft leather cushioning makes me want to never get up again.

"It was when he banned me from seeing my friends," I say, shrugging. "Back in Miami, just before the residency started. I knew something didn't feel right, but I also knew I was too close to him, to my mother. I was with them a lot. Even if they didn't pay me much attention, they were always near, you know? They always seemed to be in my business. I needed space. And that's where you came in."

I can't meet his eyes.

"What do you mean?"

"You told me you were ex-CIA. I figured I might be able to use that."

"Right." Isaac shifts uncomfortably, while I try not to look up at his incredible form all decked up in the sexiest suit. And I *know* he's packing beneath it. For me. Which makes me feel all kinds of things I shouldn't. "The stalker note..." he says. "If that woman wasn't behind it, like I thought..." He turns his head and gives me a sidelong scrutinizing stare. "Then, who...?"

"It was me," I say, giving the answer he fully expects. "I faked it. I knew you'd move me here, out of Miami. I knew it would give me the space I needed. And the opportunity to ask for your help."

"But, you didn't ask, I offered..." Isaac says, frowning.

"Yeah, you did," I agree. "After I told you about the suspicions I already had at that point."

I can see the cogs turning behind Isaac's eyes. "And you saw something in the bank statements?"

"Yes. I saw money being funneled out to unknown accounts. They turned out to be his and *hers*. I saw huge transactions for properties he paid cash for. I found out exactly who and what was on our payroll, then I was able to quickly identify any anomalies. But I needed more proof."

"So you asked me for passwords."

"Yes. And that's when I discovered Chuck's plans to sell the rights to my music so he could run away with his other family and start a new life in the Caribbean. It was all in the emails."

"He was really so stupid as to not protect any of this stuff?"

"He figured I was too young and naïve to know any better," I shrug again.

"Man," Isaac breathes out. "More fool him."

"You're not mad at me?"

"Why would I be mad at you?" Isaac replies, surprised.

"I lied to you. I used you for information."

He leans over the desk, bringing his face unbearably close to me. "Don't you worry baby, I got mine."

He winks and I relax instantly, grateful to him for lightening the mood.

I can't believe Chuck has gone. He's no longer in our lives. It feels strange, as though his form is still in the room, lingering, like it has for the entire course of my career. It sounds ridiculous but, despite his treachery, I'm going to miss him.

"I wonder what they'll do now," Isaac ponders. "Chuck and the lucky lady."

"He's got enough properties to keep him going. That is, until he has to sell them to pay legal fees when I sue his ass to hell and back."

Isaac laughs out loud and punches the air. "Awesome!"

He stares into space, thinking. Then he asks, "Do you think she's here? On the Key? Right now?"

"It's entirely possible. She's been here plenty of times before. That's how she got in, by the way. She had Chuck's ID so you guys would have been none the wiser."

Isaac's eyes narrow. Those beautiful pools of darkness I'm going to miss seeing every night and every morning.

"What do you think they were planning to do? If the money had transferred like they'd expected? How would they have got off the island?"

I hadn't even thought about that. But it takes less than a second to hit me.

"My boat. The Esmeralda. That's why he brought it here."

We stare at each other for a split second, then we both fly for the door.

The room has been almost entirely evacuated when we shoot through it to the corridor. I don't let my high heels stop me as I sprint after Isaac down the stairs to the concert hall. We run down more corridors, leaving onlookers to stare as we flash past them.

"I know a shortcut," Isaac shouts back to me, and we burst out onto a back road, one I haven't seen before. "This way." I run after Isaac along the sandy pathways.

My heels start to sink into the sand. "Isaac, wait!" I stop to pull the boots off my feet then fling them to the path and start running again. Isaac's hand reaches backwards and I take it, letting me him pull me along the hidden path to the marina. With my performance exertions and Isaac's unrelenting sessions in the gym, we are both fit and fast, and we fly along it until the boats come into view.

"It's there!" I gasp, seeing the Esmeralda lit up in all her beautiful glory.

Isaac's hand pushes me slightly behind him and he whips out a gun. I'm thankful my show-honed body can withstand most things, as I really don't need my jelly-like legs to collapse. I have never seen Isaac like this and thank God I hadn't. I would never have been so strong as to leave him lying on the villa deck after we'd had sex, to walk away. He wraps an arm around my waist and guides me forward, towards the boat that I bought, with money I earned, that I named after my beloved grandmother. His warmth and scent threaten to send me reeling but I can't let my mind surrender; I need to focus.

There's movement on the boat. Isaac moves us into a shadow and unwraps himself from me. His eyes burrow into mine and there's so much indecipherable emotion behind them it makes me feel lightheaded.

"What do you want?" he whispers, his breath grazing my face.

My eyes drop to his lips and I mentally shake my head. If this is real, this chemistry, this bond we've built… he'll let me return to him. I flick my eyes upwards again.

"I want my boat back."

CHAPTER THIRTY-ONE

saac

I COULD HAVE STOOD like that forever, one arm stretched out behind me, my gun poised to threaten the people who almost ruined her life, the other wrapped around her waist, her eyes locked on mine. But those words, that final request, filled me with resolve. If they hadn't, the sound of Chuck's fumbling feet on the gravel behind us, and his gruff yell to "Start the fucking boat!" would have done the trick.

I whip around to see Aurelia's overweight, unfit ex-manager ambling along the pathway towards the marina. At the sound of Chuck's voice, the blonde woman appears on deck. She's dressed in a floor-length gold number with jewels glittering in her ears. We're about three hundred yards away but the giant diamonds are visible even from this distance.

"At least she dressed for the occasion," I mutter, grabbing Aurelia's hand. We cut across the grass and over a few small dunes, to the main pathway, hot on Chuck's heels.

"Just stay where you are, Chuck," I shout.

"Chuck!" The woman screams, pointing a glittering finger in our direction.

Chuck skids to a halt and braces himself. "Get the hell away from me. You've got everything, Aurelia. You never even use this damn boat."

"It doesn't matter!" Aurelia shouts. "It doesn't belong to you. I paid for it myself, just like I did the clothes on your back, and probably hers," she adds, jerking her chin towards the woman.

I Look back to the boat and the woman is scrambling. "How do I work this thing?" she screeches.

Chuck spins back to face her. "Just switch on the damn engine, Joan!"

"Where is it?" She's clambering across the deck in spiked heels of all things, wobbling frenetically.

"In the helm! Up top! It's right there! Jesus Christ, Joan…"

"If you get on that boat, I'll put a hole in your leg, Chuck."

Chuck spins and bares his teeth at me. "Then you'll go to jail."

Man, he really doesn't know anything. "No, I won't," I half-laugh. "And even if I did, I'd see you in there. You're already going down for theft and fraud. How big of an idiot are you?"

Chuck's lady friend stops, finally inside the helm, searching for the ignition. "Chuck?"

"Don't listen to him," Chuck throws back at her. "He's talking a load of crap."

I raise my eyebrows. "Well, that's a little offensive," I mutter under my breath.

"Turn on the engine, Joan!" he yells again.

"Chuck, the cops are going to be here in a couple minutes. You may as well give up now. Get your woman off the boat. They'll want to speak to her too."

Her head shoots up again. "What?"

I turn to her. "That boat goes anywhere with you on it, they'll want you for theft too."

"Chuck?" Her voice is fragile now.

"Don't listen to him, honey. This is our last chance. The cops won't come after us on a boat. We're gonna start that new life remember?"

I sense he can smell her weakening and he's throwing out whatever he can to persuade her. Just turn the key, Joan, and we can be out of here." He throws his arms up in desperation. "Just do it, for fuck's sake."

She grabs onto the boat's windshield for stability and leans further into the helm.

"Haven't you done enough?" Aurelia yells, to both of them, halting the woman in her tracks. "You've come into our lives under false pretenses, you've duped my mother into thinking you loved her, for crying out loud. You commandeered my entire life for nearly five years. You've let those two precious, beautiful girls believe you're their father." She faces the woman. "And you've put up with this? With him living a double life? All for the promise of money you're not going to get? Do you have any self-worth *at all*?"

The woman freezes, her gaze flicking manically between Chuck and Aurelia.

"She's playing you," Chuck yells. "For the last time, Joan, start the fucking boat. Otherwise…" I can see him mentally grasping for anything he can use to convince her. "Otherwise, the boys will grow up without a father."

It works. The woman disappears into the helm and the otherwise still night is burst apart with the roar of the boat's engine. Her face peers through the windshield as she seeks her next instruction.

"Put it in reverse," Chuck yells, turning to run along the deck towards the boat. I release Aurelia's hand and take off after him.

The woman's head disappears again and the boat begins to move slowly backwards. Chuck reaches it and starts unwinding the rope. "Ok, now forward and turn!"

For someone who's apparently never piloted a boat before, the woman is doing pretty well. Probably more testament to the boat. It really is a beautiful thing. She manages to turn the boat slightly, enough to point it to sea and allow Chuck space to leap up. Only, Chuck is not fit. I almost want to stand back and watch the spectacle about to unfold, but I can't risk it, even if there's only a two percent chance he's actually going to make it up onto the deck. I keep running, pointing my gun at his thigh.

"If you don't stop now, Chuck, I'm going to shoot."

He continues, determined, and I hear Aurelia suck in a breath behind me. Just as he jumps up, the boat pulls away by half a foot and, just as I expected, Chuck slides down its edge into the water.

"Joan! Stop!" He yells, his arms flailing about in the water for something to hold onto.

"Shit," Aurelia says, her voice panicked. "What should we do?"

"Chuck!" The woman appears back on the deck and hobbles, still in heels, to the edge where Chuck is floundering against the side of the boat. Thankfully, the gap between the boat and the deck is widening, so Chuck might escape being crushed. Wait, widening?

I run towards the edge. "Aurelia, throw him a ring!" I shout, pointing to where several are stored at the side of the marina. I try to grab for the rope but the boat has drifted too far.

"Turn off the engine!" I shout up to the woman.

"I… I… how? I mean, no! Get Chuck out of the water!"

The boat is picking up speed and moving further and further away from the marina. *How the hell has she managed that? Has she weighed down the accelerator somehow?*

"Joan, I can't until I've secured the boat. Turn off the engine. Now!"

She stands up straight, seeming to realize she has something of an advantage. Her hands perch on her hips, her eyes narrow and her lips purse. "No."

The boat continues to move away, picking up speed.

I see Aurelia throw a ring down to Chuck then return to my side. "Isaac," she whispers. "She doesn't know how to pilot."

"Joan…" I try once more. "This is your last chance to stop the boat." I raise the gun and aim it at her. It's purely for effect; I don't intend to shoot. The next few seconds happen in slow motion. The softly undulating waves and a harsh view down the barrel of my gun spurs Joan into action, but not the kind of action she'd hoped for. She steps backwards and the heel of her golden shoe snaps in two, throwing her off balance. She thumps down onto the deck and reaches for something to grip onto. But, that's the beautiful thing about the Sunseeker 100—it's surface is as smooth as silk and she slides down it, clean through the railings, dropping fifteen feet into the water. I hear Aurelia run back to the life rings to grab a second, while I watch, helplessly, as the boat sails out to sea.

Less than ten seconds later, I hear another engine roar to life and one of the Starling Key dive boats appears around the mangroves to the west. Heavy footsteps on the deck make me turn.

"We got it," Jax shouts, running past me to the edge of the deck.

The boat pulls up alongside and I see Luca sitting at the helm. He throws me a mock salute as Jax jumps in beside him. Then they roar off towards the now-rapidly accelerating yacht.

"Isaac!" Aurelia shouts and I remember the two ridiculous bodies bobbing in the water. I turn to help her fish out the man who just tried to take everything she's worked so hard for. I want to connect my boot with his face and send him right back into the freezing water, but I know Aurelia will kill me if I do that. I reluctantly reach down and grab his arm. His small, beady eyes look, for once, humble as I yank him up and drop him on the deck like a sack of potatoes.

"She's floating out," Aurelia gasps. I look up; she's right. Joan is being carried further and further away from the deck, away from the life ring Aurelia threw to her. And, adding insult to injury, it doesn't appear she can swim. *What the fuck was she thinking, trying to escape on a damn boat?* I don't have time to figure it out; I dive into the water, tux and all, and swim towards the flailing woman. It takes me a minute to reach her, then I'm engulfed in gold as her dress floats up around us. For a moment I think she's about to stubbornly reject my help, but then she thinks better of it and takes the arm I'm holding out to her. I roll her onto her back, resting her head on my shoulder and slowly swim back to the deck.

I'm relieved to see the cops have finally arrived and Hud is escorting them down the deck. Chuck doesn't even fight as they handcuff him. Hud reaches down, hooks his hand under the woman's arm and effortlessly pulls her out of the water. Aurelia watches, practically dancing on her tiptoes, as

I climb out after her. No sooner am I standing on the deck than Aurelia's arms are around my middle, squeezing the air out of my lungs. I really need that air right now but I don't want to unwrap her just yet. She's leaving in a couple of days and I want to inhale as much of her before then as I can.

"Here, dude." I look up to see Axel strolling towards us, brandishing a fresh, dry pair of combat shorts. "Hud's orders," he shrugs, in explanation.

"Thanks man." I sigh my appreciation and reluctantly step out of Aurelia's embrace. It'll be a much better experience for her if I'm at least dry.

The cops lead Chuck and Joan back down the deck while I strip out of my sopping wet uniform. "Anything else we can get you?" Hud asks.

"Nah, this is great, thanks guys. I'll catch up with you in the morning, ok? Connor's team meeting?"

"Sure," Hud replies, slapping Axel on the back. "Catch you later." They both walk away leaving me and Aurelia alone on the deck.

I fold up the jacket and shirt, then step out of my pants, feeling Aurelia's eyes lasering into my skin.

I look sideways at her, cheekily. "You enjoying this?"

She grins and shakes her head in despair. "I'll give you some privacy."

She does turn away and I'm thankful as I roll down my tight, wet boxers. I'm getting hard, despite having just dunked myself in ice cold water. The look she just gave me set everything on fire.

I pull on the combats, commando. "Ok, all done."

She turns around and her eyes go immediately to my bare torso. I watch her swallow, and try my best to curb the erection I know is desperate to make an appearance.

"Come on." I jerk my head east, towards the boardwalk. "It's been quite a night, and we have a birthday to celebrate."

She catches up and takes hold of my hand. I feel warm everywhere. We walk together, as though we're a couple, along the beach. I don't know if it's just me but I feel like our strides are getting shorter, the pace slower, as if neither of us want to stop walking. I open the gate, still holding her hand, and we walk through together. I still don't let go as I take the key card and swipe open the door. I still don't let go as I lead her across to the couch and pull her down next to me.

"I've been thinking." Her voice is quiet and she looks past me as if too nervous to address me directly.

"That's dangerous."

She grins. "I'm going to need to build my own team now, from scratch. And that includes my security."

I listen, even though I know what's coming next.

"Would you want to work for me full-time?" Her eyes flick to mine hopefully.

I stare into them, marveling at how clear and courageous they are.

I shake my head. "No."

Her lips pull up at the corners a little. She knew I would say that.

I don't think. I just lean towards her and press my lips to hers. She opens them for me and lets me slide my tongue into her mouth. A small moan vibrates against my lips and she licks my tongue as it roams gently. My hand slides up to the back of her head and I hold her as I lower us both down on the couch. I'm going to take this, whatever she's prepared to give me. Our limbs wrap around each other, her hips glued to mine, as we lose ourselves in the kiss. I open my eyes because I need to see her. Hers are open too, just an inch from mine, and we watch each other as we delve deeper. I curl a leg around her, anchoring her to me, and just when I feel we can't get any closer without me being inside, she pulls back.

"Are you sure you won't be my security?"

I nod and go back to her lips, sucking them between my teeth and licking my tongue across hers.

She pulls away again. "You're really, really sure?"

"Mm-hmm," I murmur, dipping into her again.

"Is this real?" It's a whisper against my mouth.

I move my lips across her cheek and nibble at her jaw. "Yes, Aurelia. This is real."

"Is it going to last?"

I stop nibbling and plant small kisses on her throat beneath her ear, then pull back to face her.

I shake my head slowly. "No. You have a new life to start, and I belong here."

She nods, her eyes taking on a watery shine. "Did you ever want me?"

I frown and pull away. "Don't ever ask me such a fucking stupid question again."

Her voice drops. "Do you still?"

I lower my lips to hers and whisper against them. "What did I just say?" I want her more than anything but she deserves better than me. I'm messed up about women, and even if I wasn't, she has a new life to build and I would only get in the way.

"So come with me," she whispers back.

I breathe against her, wishing I didn't have to say it. "I can't."

Her body folds further into me, warm and malleable. "I'm never going to meet anyone else like you," she says, nuzzling into my neck. Her breath is growing deeper and I know she's close to sleep. She must be exhausted.

"I hope, for your sake, you don't." My lips graze across her temple.

Sleep starts to take her, but not before one last thought leaves her mouth, whether she's conscious of it or not. "We're not over, Isaac."

I kiss the lids of her eyes and feel the breath of her sleep hot on my face. "You're right, baby girl. I don't think we ever will be."

CHAPTER THIRTY-TWO

Aurelia

I WAKE up reluctantly from the most amazing dream, and realize with a start, I'm not in my bed. I don't move. Instead, I allow the nerves littering my skin to detect what's pinning me down. Isaac. I slowly turn my head to the side and his sharp jaw and deep lashes come into view. He must be still sleeping. His face is peaceful, his breath soft. Mine catches in my throat. How much of my dream was real?

I lay still, watching him, taking in as much as I can before we wakes up and breaks this spell I'm under.

His lips move, making me jump. "Why you staring at me?"

My smile widens. "I've never seen you asleep before."

His eyes open and he blinks, squinting at the closeness. "Yes, you have. The time you left the villa and almost gave me a heart attack."

"Well, now that you know why I did it, do you forgive me?"

He sighs and raises a hand to rub his face. "Nope."

"You're infuriating," I bite out with a grin.

"That's my line." He pulls his arm out from under me and stretches both of them above his head, yawning. I miss the feel of him already.

I shuffle up to sitting and turn to face him. His hands are behind his head, his elbows dropping to side, and he's watching me, almost amused.

"Thanks for last night."

"Which part? You were barely speaking to me for half of it."

"That's not true."

"It's ok. I guess you had a lot on your mind up until the announcement at least. Speaking of which. We should check the papers this morning. I've no doubt the media on the monitor will have filed their stories hours ago."

"I wasn't *not* speaking to you. I was keeping my distance." I look away. "I didn't want to get in the way with… you know… Paris."

"You didn't. And, as it turned out, there was nothing to get in the way of. It wasn't happening, and it was all me. I've changed, I guess."

I don't know what to say to that. He might have changed and he might no longer be with Paris, but he also isn't willing to come with me, as my security or as a boyfriend. I never said the 'b' word but the implication was there, and it was clear.

"Well, thanks anyway. I couldn't have done it without you."

He sits up and rubs his eyes. "Yes, you could, and you did." He faces me with a serious expression. "Sure, I got you passwords and stuff, but you figured it all out yourself, you came up with a plan yourself, and unless I'm blind, I didn't see anyone but you standing up on that podium making that announcement. And that took guts. I mean, your mom…"

"Mom!" I suddenly feel a driving urge to see her. I'd almost forgotten this would have had a devastating impact on her. The girls won't remember Chuck ever being a part of their lives—they're too young—but Mom really loved Chuck, despite what he said. She's going to be heartbroken. "I need to see her. Is she still on the isalnd?"

"I imagine so. The girls stayed in one of the villas; I doubt your mom would've gone back to Miami without them. Wait here. I'll call Connor."

I stay on the couch, wringing my hands while I wait for Isaac to return. "She's here, in the villa nine. Two of your dancers stayed with her."

A hand flies up to my chest in relief. "Thank God she wasn't alone."

"I get the impression she was out of it for most of the night. Shall we go there now?"

I nod. "Let me change quickly."

It's Sasha who opens the door. She throws her arms around me before letting me inside. "I'm so proud of you, girl."

"Thanks honey."

She pulls back and holds me at arm's length. "It took guts to do that."

"Thanks. How is she?"

"She's getting better. It was a real shock to her, the whole second family thing. She's proud of you though, I can tell you that much. Come on in."

I follow Sasha inside and Isaac comes too but hangs back by the door, probably mindful of my mother's frostiness towards him that day on the beach. Mom is curled up on the sofa with a blanket wrapped around her and Tanja, another of my dancers by her side. They both turn their heads as I approach.

"I'll leave you guys alone," Tanja says, standing off the sofa. "Happy birthday, Aurelia," she adds, almost apologetically.

I smile my thanks and settle next to my mom. To my surprise, she opens her arms and pulls me towards her. To be honest, I'd been expecting to have to coax her towards me. She wraps her arms around me for the first time in as long as I can remember. It feels nice, but I know better than to get too used to it. Mom's alone again, but it won't be long until a replacement is found for Chuck, I'm sure of it.

"I'm sorry, Aurelia," she says, firmly, and to my great surprise.

"You have nothing to be sorry for, Mom."

"Yes I do. For everything. For bringing that man into our lives, and for allowing him to get away with so much deception for so long. If I had known about the houses and all the other things he'd been buying with your money, I would never have stayed with him. I certainly would have insisted he give back our name. That man is worse than the devil for taking everything from you like that. You work so hard…" She chokes out a sob and I hold her closer.

"It's ok, Mom."

She hiccups more sobs against my shoulder and I feel so sorry for her. She really did love Chuck. But then, the babies…

"Mom?"

She sniffs. "Yes?"

"The girls. How…?"

Slowly, she pulls away and puts both hands over her eyes. "They're not his. Chuck is not their father."

"I know, Mom. He told me it wasn't possible they could be his."

Her head jerks up sharply. "What? What did he mean by that?"

"He had a vasectomy. That's what he told me."

Her voice shrinks to barely a whisper. "He did?"

I nod.

"I just thought he was infertile. I asked him if we could see a doctor about it but he refused, and I just figured he was embarrassed about it. I never told him about the IVF because I wanted him to think… Oh God!" She drops her face into her hands again, emitting huge shoulder-racking sobs. "I'm such a fool."

I rub her back, unsure of what else to do. They had both deceived each other. But Chuck did it with malice, whereas Mom did it to protect his feelings, even though that didn't make it right.

"He knew they weren't his babies all along." She shakes her head and stares wide-eyed at the floor. "No wonder he wasn't interested in them. My poor girls…"

"They'll be fine, Mom," I say, trying as best I can to comfort her. "They're so young. They won't remember any of this."

"But, Aurelia… the media reports…"

"Well, yes, they'll be able to look back at articles in years to come, but we don't need to keep the truth from them while they're growing up. What you did wasn't terrible. Misguided, yes, but not a crime, and not with the intent of hurting anyone."

"It's going to come out in the papers what I did," she whispers, her voice trembling.

I nod. I'm guessing the print presses are running reports about the mysterious origins of not just the twins, but me too. But if anyone cares less about me because my conception wasn't typical, I don't them as a fan. My mom's ego is fragile though, and this will probably hit her hard.

"Maybe you should see a therapist when we get back to L.A., Mom. Meet up with some of your close friends, talk to a professional, lay low for a little while—no beach club lunches or shopping trips where the paparazzi can follow you. Stay home and enjoy the girls."

She sniffs and wipes her sleeve across her face.

"My life had become a circus, Aurelia," she says, quietly. "Nothing compared to yours, of course, but I put pressure on myself to look and to be a certain way."

"Well, think of this as an opportunity to re-set. You don't have to prove yourself to anyone, Mom. You could even back east, you don't need to stay in L.A."

She nods. "It's something to think about."

I wrap my arms around her and she collapses into me, as though she's the child who needs mothering. "You're going to be fine, Mom. We're all going to get through this, I promise."

A FEW HOURS LATER, I'm waving my mother and two sisters off again as they leave for Miami, for the last time. I've kept on some of Chuck's staff to help with the transition and they've already made a start packing the family's belongings. Mom and the girls will head back to L.A. and I will join them in a week or two—however long it takes to rebuild a team.

I've given Isaac a few well-deserved days off, so Luca is

going to take up residence in the villa. It's not really necessary anymore. There was no stalker in the first place and the blonde woman is in cuffs at the county jail, but Isaac insisted. He's adamant that while ever I am on the island and under his watch, nothing is going to come within a mile of me. But, he and I both know that the minute I leave this resort, I will no longer be his to worry about.

I don't know where he's going after his team meeting, but he's packed a bag and loaded it into one of the trucks already. I doubt I'll see him until he gets back. I've turned the kitchen counter into Aurelia Bird, Inc. HQ, with papers everywhere and my grandmother's lawyer on a permanent open screen. I finally sign off for the evening when there's a knock at the door. Luca gets it and when he returns he has a huge smile on his face.

"You up for visitors?"

"Of course! Who?" I jump off the bar stool and see Ana and Billy appear. The three of us squeal and join together, fast and furiously, into one heap of hugs.

"Oh my God! What are you *doing* here?" I pant when we finally pull apart.

"Are you kidding?" Billy gasps. "I saw the headlines at five o'clock this morning. I called up Ana—"

"*Woke* up Ana…" she corrects.

"And we booked flights there and then."

"We're so proud of you, Ray!" Ana gushes, wrapping me up in her arms again and squeezing me fast. "How did you do it all? Who's idea was it? How did you keep it a secret for so long?"

She releases me and I catch my breath again. "I'll tell you everything, I promise." I scoop them both up in another hug. "I can't believe you're here! This is so awesome!"

"Shall I get some food sent over?" Luca asks. "You guys

might as well make yourselves at home. I'm assuming you'll be staying here? In this villa?"

They both look at me. "Of course they will. That's ok, right?"

Their nods and squeals answer my question and we jump up and down, clapping our hands, like kids at Disneyworld.

"Sure thing." Luca coolly walks away to make the call and I usher my friends out to the deck.

As soon as we sit down, the questions come again, thick and fast.

"Where's Isaac?" *Ana.*

"Did he help you?" *Billy.*

"I knew he was going to be good for you." *Ana.*

"Are you guys, like, together?" *Billy.*

"Did he really save that woman from the sea?" *Ana.*

"Ok, ok, stop!" *That's me.* "Slow down a minute. I'll answer them one by one."

They both look back at me.

"Isaac has gone away for a few days. Yes, he helped me get information, but I did all the rest. Yes, he really did save the woman. I watched him do it—it was effortless and it took my breath away. But, no, we're not together. I would like us to be, but it's not going to happen. He doesn't want to leave this place and come with me."

"Hey," a voice comes from inside the villa. I turn to see Tawny making her way towards us. "I'm not intruding am I? I just wanted to see how you were doing."

"No, of course you're not intruding. Have you met Billy and Ana?"

"Briefly." She gives them a small wave and sits down on the floor of the deck. "How are you doing?"

I don't get a chance to reply because Ana is in there faster than a speeding bullet.

"She's doing amazingly, apart from the fact she's in love with her bodyguard and he's too dumb to realize she's probably the best thing that's ever going to happen to him."

Tawny's mouth falls open. "What?"

I feel my cheeks flood with heat and know there's no point trying to cover them up. "Yeah. It's not how I would have put it, but…"

"That's huge!" Tawny says, breathily. "And amazing! I mean, you two are perfect together. I never would have thought it—he's always been so against younger women, but you've changed him Aurelia. He's become a different person since you arrived."

I drop my head to keep my sadness just below the surface. "Not really. He's very much the same underneath. There was a reason he always went for the older, married type. He may not go for them anymore, but the reason is still there."

I don't say any more than that because it's not my reason to divulge. The fact is, Isaac is incapable of being vulnerable. He would sooner sell himself short with women who don't need him, than take a chance on being truly loved by someone who is human, who might have the capacity to leave, but may never want to.

Thankfully, they let me answer the rest of their questions without bringing Isaac up again, and we eat the amazing, delicious food that Arnaud sends over. I feel as though my life is starting all over again, whether Isaac wants to be a part of it, or not. And despite his refusal to come with me, I'm happy. I'm slowly but surely getting little parts of my mom back. My friends are by my side again, and for the first time in my life, I'm in charge of my own future.

CHAPTER THIRTY-THREE

Isaac

I TAKE the familiar turn down West Sycamore Avenue, and slow down as I get to number three four nine, the place I grew up.

I know she lives here. It was my grandmother's house and she left everything to my mom. The curtains are drawn, the very same ones my grandmother had fitted twenty years ago. The grass has been cut on the lawn at least, but gone are the flowers that my grandmother had tended so lovingly to. I park, step out of the truck and spend a minute stretching. That was one hell of a drive and I don't want to be away from Starling Key longer than I have to be. But I have questions that need answering if I'm going to be able to move forward with my life, with a normal relationship, and only one person can help me.

I lock the truck and walk up the short drive to the front door. I look over the age-old Ford parked up. It's covered in rust and probably barely working but the interior is spotless. I knock at the door and wait, but no one answers. I try the handle but, unsurprisingly, it's locked. I walk around the side of the house where I remember there was a loose brick where Grandma used to keep a key. Although, that was a long time ago and I used to give her hell about it. I find the brick and pull it out, almost falling over when I see a key lying there. I pick it out and walk back around the front. I half expect the key to not work—it might well have been there since Grandma died. But it unlocks the door easily.

I step inside and immediately smell cleaning fluid. It's so strong it feels as though my nostrils are burning. I step through the porch and look right into what used to be a laundry room, and there I see the culprits. Lots of them. What looks to be hundreds of bottles of bleach, floor cleaner, woodwork polish, floor wax, and a lifetime's supply of cloths, sponges and rags. I head on past into the living room. It's too dark to see much, so I go to pull back the curtains when I hear a groan behind me. I quickly draw back the curtains, then turn to see a lone couch at the back of the room, and on it, my mother, covered in a blanket I recognize well.

"Isaac?" Her voice is croaky with sleep.

I check my wristwatch. "Mom, it's two o'clock in the afternoon.

"I know, honey. Thanks for waking me. I can happily survive on only two hours sleep." I smile inwardly. That's clearly where I get my sarcasm from.

"Why two hours?" She better not still be partying. She's nearly in her sixties for heaven's sake.

"I've been at work."

I try and fail to hide the surprise in my tone. "Work? Doing what?"

She drops her feet to the floor and looks up at me,

wearily. "I'm a cleaner, Isaac. I clean offices, peoples' houses, whatever I can." She sighs and rubs at her face.

"What about the money? Where did it go?"

She stops rubbing her face and closes her eyes as if hoping when she opens them, I might have gone. I persist. "I know you got the money, Mom. What did you do with it?" I look around the sparsely decorated house. Pretty much all of Grandma's beloved furniture has gone and all I can see is a small dining table, one wooden chair and the sofa on which my mother is sitting. "Why are you living like a pauper when you've just been given fifty grand?"

She sighs heavily and drags open her eyes. "That money was never mine," she says, slowly, as though she knows I can't feel any more exasperated with her.

"What do you mean?" I shove my hands into my pockets so she can't see me clenching them.

"It was a debt I owed to someone from way back."

"A debt? To who?"

"No one important," she sighs again. "Anymore."

"What do you mean by that? Tell me the truth, Mom."

She stands and walks into the kitchen where she flicks on a small kettle on the same counter I remember from my childhood days. There's barely anything else here though, no pots and pans that I can see. Nothing on the drainer.

"I'm an addict, Isaac," she says, without looking at me, even when I suck in a sharp breath.

I force myself to swallow. "To what?"

"It started six years ago. I was addicted to painkillers. I'm clean now."

"Why were you taking painkillers?"

"To manage the pain I had when I broke my leg."

I shake my head in surprise. "When did you break your leg?"

"Six years ago," she says, finally looking at me. The only word missing from her tone is 'duh'. "I was drinking pretty heavily. I fell down the stairs. The break didn't heal for a long time so I had all kinds of pain from over-compensating and simply trying to get around."

"Why didn't you call me?"

She opens a cupboard and takes out one cup. It's the only cup in there. Then she spoons some coffee grounds into it before turning to face me again. "The same reason I've *never* called you."

"Which is what?"

"I didn't want to bother you. Not after everything…"

We stand in silence as the kettle boils and then she pours hot water into the mug, adds some creamer and hands the cup to me.

"No, you have it," I say, pushing it back to her.

"You need it more than I do," she says, arching an eyebrow and casting a critical eye over my appearance.

"Well, I have been driving all night," I say, taking the mug. "But then, you've been working all night… Is that what you do all the time?"

She jerks her head towards the back door. "Let's sit outside."

I follow her out and the second I step foot in the back yard, I gasp. The front of the house looks as though no one has loved this place for a very long time, but the back tells an entirely different story. There are flowers everywhere—flowers planted by Grandma and new ones in pots and borders, all different colors of the rainbow. There's a small fountain in the far corner and small fruit trees dotted along the back.

"It's stunning out here. Did you do all this?"

"Don't sound so surprised," she says. "I had to inherit at least one decent gene from your grandmother."

She leads me to a wooden bench and we both sit, a little awkwardly.

"So?" I press. "This cleaning job…"

"I've been cleaning for years," she explains, resting her hands on her knees. I'm shocked at how small and leathery they've become. She notices me noticing them and shoves them between her legs. "I do whatever job I can get. At the moment, the council offices and Gunners, the new heating company in town, are my biggest jobs, but they're both overnight. They pay ok though, so I can't complain."

"And the fifty grand?"

"It paid off my last debt to the guy who used to get me my painkillers."

I can feel my blood start to boil. "Who is he?"

Her head spins to look at me and for the first time she looks authoritative, possibly out of fear. "Isaac, it's none of your business. It was mine, I've dealt with it, it's gone away. He got me those drugs because I begged him to. He gave me a lifeline when I didn't have any means to pay for them. He didn't mark up the debt too much—he didn't play me like some of the dirtbags out there. But, he got ill and didn't have health insurance."

I roll my eyes to the ground. "I guess it's hard to come by in that line of work."

"Exactly," Mom smiles. "I owed him, Isaac. He needed all kinds of treatment and he was out of pocket because of me. I had to get him the money. I'm so sorry I came to you but I had nowhere else to go. Cleaning all night and sleeping all day doesn't leave much time to make friends."

"And that's it? You don't owe him anything anymore?"

"No, nothing. That's it." She looks back at the little slice of happiness she's grown for herself out here. "Anyway, I thought you gave me that money on the proviso I was not to contact you again. I figured it was because you didn't want anything more to do with me. So, why are you here?"

"I need to ask you some things."

She shakes her head and growls under her breath. "Ugh, Isaac. I should have known this time would come. I was half-hoping I'd be dead before you got around to wanting this conversation."

"That's morbid."

"Yeah, well, a lifetime of being a shit daughter, a shit wife and a shit mother will do that to you."

I sigh and focus my gaze on the water fountain. It's soothing and I feel weirdly at home again even though Mom's clearly sold everything that used to belong here.

She gets to her feet, unsteadily, then heads for the back door. "There's something I never showed you. You deserve to see it."

She returns holding a folded piece of paper. It looks very well-thumbed, fraying at the folds and slightly yellowing. I don't recognize the handwriting but my name sits at the top of it. As I read, my hands start to shake. I look up at my mother. "Is this…?"

She nods, her eyes filled with tears. My dad's suicide note. Addressed to me.

I take a deep breath. It's short, it's clear, it's heartbreaking.

Isaac.

Buddy, your mother and I have been having a lot of problems. You won't remember this, but we argue a lot. I don't do enough for her. I don't support her enough. I'm selfish. I don't earn enough money. I like the bottle too much, buddy. I get a job but I can't hold it down. Your mom yells at me 'til she's blue in the face. She's working too but, kid, I keep drinking the money. I can't help it.

If I stick around, this isn't going to end well, for any of us, and you deserve to live a life without constant arguing in the background and without a drunk for a father. I hope, by the time you're old enough to read this, your mother has moved on and found someone who really deserves her, because it ain't me. The only good thing I've done in my life is give her you. She adores you, kid, and seeing you two together makes my heart swell. But when I enter the room, everything changes. You cower, she braces herself for a verbal battering. I don't like my reflection in your faces. I'm too big of a coward to just walk away and hope you'll find me when you're all grown up. I don't think I could face you. So I'm not going to give myself the chance, buddy, I'm sorry.

You're going to do great things Isaac D'Amico. I'll be watching from up high. Make sure you put on a good show. Live the life I drank away.

And always remember, I never left you, kid. I just left me.

I CAN'T SPEAK. I sense my mother sitting next to me, putting an arm around my shoulders, pulling my face into her shoulder. I'm giant compared to her but she still manages to command me as though I'm a kid. I guess because I feel like a kid right now. I feel like the four-year-old who woke up one morning to find himself in his grandmother's house, wondering for the first time of many why he's never going to see his dad again.

"Why didn't you give me this before?" I ask, wiping my face with the back of my hand.

She lets me go and hugs herself tightly. "I was selfish, Isaac, I'm sorry. I kept it for myself. I had always meant to give it to you, but the more time that passed, the harder it was to show you—you'd have known I'd had it all along."

"Did he leave one for you too?"

She nods and tears roll down her face. "I burned it."

"What?"

"I was so angry, Isaac." Her voice is a whisper, a narrow, seething whisper. "He just left us both, just like that. I was twenty-five years-old and he'd left me alone with a four-year-old son. I had to find more work. I had to leave you with your grandmother while I went out to work all day and most nights. I saw you and my mother forming such a close bond and I hated it. I hated that you were growing closer to her than to me. So, I started staying out late, hanging out with guys in town I shouldn't have. I got into drinking and taking some small-time drugs. But before I knew it, days, sometimes weeks, would pass and I hadn't seen you."

She sniffs and wipes her sleeve across her face, still staring out at the garden. "It killed me that you could carry on without me, so I just did it more and more, like I was trying to prove to myself I wasn't worth anything to anyone. Then one day I showed up to this house. I was a little worse for wear—actually, I was a lot worse for wear. I'd been drinking all day, my clothes had gotten ripped from the motorcycle I'd been tearing around on with the latest guy. We'd had a fight so my makeup was all over my face. Mom told me to leave. She didn't want you to see me like that. I said that if I left I would never come back. I know now it put my mother in an impossible position. She was trying to protect you, and in a way, by not letting you see me, she was trying to protect me too. But, I didn't see it that way. I walked out and never came back. But it killed me, Isaac. Every day I was away from you, knowing you were getting bigger, making friends, doing so well in school, it killed me that I wasn't a part of it. It killed me that I was hurting you by not being there. But I couldn't come back. I promised my mother."

We sit in silence for several minutes. It's an insane amount of information to digest. "So, you didn't leave me because you didn't want to be saddled with a kid when you wanted to party instead?"

She almost chokes on tears. "No! God, Isaac. I partied because I felt like I was no longer needed. I was young and stupid. I should have known that you having such a strong bond with your grandmother could only be a good thing for all of us. But I didn't see it that way. I was jealous and I rebelled. I was hurting so badly and I didn't know how else to make the pain stop. Every time I thought about you, I felt as though my insides were falling out. It was easier to numb myself with drink and drugs. It was only when I stopped all of that I realized what I'd done, but it was too late. And then she passed."

"Grandma?"

Mom nods. "We hadn't spoken since that day I walked out. It had been twenty years. I can't tell you how much I regret leaving, or how much I regret cutting all ties with you both. My life is just one giant regret. If it weren't for the fact I gave birth to you, the world would have been better off had I never been born."

It's my turn to put my arm around her. I pull her close and let her cry it all out on my smelly two-day-old shirt. Despite the pain of reading that letter and hearing about what my mom and my grandmother lived through, I feel a million times lighter. I feel as though, for the first time in my life, I have answers. My grandmother couldn't tell me any of this. It wasn't her story to tell. She never talked badly about my mom and that meant never telling me the truth, so it was always in the back of my head that I deserved it somehow. I took whatever basic facts my grandmother had given me and read generously—or not so generously—through the lines, adding my own pitiful narrative. It was my fault my mother had left me. That if she couldn't stick around for her only son, then I was, basically, unlovable.

We sat like that, without speaking, until the sun went down. I resolved, without saying anything, that I would rebuild this bridge. I wanted my mother back in my life. I wanted to get back the years we'd lost. There was no chance I would ever get my father back, or my grandmother. But my mother was still alive and atoning for mistakes she'd made years ago. She didn't deserve to be disowned, and I wanted to know her. I wanted a mother.

I WAKE up the following morning and my back is positively screaming at me. The floor of my grandmother's house is not the most comfortable place to sleep. I clamber to my feet, still dressed in everything I wore to get here. Mom and I were so cried out by the end of the day I couldn't bring myself to get my bag out of the truck so I just curled up on the floor of my old bedroom and fell asleep. As far as I know, my Mom is on the couch.

I tiptoe past her and hop into the truck. I return with a bag of groceries and busy myself making bacon, pancakes and a decent cup of coffee while she wakes up.

"What's all this?" she asks when she walks into kitchen that probably hasn't seen any action in years.

"Food!" I say brightly. "And I took the liberty of buying you some new plates and a few more mugs, since you appear to have virtually nothing."

"Thanks," she says, although I detect a grumble.

I dish out pancakes, top them with bacon and pour a liberal amount of maple syrup over them, then nod to the back yard. "Let's eat."

We sit and inhale the food as though we've been deprived for weeks. My mother might well have been.

"Are you working tonight? Do you need to sleep today?"

"I've already called in. I'd prefer to spend the day with you, if that's ok?"

I smile to myself before shoveling the last piece of bacon into my mouth. "I was hoping you would."

I DRIVE BACK to Florida feeling like a completely different person. Aside from the relationship I'm going to rebuild with my mother, I know what I need to do when I get back to Starling Key. I know what I want to do, and it's the total opposite of what everyone expects me to do. But fuck it. I never wanted a normal life. I want excitement, adrenaline, pace, change and Christ, I want passion—lots of it. Raw, authentic, unfiltered, unfilled and uninhibited passion. And I know exactly where to get it.

I can only hope it isn't too late.

CHAPTER THIRTY-FOUR

Aurelia

I TRY NOT to feel disheartened as the fourth supposedly highly-qualified talent manager leaves the room. Actually, that's a little unfair. They have all been highly qualified and, in many cases, heartily recommended by other people in the business I respect. But, there's something I can't put my finger on with each of them. I think back to the relationship I had with my former manager and the hold he had over me—one I eventually rebelled against. One thing I'm now clear on is this is *my* career, and whoever takes me on needs to respect that.

I'm no longer going to work back-to-back and tirelessly for every single potential dollar. I'm going to have a life, otherwise, how can I come up with new, original material, or give my fans the best possible version of me? I want to be managed by someone who respects that but who also isn't afraid to speak their mind and object if they think I'm wrong.

I want someone who sees me as the grown-up billionaire pop star I am, but isn't afraid to challenge me too. All the managers I've spoken to have been either slightly too arrogant about their experience, or far too eager to please.

I look down at the schedule my personnel advisor prepared. There's been an addition. I click on the app and read down the list. Apparently I haven't finished up for the day; there's one more candidate to see. I don't have time to click through for more details when a knock comes at the door.

"Come in," I call. I try to muster some energy, but the problem is I'm tired of talking about myself, but that's kind of what the job is about.

I sift through the resumes on the desk. This one really is last-minute because there are none left I haven't already been through with a candidate.

I plaster a fake smile to my face and look up to greet the fifth and final candidate of the day, and freeze, not knowing whether I should laugh out loud. "Isaac?"

"Miss Bird," he replies, formally, letting the door swing closed behind him.

"Can I help you?" I'm smiling and my heart is thumping like it's on steroids, but my frown must give away a huge amount of confusion.

"I'm here for the interview," he says, calmly. "Talent Manager."

"What?" I look around, which is silly really because the room is small and there's no one else in it.

"I'd like to interview for the job," he says. His eyes bore into me, willing me to take him seriously.

"Ok," I say, shaking my head lightly. *This is going to be interesting.* "Please, take a seat."

He pulls out the chair opposite and sits down, pushing a

sheet of paper towards me. It's every hiring manager's dream. Clear, to the point, no longer than two sides. I look over it but barely take anything in.

"So, Mr. D'Amico. Where to begin?" I roll my eyes upwards, genuinely *not* sure where to begin. "Have you had much experience of managing musicians before?"

"Yes," he replies. "I managed a band called the Blue Hides when I was in school. They went on to perform at the local student bar several times and I ensured, with ticket sales and various, um, forms of merchandise, they had turned a profit by the end of each night."

I take a deep breath and bite down on the inside of my cheek to stop myself from laughing. "Ok, um, great. Ok, so further to that, have you had experience managing people or teams in other professional areas?"

"Yes, ma'am, I have."

"Can you give me details? Any examples of scenarios where, perhaps, you've had a disagreement with someone you've managed, and you've been able to work through your differences to reach a satisfactory conclusion?"

"I do have examples, ma'am, but I can't tell you."

I'm not sure I heard correctly. "You can't tell me?"

"They're classified."

I bite my cheek again. "I'm sorry," I say. "This is an interview for my new manager, not a scene from *Top Gun*."

"I understand that, ma'am."

"Also, we have already established I don't like to be referred to as ma'am. We're not getting off to a great start, are we?"

"I apologize, ma—, sorry, Miss Bird. I am genuinely interested in the position and I'll tell you everything you need to know. That isn't classified, of course."

I roll my eyes and fail completely to hide a smile. "Are you really here for the job?"

Isaac leans forward, so far that I can smell him—that distinctive smell I love, and have missed, even though it's only been a few days. "I am. I'm being serious. I don't want you to feel obliged to hire me, but I think I could do a good job as your manager. You know I respect and admire you. You also know I won't hesitate to challenge you if I question some of your ideas." He says the words as though he knows my exact brief. "I might not have had experience managing musicians specifically—Blue Hide aside," he smiles, sheepishly, "but I don't think I need it. All I need is the desire to help you be the best you can possibly be."

He sits back in his chair, the confidence I've come to love about him sneaking back to the fore. "And I think I have more of that than anyone else you'll ever speak to."

I'm stunned, and speechless. And my brain is strangely devoid of questions.

"I thought you didn't want to leave Starling Key."

"I thought that too. I just didn't want to leave to do the same job somewhere else. But I can do a different job somewhere else. Something that keeps me interested and challenged. And..." he looks down at his hands which are twisting and turning on the table. "If it means I can carry on this fairytale journey with you, and I can be useful, I'm happy to leave this place."

My lungs suddenly feel a little shallow. He wants to come with me. I want to feel elated but my barriers are still up. I stare at him blankly. "What's made you change your mind?"

He drops his hands into his lap and takes a deep breath. When he looks back at me, there's no arrogance, no swagger, just pure, authentic Isaac.

"You were right, Aurelia. I did have some soul-searching

to do. It turns out I had a lot of questions about my parents, and no answers. Those few days I took off? I went to find answers."

My heart is in my mouth. "And did you get them?"

"Yes. I got answers and a hell of a lot more."

"What do you mean?"

His eyelids lower, showing me an Isaac I've never before seen. Innately confident and assured. "I learned who I am, and who I am not. I learned that no one left me. Not my father, not my mother. They left themselves and each other, not me. You were right; I've been running from this all my life. It's time for me to do what every fucker on this planet has to do."

"And what's that?" I smile.

"Take a chance. Be vulnerable. Let someone in." He throws his hands up and looks almost joyful. "I have to put my heart on the line. You might break it, I know that. But nothing is going to hurt as bad as anything I've already been through. And none of that was my fault."

"That's amazing, Isaac," I say, softly. "I'm happy for you."

He drops his gaze again. "You've probably moved on. I wouldn't blame you. You're young and you can do a lot better than settle for some older guy, bodyguard or no bodyguard." He looks up at me through his dark lashes, cheekily. "But I'm willing to invest time and effort… "He straightens his posture and his face. "One hundred and ten percent effort, no less, in convincing you I am the right and only man for the job."

I want to burst out laughing. He's giving me everything I ever wanted. Himself, on a platter, and a kick ass manager, all rolled up into one sexy-as-fuck package.

"What's your notice period?" I ask, straight-faced.

He tips his head back and gazes down at me, cocky. "One week."

"I'll need impeccable references." I raise one eyebrow.

"I can have those to you by the end of the day."

"This job will be based in Miami, but with around eighty per cent on the road. Does that work for you?"

"I like traveling."

"Some assignments will take you abroad…"

"I can speak most languages."

"…to some pretty cold climates." I graze my eyes over his Italian blooded body.

"I can find plenty of ways to keep warm."

I am now chewing my cheek, the urge to laugh out loud almost getting the better of me.

"Do you have any other questions, Miss Bird?"

"Only one." I cock my head. "I've yet to hear your elevator pitch. That would really be the deciding factor, I think."

"My elevator pitch…" He narrows his eyes and places his hands on the arms of his chair. He slowly presses onto his feet, pushing the chair backwards, then straightens so he's standing over me. Blood is thundering through my veins. I don't think I've ever felt so turned on, and definitely not in an interview. My eyes track him as he saunters around the desk. He reaches a hand out to the back of my chair, bringing his chest perilously close, then he spins me around to face him.

"My elevator pitch," he states, again. "How's this? Of all the managers you've seen, not just today, but in your entire life, your entire career… *I* am gonna manage you… *better*."

My mind immediately darts back to the afternoon we fucked on the deck of the Morrison villa. I fill my chest with air. He sees it and wets his lips, his eyes dropping to mine.

"What else can you do better?" My voice is throaty but I strain out the words.

He places both hands either side of my chair and brings his face closer. "Oh, there are a lot of things I do better. You haven't seen a fraction of them yet."

I feel a surge of heat between my thighs and I'm high on this feeling. This taunting. "Perhaps, um, we should arrange some sort of induction."

He nods, his face serious. "I think that's an excellent idea, so I can be certain as to exactly how you like to be managed."

I swallow, my need overriding my brain. "I can certainly arrange that. And…"

I don't get to finish my sentence as Isaac's hands hook beneath my arms, lifting me onto the desk. Then he sinks to his knees. "Go on."

"And maybe some kind of orientation," I suggest, looking down at him on the floor. "You know, of the premises." He puts his hands on my knees and spreads my legs apart, looking hungrily at the largely transparent underwear I threw on that morning.

"That would be very helpful," he says, nodding his approval. "I can already tell the reception area is quite welcoming."

I can't help the blush that floods my cheeks. He's so damn good at this. "A lot of effort went into the décor," I reply, knowing he's referring to my recent Brazilian wax.

Seconds pass as I watch him breathe me in. No words are spoken for the moment but a whole lot of meaning passes through our connected eyes. We are both raw and open, knowingly vulnerable to being hurt but, more than that, eager to live our lives. In Isaac I see adventure, laughter, wisdom, safety. God knows what he sees in me but there must be something, otherwise he wouldn't be kneeling in front of me declaring his unwavering support for everything I stand for.

"You can tell whoever did the décor," he says, a wink in his eye, "they're hired." And with that, he dives in, making me jump in surprise, before I melt at his decadent touch.

"Oh!" I cry out, the second my body realizes what's going on. He's lapping at my clit, quickly, hungrily. I'm spinning. My climax is right there, waiting, on the surface of a calm ocean. Only it isn't calm anymore. It's raging. I want so much of Isaac, I don't think I'll ever get enough. I pull him deeper and feel him suck my clit between his lips, circling his tongue around the nub, then diving into me, his nose grazing my flesh. I can't take it. I part my legs further and lean back on the desk, presenting myself.

Then he stops.

I raise my head which is heavy with lust and shoot him a questioning look.

"Isn't this a little unethical?" he asks, innocently. He licks his lips slowly. "Eating out the boss, I mean."

I reach forward and put my hand to the back of his head.

"Don't be so presumptuous," I smile. "I haven't hired you yet."

His eyes light up before he dives back down, plundering me with his tongue. All I can do is collapse backwards, revel in his expert touch, and surrender.

CHAPTER THIRTY-FIVE

Isaac

WE PICK our way around the edge of the northeast wall, Aurelia's hand gripping mine as I lead the way. It's completely dark—even the stars don't cast a great deal of light this evening. And, surprisingly, there is total quiet as we make our way to the staff beach. It's Aurelia's last night on Starling Key and this is the only place I haven't yet taken her to.

We round the corner and while I'm pretty sure Aurelia is totally oblivious, I can see the shadows of around eighty bodies crouching behind beer kegs, chairs, palm trees and sand dunes.

"SURPRISE!"

Lights switch on all around us, and every single person jumps to their feet, cheering and shouting Happy Birthday to Aurelia, who I'm pretty sure has just died of shock behind me. Even I, who knew this was going to happen, feel a little shell-shocked. Seconds later, loud hip hop kicks in, bottles are opened, drinks are poured, and people crowd us to give their best birthday wishes to my girlfriend, and unbeknown to anyone else just yet, my new boss. I stay by her side as she returns hugs and good wishes and good-naturedly poses for selfies with the team. Then, almost as quickly as they descended upon her, they filter away, shaking their asses to the music and smashing beer bottles together. It's the end of the season and this is our traditional staff beach party. A few of the team had the idea of using it to honor and thank Aurelia. That was before her dramatic announcement. Following it, they were insistent. They wanted to celebrate her, show her respect for making such a bold move. They wanted her to know family didn't have to be like that; it could be like this.

I look around at everyone as they finally kick back after a long, hot, busy season, and feel my heart swell. These guys were here when I needed a family. When I divorced myself from my CIA brothers and sisters and came looking for others to embrace me. I might have been thirty years old but I hadn't had family since my grandmother died. Starling Key gave that to me, and more. Right on cue, Connor comes up behind us and slaps me on the back before wrapping me in a bear hug.

"How'd it go?"

"Great," I reply. "Better than great, actually. I got to bury a few demons."

"That's fantastic man, I'm happy for you."

"It also made me think about the future," I add. I feel strangely emotional, knowing now is the time. I'm handing in my notice.

"I'll come find you," I say to Aurelia who nods, knowingly, and heads in the direction of Tawny and Seleste, not before gripping my hand tightly, which gives me more courage than she'll ever know. "Connor, I need to talk to you."

"Uh oh, not you too," he frowns. "Bit early for a proposal, isn't it?"

"What?"

"Well, the last time one of us said that, we were looking for proposal advice."

"Oh, yeah, right. No. It's not that." I steer him to a dune away from the crowd and sit him down. Before I can open my mouth, Carter and Luca are beside us too. Hell, they're going to find out anyway. "Guys," I start. "Connor, I'm leaving Starling Key." I grit my teeth and wait for the verbal clobbering, but it doesn't come.

"We guessed," Connor says, after an unnerving stretch of silence.

"You did?"

"Yeah," Luca adds. "You came back from your mom's, went straight to Aurelia and didn't resurface until, well, this morning. We knew something was cooking."

"You were spotted waiting outside the interview room for Talent Managers," Carter says, blinking his long eyelashes, innocently.

"So you guys have had your suspicions about this for three whole days and you haven't said anything?"

"You were clearly enjoying your moment," Connor says, kindly. "You know, that time between when you make a life-changing decision and the time when the whole damn world knows. I would say that figuratively, but in your case, the whole damn world will actually know, sooner or later."

"Yeah," I nod.

"Are you ready for the kind of attention and scrutiny

you're going to get being in Aurelia's life in the public eye?" Carter cocks his head.

I let out a long breath. "I don't care what people are going to say about me, and if they have an issue with the age gap, they can go freaking jump. But I care what is said about Aurelia. She's thick-skinned though, and she has some great ideas about creative direction and trying new things. She's prepared to lose fans along the way if she has to."

"So, you're really leaving?" Luca asks, quietly.

"Yeah," I sigh. "I can't believe I'm saying it, but yeah. I'm really gonna fucking miss this place."

Connor slaps me on the knee. "This place is really gonna fucking miss you."

"Nah," I laugh. "You have the child prodigy now—Axel."

"It won't be the same," Luca says, sadly.

"I won't be far away," I say, as much to make myself feel better as them. "I'm going to be based in Miami. I foresee a lot more beers and beach parties in our future."

"Hey dudes and dudettes, what did we miss?" Hudson is standing over us, with Jax and Axel close behind him.

"Isaac's leaving us," Carter replies, patting the sand next to him. All three sink down next to us and start firing questions at me. I do my best to answer them all with the little information I have. Aurelia and I still have a lot to work out and I don't have all the details yet. All I know is, as painful as it's going to be leaving my life here behind, my future is definitely with Aurelia. Nothing has felt quite so right before.

"That reminds me," Luca says, when I've finally explained everything I can, and received kind congratulations from the guys. "Aurelia promised she would sing for us, for the team. A private, exclusive performance. I think she owes us now that she's taking you away."

"I'm sure she'll be happy to," I grin. I've been watching

her for the last thirty minutes as she talked to Tawny, Esme, Maisie and Seleste. Her eyes kept flicking towards me and I know she's been itching to come over. I call her name and they all make their way towards us. I hold out a hand and pull her between my thighs. It's the first time we've ever been openly 'together' in front of anyone, and I feel so proud I could burst. The soft breeze is blowing her baby blonde hair about her face and I tuck it behind her ear as she looks nervously around at the guys.

"I'm really sorry," she squeaks, and they all crack up.

"Yeah, Aurelia. You're taking away our boy," Luca says, wagging his finger. "You know what this means, don't you?"

"You want me to sing?"

"Wow, I thought you'd be harder to persuade than that," he says.

"No way. I would love to sing for you guys."

"The whole team?" I ask, checking she's comfortable.

"Yeah, of course. Now?"

We all stare at each other. "Uh, yeah," Connor says, speaking for everyone. "Carter, go switch off the music. Luca, Hud and Jax, go round everyone up. Axel, use that big booming voice of yours to get everyone's attention. Isaac… you just sit there and look pretty," Connor winks.

"Asshole," I mutter.

Axel's voice is indeed booming and as soon as the music is cut, there is not one person on the staff who didn't hear his announcement to shut the fuck up and gather round.

"You sure you're ok about this?" I whisper to Aurelia.

She squeezes my hand. "Absolutely."

As soon as there's silence and everyone is still, Connor makes his announcement.

"You all know we say goodbye to Aurelia tonight, after what I'm sure you'll agree was the best, ass-kicking residency this state has ever seen. Well, we're not letting her go empty-handed. She's taking our good friend, our brother, Isaac, with her."

There are a few murmurs in the crowd and I catch a few pointed glances from the likes of Elija and Arnaud. "But she's leaving us with something too," Connor adds. "Over to you, Aurelia."

I don't think my heart could swell any bigger as I watch Aurelia get to her feet and look out over the Starling Key staff.

"I just want to say thank you," she begins. "You've all made me feel so welcome here and supported every step of the way. You've given me the best birthday celebration I've ever had, and you've also given me an incredibly special person in this one here." She peers down at me and I wink, hopefully conveying everything I feel in that one small movement. "I'd like to dedicate this song to every one of you. You are each as unique, and as strong, and as beautiful as the island you look after every day."

And with that, she launches into the most heartbreakingly beautiful rendition of Dolly Parton's *I will always love you.* And my God, she would give Whitney Houston a run for her money. Everyone listens in utter silence and rapture as she holds the notes, her lone voice in the still air carrying such power and grace it is mesmerizing. When she finishes, there's a moment of stunned silence before a slow clap spreads across the crowd.

I look out across our team, our large flawed family, and see not one dry eye amongst them. I wipe at my own and tug Aurelia back down to me. She immediately presses her lips to mine and I cry into them. That was the most beautiful thing anyone has ever done for us, and I can't believe how lucky I am to be the one who gets to spend a lifetime trying to repay her for making us feel this seen and appreciated.

"You've done it now, Aurelia," I whisper into her ear. "You're one of us."

She turns to me and puts both hands to my face. "I can't think of anything else I'd rather be."

EPILOGUE

Isaac

Eight months later.

I step out of the limo and stretch every limb, then I turn and hold my hand out to Aurelia as she steps out behind me and takes a deep, cleansing breath.

"Mmm, it's so good to be back."

"Back to where it all began," I grin, wrapping my arms around her. She melts into me, pressing her lips to mine, and as always, it feels as though time stops. Since I offered myself to her in all my raw, uncoated vulnerability, it's like I feel everything a million times stronger. The feel of her lips alone is enough to send me spiraling into a pool of yearning, and I know we can't attend to that right now; we have work to do.

"I can't wait to see everyone," she says, lighting up as I take her hand again.

"Walk or buggy?" I ask.

"Where are we staying?"

"Not the Morrison, unfortunately. We'll get the same level of luxury in one of the garden villas at half the price," I say, ever mindful of the numbers. "So, we're in villa six, not far from Reef Street."

"I'd like to walk."

"Me too." I lead her onto the path and we head south past the northeast wall.

"Do you miss living over there?" She says, nodding towards the dorms.

"Sometimes," I reply, honestly. "It was fun. It felt a bit like being at some kind of boarding school, but one where people genuinely work hard and party even harder. But there was always something missing." I squeeze her hand. "Living with you is better." I bend down to kiss her on the lips. "Much better."

"And working with me?" She presses.

"Yeah, that's ok," I tease, which earns me a playful smack on the arm. "I mean, you're a hard taskmaster."

"That is so not true. I've kicked back way more since Chuck left. If anyone's the taskmaster it's you. You're like a Trojan, you never stop working. I think the rest of the team suspects you're bionic."

"Maybe I am," I say, plastering a serious look to my face.

"It would explain a lot," she mutters.

We make our way straight to the reception building. Familiar faces approach, giving us bear hugs and backslaps. It feels as though we never went away.

"Connor here?" I ask Tawny who jumps down from behind her desk to greet us.

"He's on the beach, supervising the set-up." A sizeable diamond glitters on her ring finger. "I feel for the guys building the stage. He's in one of his perfectionist moods."

"Uh oh. We should go and rescue them." I wrap an arm around Aurelia's waist. I know she's right there but I can't keep my hands off her, especially now that the world knows and we've got nothing to hide.

"Can you rescue Luca while you're at it?" Tawny asks with a small frown.

"He's taking it badly, huh? Autumn's wedding next week?"

"Yeah, as can be expected."

"When did she leave?" Aurelia asks.

Tawny faces her. "This morning. We all waved her off. None of us are going to the wedding unfortunately; it's our busiest time on the resort."

"When will she be back?" I ask, my brain automatically shifting into personnel management mode. I feel an Aurelia shaped elbow in my ribs.

"Three weeks," Tawny replies, then grins up at me. "Don't worry Mr. Finance. She took some unpaid leave."

"And you have cover?"

"Yes, we do. Anyway, this is not your problem to worry about anymore. You're a hotshot talent manager now, not a lowly security guard-come-finance guy." She winks at Aurelia.

"Come on," Aurelia says, tugging me towards the exit. "We don't have all day."

"Yes, Boss," I reply, rolling my eyes at Tawny. I follow my girlfriend out of the building, my eyes held hostage by her pert little bottom taunting me through ripped shorts as she strides out onto the lawn. We see the stage immediately, reaching majestically from the sand up into the sky. It's surrounded by set-builders, technicians and roadies running around like their life depends on it. And in the distance, I see Connor, orchestrating the whole performance, with Carter and Luca by his side.

We walk across the grounds towards the beach. Carter sees us and waves us over.

"Hey man, how are things?" I say, slapping my brothers on the back.

"Great," Carter replies, monotone, then he lowers his voice to a whisper. "Turn around now, save yourselves."

"Hey," Connor grins. "It's all good. We're right on target. You'll be able to get a decent rehearsal in before the crowds arrive."

"If the roadies haven't collapsed from exhaustion by then," Luca mutters under his breath.

Connor whips around. "So get them some water." Then he turns back to us, a bright smile plastered to his face.

"Still running a tight ship, huh?"

"Always. Good trip?"

"Great. We've had a couple days to get over the jetlag after the European tour."

"Sure. Must have been amazing though—all that traveling."

I look down at Aurelia who's smiling her big hazel eyes up at me. "We mostly only see the inside of hotel rooms."

"Alright, man, don't rub it in." Luca stomps off to help one of the roadies carry some heavy equipment up onto the stage.

"I didn't mean it like that…"

"Ignore him," Connor says, looking back at Luca over his shoulder. "He'll be right again in a few weeks. He just needs to get over Autumn."

"If it isn't Mr. Lover Man himself." A giant voice booms

from up the beach and we all turn to see Axel's seven-foot-tall frame strolling towards us.

"Hey, how's it going?" I ask, leaning into our handshake. "Enjoying the job?"

"Love it, man. Best thing you ever did, getting shacked up with this one and leaving it all to me." He winks at Aurelia and my hand grips hers more tightly. I still don't one hundred percent trust the guy.

"Isaac!" I look past Axel and see Jax and Hudson walking towards us. My chest expands at the sight of all these guys, my best friends, all in one place. As much as I love being with Aurelia and being her manager, I do miss this. I wouldn't want to be back here all the time again, but I definitely need to come back more often. I give out more hugs and fist pumps, then Aurelia pulls at my hand.

"I'm gonna head off and see the sound guys. See you backstage in an hour?"

"Sure thing." I bend down and press my lips to hers, and immediately, I'm lost. I sink into her, oblivious to everyone standing around us, until Carter coughs, indiscreetly. "See you soon." I squeeze her hand and the lust in her eyes mirrors the lust I feel everywhere. I can't wait to watch her perform this charity gig, but I can't wait to get her back to the villa afterwards even more. We have some pretty hot memories to re-live.

Once Aurelia is out of sight, we all sink to the sand.

"How's Saf?" I ask Carter. "Sleeping yet?"

"Yes," he sighs in relief. "Finally. It's not all that bad you know, being a dad. Y'all should try it."

Carter's comment is met with a collective, resounding, "Nah, nuh uh, no," and I resist chuckling. I *know* Connor is going to be hot on his heels; he still can't keep his hands off Tawny.

"Any other gossip?" I ask, my eyes cruising across them all as they tip their heads back and soak up the last of the afternoon's rays.

"Hud's sis is going to come work here next season," Connor says.

"Parker?"

"Yeah. The sooner she's out from under our folks the better," Hudson grunts. I remember Hud telling us about his abusive father, how Hud stood up to him one day and how his mother turned on him too. He's been dying to get Parker, if not to Starling Key, then somewhere else he knows his father can't reach her.

"How old is she now?" I ask.

"Just turned twenty-one. She's been at school the last three years but I don't want her going back under that roof."

"Twenty-one," Jax whistles through his teeth. "The last time I saw her she was twelve, something like that."

Hud shoots him a glare. "Don't be getting' any ideas, bro'."

"Never," Jax snorts. "Do I look like I have a death wish?"

We all exchange a look, silently. Only Carter smirks.

"What?" Jax pouts.

"'Course you have a death wish, man. Why else do you have that scar across your skull?"

Jax shakes his head and lies back on the sand, ignoring us.

"What else's happening?"

"We should be asking you, Isaac," Hud grumbles. "You're the one living it up with a popstar."

"All work, no play," I wink.

"What happened to you, man?" Hud whines. "You were never this tight-lipped about your women."

"I'm serious about this one," I say in a serious tone, with a serious look on my face. Because I've never been so serious about anyone in my life. "Anyway, what about you, Hud?"

He buries his hands into the sand, avoiding my eyes. "Still playing the field, sowing my seed, you know."

"Waiting for (cough) Blue to come home," Jax smirks, rolling quickly away before Hud's left hook gets him in the shoulder.

"Still?" I laugh. "Didn't she blow you off last summer?"

"He's persistent," Jax says, leaping to his feet as Hud lunges for him. I watch them both race off down the beach, then I turn to Axel.

"How about you? Any lady friend on the scene?"

"Hell, no. I'm going to slip happily into your shoes. Lots of beautiful women on the Key wanting a little companionship. And I'm perfectly happily to oblige."

I cast my eyes over him. He's one giant muscle, covered in tattoos, with a permanent scowl on his face. But, some women like that shit, I think, so good luck to him.

We sit for another hour and the guys catch me up on the latest with Bianchi and Starling and the rest of team. Turns out I haven't missed a whole lot, thankfully.

"Isaac D'Amico." I turn in the direction of another booming voice and squint to make out who it is walking towards us with what appears to be a wife and two kids in tow. "There you are, you prick."

"Emerson," I grin, jumping to my feet.

"Had to come and see what all the damn fuss was about. Appears I am five years too late though, huh?"

"I'm afraid so, sir."

"From the CIA to MTV. You are a constant freaking surprise, D'Amico."

"You know how I like to mix things up. Are you staying here?"

"We certainly are. I mentioned our connection to your good friend Connor here, and he very generously honored that discount you offered all those years ago."

"Glad to hear it. You coming to the concert?"

"Of course." Emerson jerks his head back towards two teenage girls who are, weirdly, staring at me and don't appear to be blinking. "My life wouldn't be worth living if we came all this way and then missed that," he says, with gritted teeth.

"Sandy." I lean past him to shake Mrs. Emerson's hand. "It's been a while. You're looking well."

"Thanks Isaac, so are you. Your new life suits you. This is Jessica and Britt. They haven't talked about anything else for weeks."

"Well," I address the two girls, "how about you come backstage afterwards? I can introduce you to Aurelia."

"Wh—what?" Jessica stammers, her blonde hair, cut exactly like my girlfriend's, bobbing about her face. "Really?"

"Sure. She'd love to meet you."

"Oh my God!" her sister gasps, and they both jump up and down, holding each other's hands, shrieking.

"Don't use blasphemy," Sandy says, but it's lost amongst the squeals.

"Speaking of Aurelia," I say, apologetically, "I need to go and check she has everything before the show starts. Good to see you Emerson, let's talk tomorrow."

"Sounds great."

I LEAVE Connor and Carter discussing work with Axel, to go see my no-so-anymore boss. I find her warming up her vocal chords in her dressing room. Before she notices me, I take a few seconds to run my eyes appraisingly over her outfit, deciding she looks far better in fishnet stockings, a tasteful leather corset and patent, buckled boots than my last boss would. Picturing Connor in this get-up makes me smile.

"What's so amusing," she asks, catching my eyes in the mirror.

"Nothing," I shake my head and walk up behind her. I smooth my hands down the side of her corset and run them over the top of her hips. "How long before showtime?" I whisper, tickling the skin below her ear with my tongue.

"You tell me," she replies, her voice suddenly breathless. "You're my manager."

"Fuck it. You can be fashionably late."

"Why? What's more important?" she moans, tipping her head back to my shoulder, exposing her neck like a rag to a bull. My tongue laps at her soft skin and her hand curls behind her back, then finds me rock hard beneath my jeans. One perk of this job is I can wear what the hell I like. Her fingers cup my girth beneath the denim.

"I think you know," I groan, unraveling as she rubs me firmly, whisking my breath right out of my throat. I run my finger along the edge of her corset down to the apex of her thighs, my head is bent over her collarbone so I can see exactly what I'm doing. Her legs part, allowing the tips of my fingers a frictionless entry into the gusset. Her breath chokes out as I rub her gently, back and forth, dipping into her wetness then spreading it back out over her clit.

"You were ready for me, baby girl."

"I'm always ready for you, Isaac. Let me into your pants."

I use my free hand to rip open my fly and tuck her hand inside my boxers. She wastes no time in curling her fingers around me, skin on skin. *Fuck, yes.*

I continue to lick at her gorgeous neck, the curve of her throat and the soft dip below her ear, as I stroke her gently, persistently. I look up and catch her eyes gazing down at me so I raise my head fully and take them in as she sinks further and further into a lust-filled haze.

"Lick your lips. They're dry." She does as I say and my cock lurches for her.

"Trojan," she replies, smiling.

"You're so wet," I say, glancing down to where we can both see my fingers pushing into her. I rock her back and forth, loving the feel of her perched on my hand, my fingers knuckle-deep. My thumb massages her clit, getting wetter by the second.

"That's it, baby," I say, clasping my hand around hers and rubbing it up and down my cock. She's about to come and I need to keep up.

"Oh fuck, Isaac," she says, her knees buckling. Her free hand comes down to the dressing table and she leans on it. I ride us both to the end, rubbing her hand up and down my cock and fucking her with my fingers. The sight of us in the mirror, panting, hot and sweaty, ever hungry for each other, is so sexy I can't hold it in any longer.

"Aurelia," I choke out, tightening my hold on me and her. I come forcefully inside my shorts and feel her do the same over my fingers. I keep rubbing until we are both completely spent, then I stop, my hands still.

"Jeez," she breathes out, slowly looking up to face my reflection. Our eyes meet and we say nothing. We don't need to. That one look which passes between us says everything.

I've traveled a long way to get here. I'm now thirty-five years old and finally feel like I have the answer to life. And what is that answer? That we never really find out how it all works. We just have to take the risks. It's the only way to live. Otherwise, we're not really living at all.

I'm Isaac D'Amico and I'm in love with someone fifteen years my junior.

And I'm the luckiest fucker in the world.

The end.

EXTENDED EPILOGUE

uca

I WAKE UP, still clutching the bottle of tequila I took to bed with me, but with a raging headache in the same place my rational mind used to be.

I feel worse today than I did yesterday, if that's possible.

This is it. This is my life now. It's official. I will never be happy. I just need to get the fuck on with it.

Maybe she won't come back here after all. She'd been talking about getting work on Miami Beach. It would make more sense, since Mr. Stiff in a Lamborghini lives up there and that's where they'll be having and raising lots of little Stiff Lamborghini children. Probably.

I go to sit up but the room actually tips up on its ass and then the whole of yesterday's nutritional intake along with the contents of the tequila bottle and several beers comes flying up out of my stomach onto the floor. I think it's the floor. Could be the ceiling.

I lie back down and squeeze my eyes shut and pray for more sleep.

Maybe when I wake up this will never have happened. Or better yet, I might never wake up. Death might actually be preferable to this nightmare.

Because the universe hasn't kicked me *quite* hard enough, sleep evades me and I try sitting up again. It's not too bad this time. The room stays the right way up at least.

I chug down a couple bottles of water and try not to barf at the barf already soaking into the floor, then I haul myself into the shower. As I try to scrub away my entire identity, my mind roams aimlessly around the last three and half years.

The first time I met Autumn Lockhart was over the phone. She'd been to visit the Key, Connor had given her a job, but she had a few things to care of in Miami before she moved in with the rest of us. This all happened before I'd even laid eyes on her. Then she'd gotten cold feet. She'd tried calling Connor to decline the job offer, but I answered the phone. I remember the conversation like it was yesterday.

The line was silent when I answered. "Hey, is anyone there?"

"Um, yeah, um. Sorry, it's, um, Autumn Lockhart here. I was supposed to start work in the dive center this week."

"Right." I remember mindlessly flicking through the pages of a magazine on Connor's desk while only half-listening to the call.

"Yeah, um, I don't think I can take the job after all."

I stopped flicking through the magazine and racked my brains. What job was she talking about? "The admin job?"

"Yeah. I don't think I can do it."

I thought quickly. I knew we needed to fill that post fast because we'd just taken on the trips for a neighboring resort. "Is there anything I can help with?"

"Sure, if you can perform a parent lobotomy or build a time machine so I can go back and be born, like, ten years later."

"What?"

"I'm sorry. I just… my parents are gonna think I'm a total bum taking this job, especially after my younger sister just won herself a BAFTA, the freaking high achieving bitch."

I grinned to myself.

"I'm sorry," she added, quickly. "I really don't mean that. I love her to bits, but you know, she's set a precedent for our family now, and, well, me taking some admin job on a beach resort doesn't look anywhere near as good as BAFTA-winning actress, does it?"

"I'm not going to argue with that," I said.

"What would you do?" she asked, putting me well and truly on the spot.

"Hell, I'd take the job, just to piss everyone off." It was true. It was the rebel in me.

She laughed and her voice sounded like glitter pouring out through the phone. I almost dropped it in surprise. "I like the sound of that. Are you close to your family?"

"Um—" I stalled, feeling disarmed by the personal question. "Kinda. It's pretty big. My parents had a lot on their hands so I guess we got away with a lot."

She sighed, wistfully. "That sounds so nice."

"Yeah, sometimes." I didn't say anything else because no one's family is perfect really, and the call was about her, not me.

"I guess I can always leave if things don't work out," she said, almost to herself.

"Sure you can. Just hit me up when you get here. We can talk."

"Ok, that sounds good. What's your name?"

"Luca. I work with Connor."

"Luca..." She said it back to me, slowly. "Well, you know my name. Autumn."

"Yeah, hey Autumn."

"Hey Luca."

A strange silence followed, then we both spoke at the same time. *"Well, I guess I better..."*

I laughed. "Yeah. I'll look forward to meeting you."

"You too, Luca."

I was about to hang up the call when she said, "And Luca?"

"Yeah?"

"Thanks."

I found myself watching the gate after that, for one Autumn Lockhart to arrive. I mean literally. I positioned myself in the CCTV suite for three days straight and didn't take my eyes off that damned entrance. I must have missed her though, somehow, because she showed up at the door of my dorm with a basket of muffins and a thank you card she'd made herself. I hadn't expected anyone that afternoon, not least Autumn Lockhart, so I was dressed in freaking pajama pants with nothing up top.

When I opened the door to see what may as well have been Pamela Anderson's better looking twin, I gave the worst first impression known to mankind. I grabbed the muffins and held them about waist height so she couldn't see my growing erection, then I mumbled something about being on shift in thirty minutes and needing a shower. Damn right. I needed an *ice cold* shower. When I closed the door on her, I almost shrank down into the floorboards. *Who. The fuck. Was that?*

Only now do I know the real answer. That was Autumn Lockhart, love of my goddamn life.

I VAGUELY DRESS myself and head out of the dorms. The sunlight is blinding, so I pull my Oakley's down over my eyes and open the gate letting me out of the northeast wall. I make my way slowly, and pitifully, to the reception building. I know I'm on shift today, but for the life of me, I can't remember where. So, first stop, Connor's office. I don't get that far.

Carter comes racing through the doors. "Luca! Did you hear?"

"Hear what?" I groan.

"About Autumn!"

"What about her?"

"Where's your phone, man? She's probably been calling you."

"I've got no freaking idea. I barely know my own name right now."

"She's coming back here," Carter says, almost out of breath.

"What? Why?"

"She didn't get married."

"What? Why?" This is way too much for my brain to handle so I appear to have morphed into a broken record.

"The asshole left her at the altar, man."

I squeeze my eyes closed. I need to understand this. I need to process this, and fast. Autumn. My friend. My best friend…

"I don't understand…"

"Look at me, Luca," Carter says, gripping my face between his hands. "She's coming back, dude."

"Why?"

Carter lets go of me, stands back and eyes me seriously. “You need to check your phone, man. She’s going to need you. Autumn just got jilted.”

The end.

THE BROKER

Autumn Lockhart, best friend, dive master extraordinaire and secret love of my life, *jilted at the altar.*

Words I never thought I'd hear.

That was six months ago. Now, her ex is back, enjoying a honeymoon with Autumn's ex-best friend and bridesmaid right here on Starling Key.

So, when Autumn asks me to be her fake boyfriend for two weeks, I don't even need to think.

But it's all for show: the staged kisses that go on a little too long, the accidental thigh grazes that inch a little higher each time, the romantic couples' day trip on a boat that… breaks down.
Being trapped on a tourist boat with her ex not only sends Autumn flying into my arms, it forces him to reveal exactly who he is: a guy who'll do whatever it takes to screw over Starling Key.

He thinks blackmail is a legit form of negotiation, but he's never met me. And they don't call me The Broker for nothing.

But negotiations have limits. After that, the only solution is war.
And if Autumn Lockhart's life is on the line, the last thing I plan to do is lose.

ACKNOWLEDGMENTS

Writing a series like Starling Key is no mean feat. While I love to escape each time into the vibrant landscape of the Florida Keys and catch up with all the characters in my head, the responsibility to stay true to the setting, the character arcs and the long term storyline seems to intensify with each instalment. The Banker is my first age-gap romance and I have to thank every other author of the trope that has gone before me, for having the courage and providing the inspiration to write a much-loved, very specific arc.

I wrote most of this book while sitting in the hippest cafe around—The Forge in Ringmer, so I'd like to thank all the staff there for putting up with me sitting in a corner for many hours, asking for "long flat whites with one shot" which later transpired to be simply a latte. (Doh.)

And, as ever, I need to thank my wonderful beta readers for pushing and challenging me to go further into the trope. Kristen, Sara and Elke, I'm so lucky to have you and I really don't know where these stories would be without your input.

I would also like to thank an array of fellow authors who very generously offered to help me spread the word about this book. Elle Thorpe, A.L. Jackson, Kandi Steiner, Miranda P Charles, Poppy Parkes, I am forever grateful. And Zoe Blake gets a special mention for going even further with her invaluable advice. It really means a lot.

Finally, a huge thank you to Wander Aguiar and Felipe

for the amazing cover photo. You have helped me capture Isaac perfectly!

And of course, I couldn't sign off without thanking my husband, Chris. You are my rock, my inspiration and my enabler - in all the best ways. I say this every time and you still don't believe me, but it's true: I couldn't do this without you. And I promise I'll try to get the phrase "throbbing member" into one of my books, somewhere. One day. Maybe.

And thank you to all my readers for enjoying the stories I write and for inspiring me to continue to write them.

Much, much love,

January xxx

ABOUT THE AUTHOR

January James lives in the smallest cottage in East Sussex with her husband, daughter and crazy sprockapoo (she finally got one!) Until recently, she inhabited the fast-paced, adrenalin-fuelled workplaces she writes about, as a communications professional. Now she spends her days dreaming up new characters and stories and trying her best to avoid indoor soft play.

instagram.com/thejanuaryjames
facebook.com/januaryjamesauthor
goodreads.com/januaryjames
bookbub.com/authors/january-james

ALSO BY JANUARY JAMES

Square Mile series

A Class Act

He Turned

Chasing Flames

Fémmes Féroces standalones

Man Eater

Dirty Diana

Starling Key series

The Brain

The Brawn

The Banker

The Broker

The Blue Blood